GANGARIDAI

Arman Chowdhury

GANGARIDAI

ii

ISBN: 979-8-9916342-0-5

For the Children of Gaza

"By the blood that you, Alexander, have spilled on these lands, you shall have no more nourishment from this soil - not food, nor water. How long your transgressing soul lives depend on how fast you can reach your ill-gotten lands to the west where you may have nourishment again. But not here. This Dharani (Earth) is done with your kind. I have spoken on Her behalf"

- Aarohan (King Hasti)
May 5, 323 BC

Forward

Philadelphia, Jan 2017 CE
Or
Gangaridai, 323 BCE

My friend and I went for a run. At the end, he yelled out "Sparta...aahh" to cap and express his elation after the final sprint. At that time, the movie "300" was fresh out in theaters. To that, I yelled "Gangaridai" as I best him. My friend stopped, looked at me, and laughed... "What the hell was that?"

... "That, my friend, is the nation that made Alexander turn on his heels and leave India... probably they gave him a whooping..." I chuckled.

My friend was now skeptical. "Right," he said. I replied, "Yeah, probably that's why he scrambled through the desert on the return leg, lost most of his army, and died within months as he reached Babylon... probably from a battle wound." My friend said, "BS. Where do you get all this nonsense?" I said, "Historians often bend history and truth to favor their kings, especially when their necks are on the line, but they often leave clues to the truth. Look up Gangaridai, and you will see I am not making this up. Ready for another run?"

That was about eight years ago.

There are many epics that history reveals to us, yet the most astounding ones are the stories that remain hidden, buried beneath layers of forgotten time. They are there, under our feet in plain collective memory.

Akdoom Bakdoom

Ghora doom Shajey

Dhak Dhol Jhajor Bajey

Bajte bajte chollo ddhuli

Ddhuli gelo Komola fuli

Komola fulir Biyeta

Surjyi Mamar Teeyeta

What you have read above is a very old nursery rhyme from Bengal, a most ancient culture. This nursery rhyme is uttered by almost every Bangla speaking toddler and taught by their parents and nannies. But what one misses is that this is not a nursery rhyme, but .... A war cry. It is a 'Haka'.

Let me explain further and translate the rhyme for you:

Akdoom Bakdoom

> "akdoom bakdoom" these are war drumbeats

Ghora doom shajey

> Horses in battle gear

Dhak Dhol Jhajor Bajey

> Drums beat Trumpets bugle

Bajte bajte chollo ddhuli

> With the drum beat the drummers march on

Ddhuli gelo Komolaphuli

> Drummers go to Komolaphuli, (this is an ancient settlement in the present Aligarh location in India)

Komolphulir Biyeta

> The wedding at Komolaphuli (referring to an event)

Surjyi Mamar Tiyeta

> This is where everything blows up in a single sentence. We have to break the last phrase down word by word. Surjyi Mama literally translates to "Sun

Uncle". In the Bengali norm 'mama 'apart from the 'uncle' annotation is often meant for anything that is fearful or potent. As an example, the fearful Royal Bengal Tiger is referred to in the colloquial tongue as "Baag mama 'or 'Tiger Uncle', a creature that one does not mess with. Surjyi Mama is a reference to the fearful Sun Uncle. So, who is this Sun Uncle? Sun Uncle is the same character in history we know of as Alexander of Macedon, or as they will say in the Bengali culture, "Eskander". Note, I have not penned Alexander as 'the great' , and I will come back to this 'great' notion later. But for the time being, the Sun emblem was front and center of Alexander's insignia and regalia of his chest armor (https://en.wikipedia.org/wiki/Vergina_Sun). Alexander is the approaching 'Sun Uncle' feared by the masses of India. But it does not end here, Surjyi mamar tiyeta means the 'Parrot of Alexander'. This 'Parrot' is Nothing but the brilliant red Greek Feathers of Alexander's helmet! In other words, this last phrase is asking for Alexander's neck or even more so the Vanquishing of the idea of Potency that Alexander the Macedon represented _the fear, the virility. "Who will bring me the parrot feathers of Alexander.... who will kill Alexander for me?" This is a battle cry to the youth of Gangaridai to rise and assemble to counter the Macedonian threat!

But who gave this battle cry?

What has history and historians to say about the Gangariddis at the time of Alexander's conquest? Only of great admiration and then a convenient silence. The reason for this silence? Megasthenes from the time of Alexander writes in his book Indica "Other nations feared Gangaridai's huge force of the biggest elephants, and therefore, Gangaridai had never been conquered by any foreign king." *(McCrindle 1877, p. 33-34)*. Greek historian from antiquity Diodorus Siculus states "First came a desert which it would take twelve days to traverse; beyond this was the river called the Ganges which had a width of thirty-two stadia, and a greater depth than any other Indian river; beyond this again were situated the dominions of the nation of the Prasioi and the Gandaridai, whose king, Xandrammes, had an army of 20,000 horse 200,000 infantry, 2,000 chariots and 4,000 elephants trained and equipped for war". *(Dr R.C. Majumder, p.170-72/234)*. Kosmin writes "Megasthenes emphasizes that no foreign army had been able to conquer India (since Dionysus) and Indians had not invaded a foreign country either. This representation of India as an isolated, invincible country is an attempt to vindicate Seleucus' peace treaty with the Indian emperor". *(Kosmin 2013, p. 103-104)*. Thus, there are a great many indications of a show down between the forces of Alexander and that of an unknown hero from Gangaridai, probably the voice that coined the war cry. But History is conveniently silent on these matters. Why did Alexander turn away from Gangaridai at the prime of his conquests? Was it the revolt in his army or was there a better reason? What was his army afraid of? Why did he split his army and one 'scrambled' to the ocean and the other took to the deserts only to be decimated by four fifths of its number? What compelled him to take this route? History records this event as the greatest blunder of Alexander. Let's ponder about this for a moment. Why would the 'greatest' general and military strategists in history make this obvious mistake of leading his army into the desert of Gedrosia (Plutarch, Life of Alexander, p 66), modern day Baluchistan?

These maneuvers of Alexander do not make any sense. One would argue that in fact he was compelled to do so, he was driven into the desert after he was not able to dispatch all his army through the sea. He seems to be on the run. And chased by whom?

Let's move away from our Euro centric historical narrative of Alexander. The greatest dynasty in Indian history, the Mauryan dynasty was established right after the time of Alexander, but here is the more interesting part. The great advisor, philosopher, strategist & mentor to the founding emperor of this dynasty, was none other than Chanakya or Kautilya, the Indian Philosopher. People who are not familiar with Chanakkya should know that he is comparable to Plato in Indian culture and his treaties "Artha shastra" a commentary on all matters of governance, politics and warfare, is comparable to Plato's "Republic". And Chanakkya is Alexander's contemporary and younger to him by five years. He was at Taxila when Alexander was there. The young Chanakkya, the future power behind the throne of emperor Chandragupta, witnessed all the Hegemony of Alexander and the Macedons yet again, he is consciously silent about this in his treatise. How can you remain silent on the most important & potent threat in history as in Alexander? Why would you remain silent? What did he see? And why did he choose not to report on it? Thus, my readers, this is the story of the 'what' and 'why' of the end of Alexander and the person who challenged him successfully. All major events in this story are factual based on history. The fillers are fiction and the story line _ a probable projection. But the main events are true and factual.

Before I end this forward, I pose a simple question. Why is Alexander considered great? He was nothing but a war monger, destroyer of nations, spiller of blood, rapist of women and young lads. What's so great about that? The idea of conquering generals to be considered a hero is very much a western concept. Eastern philosophy seldom celebrates war lords as heroes. Thus, you have so many kings in the east turning priest or sadhus. Violence is shunned upon in, once you have protected your own lands there is no need to conquer others. That's why India never came out and conquered other people's land. I will state this out clearly, this book is about that spirit, that person, that exemplar to Chanakkya who stood up against Alexander the hegemon, who united the warring chieftains of India into the seed of the first great dynasty of India and who in the end did defeat Alexander.

His name? Aarohan.

Hope you enjoy this fiction based on actual historical events.

Arman

Philadelphia, Pennsylvania, 2017.

Prologue

Gangaridai, (313 BCE)

Akdoom Bakdoom
Ghora doom Shajey
Dhak Dhol Jhajor Bajey
Bajte bajte chollo ddhuli
Ddhuli gelo Komola fuli
Komola fulir Biyeta
Surjyi Mamar Teeyeta

AKDOOM BAKDOOM (BEATS OF BATTLE DRUMS)

Horses in battle gear
Drums beat, Trumpets bugle
With the drum beat the drummers march
Drummers go to Komolaphuli
The wedding at Komolaphuli
The parrot of the Sun Uncle

The sound of the song was fresh in Chanakkya's ears as he held the bamboo slats upon which he had been writing out toward the dancing flame of the candle and contemplated the document in hand. It was nearing dark outside, and the small flame on the desk was not quite bright enough to read well by any longer. He could still recognize the form of the Pali Pakrit characters he had drawn over the last few monsoons, but they took on the hazy appearance of a babble of lines now. Still, he could clearly read the song by which he had headed his work and which he had set off in a larger type.

This was the song he'd heard children repeating in the streets. Most didn't know who wrote it; it seemed to have developed out of the people, possibly from the warriors themselves. This short work first surfaced in a letter from a student not long after the terrible war. The student had found it in Takkhashila (Taxila), that center of learning on the approach to the great passes through the Himalayas.

"Who will bring me Alexander's parrot feathers?" was the battle cry often heard.

The student had sent him the song as an amusing artifact from the days before Chandragupta, during the days of Aarohan — from the days of battle, fear, and finally victory. It was amusing for him to see it then, and he had kept it for sentimental value more than any other reason. But the song had grown roots in the minds of the people to the point where over time nearly everyone knew it by heart, though few still knew what it meant.

It was a pastiche that had evolved in real time, developed by Aarohan, though few knew that. One of the lines had been drilled into the soldiers of the army of the Gangaridai as a battle cry: "Surjyi Mamar Teeyeta!" Aarohan had insisted that the soldiers sound off those words in every drill and at every meal, in the morning and in the evening. They shouted it so often that even war elephants straightened up and readied to fight when they heard the call, even if they were gorging; years afterward, it was said the elephants might rampage if a passerby happened to sing it, so strong was the impression those words had left on them.

"Surjyi Mamar Teeyeta!"

Still, after all these years, the battle cry echoed in his mind, though he was now more apt to pick up his pen than a weapon. It was the call to kill Eskander, known in the Western world as Alexander. The call that made the Macedonian war lord, the Sun Uncle as the Gangaridai had also called him for he had the Vergina Sun emblem tapered into his chest armor, turn from the Ganges and flee through the desert of Gedrosia where they were reduced by eight in ten; to escape with his wound, back to Babylon where he died, secreted from his men in his shame. For the Gangariddis where trained with one sole objective, to tear out the parrot of the Macedonian war lord, the parrot meaning nothing but the red feathers of his Greek Helmet!

Now those words formed the basis of a nursery rhyme upon which mothers rocked their children to sleep at night and people from time to time sang absently in the streets, recalling the greatest of feats and the footings of an empire in its roots. And it was that song which he had placed at the head of his magnum opus relating the tale of

Aarohan who had stood, initially hopeless but eventually firm as the Himalayas and marshaled the people of the heart of the Ganges when the fearful 'Sun Uncle' Alexander came to enslave them. The Sun Uncle, whose name, like the fearful Royal Bengal Tiger, referred to in the colloquial as "Baag mama" or "Tiger Uncle," had become a watchword for "fear."

And yet Aarohan, the greatest of the Gangaridai, had walked away, eschewing all fame and fortune and the recollections of his feats, because he did not want his people, who had tasted blood and victory, to aspire to the crimes of Alexander, or "Eskander" as they said it, for their own gain.

At that moment, however, within the recesses of his chambers he heard a footstep in the doorway leading into the garden courtyard. He turned to find an old man dressed like a beggar in threadbare weaved clothing that was hardly enough to cover his thin but angular frame. When he saw the man at first he thought to reach for his coin purse, to give him a handout and send him on his way, but something in the man's bearing explained that he was no beggar, and with the fading daylight behind him contrasting with the relative darkness of the candlelit chamber, he found it difficult to make out the features of the man's slender face until he stepped further into the room and out of the orange light of the failing sun. A face that was so familiar from Chanakya's military days.

Aarohan !

Chapter 1

Battle of Issus

"I would rather live a short life of glory than a long one of obscurity" - Alexander / Eskander
November 5, 333 BC (Beginning of Kali Yuga)

There it was. Under the bronze ridge frames two distinct color eyes pierced through the Hellenic battle helmet. One eye blue as the sky, the other brown as the ground. As if the owner of the eyes were of two people. As if he understood both the culture, both their strengths and their weaknesses. And today he would exploit this understanding to the fullest, when he would churn up his company of soldiers, broiling with courage while create sheer fear numbing asphyxial awe within the Persian ranks. He knew how to stage such effects. In fact, he was a master of such antics.

The warm wind was blowing over the bare ball muscles of his shoulders. He could feel the wind, he could feel the very terrain of this battlefield. Every step his horse took as if he took those steps, bare feet, feeling the very ground below. As the horse cantered, he straddled along, with his red cape heaving behind. Such a magnificent flow of the cape, only to be out done by the glistening black mane of Bucephalus. The horse was large. Impressive. With a white star on the forehead. But more impressive was its rider, who matched his balancing motion with that of the horse trot. He was a large man. Able to master the will on such a large creature. He knew the horse's temperament well. And the horse knew his temper well. For they have been together for more than a decade, first as master and beast but now more as symbiotic thrill-seekers, adrenalin rush mongers. For Bucephalus had seen blood, scented blood and tasted blood. And it liked it. It liked how its master rode it, rushed it and whispered to it, calmed it, excited it, and made it mad charge into gory battles. Its mane was long and flamboyant. The only thing that was more magnificent than its mane was the parrot feathers of the Macedonian regent helmet of its rider. Here they stood, with the sun on their backs. The rider looked down from the slope on the hill they were standing. Their shadow in front. As if it was meant to cover the whole valley in front of them. There it was. There stood Alexander.

At last, he had Darius in sight. It didn't matter that there were two large armies between them.

Just a matter of inconvenience.

Alexander felt no fear for the Persian front. Only that of an opportunity. An opportunity to dare and defeat this perceived superpower. All his life Alexander dreamt of this day, the day he would dare the Persian empire. He cared not if he died, how could he? He was ambidextrous with two swords, he could best any warriors of any nation. He sincerely hoped someone would best him in his skills in one of these battles. He wore the best forged Vergina Sun body armor, the arrows would bounce off like toothpicks. His cohorts were like him, only slightly less daring. Hungry for glory and in awe of his achievements thus far. He could sense their increasing adulation by each battle. And he knew they would follow him to the very throne of Darius. So, no proximity force can harm him. As for long range javelin and arrows, he would counter them with superior battle strategy. There were battle lords who had great skills and valor, and then there were battle lords who were brilliant strategists. But there was only one battle lord who was bestowed with both these talents. So why would he die in battle? It was only glory to be dared, and he was all for it.

Alexander was a battle maker. He would walk through a battle mayhem as if it were a walk in the park. Only that this walk would come with the greatest of thrills. The war generals were great battle strategists at best. But he was more than a strategist, he was a composer of how it would play out. This he would do, on the spur of the moment of the battle, when limbs are flying, groins are severed, when all humane essence would cease. He would be at home with perfect control of all his faculty and this couldn't be replicated by the most brilliant war strategist. Alexander strategized 'On the Go'.

He could do so because he had no inhibition. No, he had no inhibition. There were great kings, arrogant and tyrants who had shown no inhibition, and there will be many more in the future. But neither had nor will have Alexander's 'dare to do at any cost' attitude. And this was no accident. This was instilled in him from very early childhood. He was the son of Zeus, so said his mother. He was a human god. This was whispered into him by his mother morning, noon and night. Such whispers of mothers have the greatest effect on men. There are many such irresponsible mothers in history. But few mothers had reinforced it through action as Olympias did. Olympias would encourage her son to own whatever he desired. This was his Zeus-given birth right. From the best of clothes to the best of gems, to the best of foods, to the best of slave tutors, to the best of weapons, to the best of horses. At first glance, this seems harmless. But it didn't stop there. He would take at will any girl he fancied, irrelevant if they fancied him in return or not. He would simply take them. And they had to oblige. Willingly was the better option. For if they didn't, Alexander would forcefully take them. Yes, rape. Though it was never framed that way. For the status of Alexander oscillated from being heir apparent to Phillip II at the least to being son of Zeus, Will of Zeus on this earth. Not a bad deal for a growing boy and his ego. Thus, he would try all kinds of sexual curiosity. From erotic to sheer abomination. He eventually settled somewhere in between.

His sexual behavior would yield to three distinct outcomes. The first: he had no frustrations and censorship in life. He took what he desired, and he not only felt he was entitled to it but that destiny was bound to oblige this entitlement. The other: his sexual acts on fellow male peers. As he grew of age, and so did his contemporaries, there was this psychological superiority that he enjoyed over them, for he rode them all. If any future challengers arose, he would simply mock them and reveal to the world how he had "enjoyed" them. The third was subtle but most significant: he lost interest in regular sex. Few things excited him to sexual arousal, for his desires and curiosities had been completely satisfied as a habit. Only the extreme — whether grotesque or poetic —could provide him with sexual excitement. Thus, he was never interested in self-gratification.

As he matured into a military man and heir apparent, his lack of interest in regular sex acts gave him an extra boost of energy and hormonal growth. If there was ever an alpha male, he was the hyper-male type—larger in ego than any man that had ever lived or ever would live. This disinterest in regular sex resulted in peculiar effects on his sensuality and desires. He soon discovered that in battle, at the sight of blood, at the sight of gory mayhem, and at the sight of men begging him for mercy, he would become sexually aroused. Few knew of this trait in him. His best friend, childhood friend, chief of the personal bodyguard, most trusted adviser, and confidante, and... lover, Hephaestion, knew of it. His tutor slave, Aristotle, knew of it too. But neither would talk of it. One would encourage it, for he was an equal partner in such desires. The other would try to moderate it and give it a cloak of civility and sanity.

Now, such a thrill-seeking maniac stood over the south bank of the Pinarus (Payas) River.

Among many things, Alexander was a martial artist, and he would sometimes employ martial arts philosophy in war maneuvering. Surprise would often take Alexander's opponents' master tacticians, whenever he employed such tactics. But what would totally escape them was the speed with which he would employ and adjust his maneuvers.

Classical tacticians didn't know how to counter such speedy changes in tactics. And most woeful for his opponents, Alexander was a battle-hardened lead general. He led by action. None of his opponents' tacticians understood this extra edge that Alexander had.

Darius stood in the center of the battle formation so that he could 'perceive' all that was going on. Alexander knew such positioning to be flawed. Increasingly battlefields were getting larger and larger, one couldn't 'perceive' what was going on at the flanks. One couldn't react quickly if there were gaps in enemy battle lines and take advantage of it. What classical strategist didn't realize, once the battle ensures, there are always gaps emerging and vanishing in the battle lines. Battles were fluid and organic, Alexander knew it. And he was amongst the few generals in history who would exploit it. So he set himself to motion, he would not center himself as Darrius did. He would lead a flank. His father's general Parmenion and the old guards would take the Macedonian left near the mouth of the river.

The night before, Alexander had told Parmenion, "This flanking arm is your arm; do whatever you deem fit. If you gain ground, slowly move up toward Darius's right from the left side. Always hold ground and move slowly. So, you bear his attention."

'You know what that means Dear Alexander?' Parmenion had said, "My troops will bleed the most."

"Yes, I know, and I know the stream is wider there, it will be cold. There, it will be a battle of tenacity rather than a battle of skills. Tell your troops to wear their heavy high boots. You will be the anchor of our battle thrust. What matters most is that you hold your ground. Our success depends on that. Also, and this is crucial, ask your men to keep an extra canteen of drinking water."

Parmenion paused and looked up at Alexander from the battle maps, smiling with admiration, unsure if the lad would actually do what Parmenion was thinking. He asked, "Why would my troops need extra canteens of drinking water when we will be right there in the river?" Alexander answered, "Because the water will be undrinkable." Parmenion smiled, "Phillip would have been proud. Where will you take up your position?" "Everywhere," answered Alexander.

Then he paused, looking over the Pinarus River. "If by midday the water is still drinkable, then recede back, which I plan not to happen. When you see the water undrinkable, thrust forward." Alexander took his most prominent parrot-feathered battle helmet and his Vergina Sun armor.

"You will draw the most attention, my lord, do you think that is wise?"

"I am counting on it!" answered Alexander.

As he was leaving the war tent Parmenion added, "One last thing my lord, regarding the thrust. How far shall I go? "Until you meet me face to face" answered alexander.

On the morning of the battle, with the sun rising in the east behind his back, Alexander took up his regent position in front of Parmenion's phalanxes, among the infantry led by Coenus, Parmenion's son-in-law. Darius, seeing that Alexander had taken the right of his flanks, gave the command of his oriental phalanx to engage Alexander. The Persian infantry began to cross the river. Alexander smiled as Darius took his first bait. The Persian "couch king," as Alexander had coined his opponent, didn't realize how cold the water was in early winter. Darius thought it would be a quick crossing to his target. But the knee-high river was the widest at that location, and the Macedonians simply held their position on the east bank of the river. The Persians were marching southeast into the headwind from the sea. Little did the "couch king" realize that marching against the wind with your shields up become quite a task after more than half an hour. And in a stalled battle that extra ounce of strength always, always, always counts!

So that the Macedonians couldn't execute a southern flanking maneuver, the Persians stretched their lines all the way to the sea. Alexander thought, "Yes, Darius, keep spreading yourself thin."

Before the slow charge of the Persians, Alexander kept himself visible with his parrot feathers, and on foot. He appeared as an easy target for Darius. Darius further strengthened his right flank with his reserve regiment. When Alexander saw how Darius had committed, he removed his prominent parrot-feather helmet and put on a regular infantry captain's helmet, then began jogging north along the east side of the river with Parmenion's phalanxes drawn out in battle formation

In the battle mayhem, Alexander vanishes.

The Persians realized too late that they were now anchored in the cold river for a while. The Persian captains still urged their infantry forward, as retreating would cost them their heads. The mercenary Greek general

Charidamus had recently lost his head for arguing with the emperor about who should engage Alexander.

Darius was not concerned at this moment. He was feeling pretty good. Earlier in the month he had cut off Alexander's supply line. He thought that was brilliant on his part. This 'Baccha' Macedonian knew nothing about war strategies. Now he had Alexander all bogged down in the infantry battle, away from his horse and away from his cavalry, where he would have been most potent. He couldn't see Alexander anymore; he was feeling elated. Had the boy king already fallen! He couldn't see the parrot feathers anymore.

Battlefield pages were updating Darius every moment, none had anything to report, they kept jogging to and fro from the right flanks to the center. What they hadn't realized is that Alexander was not an old general, he was at the prime of his youth, fit to his toe. He too jogged from the left of his flanks to the center, along with two hundred of his bodyguards under the dust of the battle. This was a general who could run a good sprint and a long run. He trained for it and so did his companions.

There Bucephalus was kept ready by its caretaker exactly the way he had instructed so the previous night. And so was his cavalry awaiting him, Hephaestion and five hundred cavalry men. Alexander mounted Bucephalus and changed his helmet to once again his prominent parrot feathers. As he did, the trumpets were blown, and Bucephalus gave a resounding 'hind legged stance front legs in the air neigh'.

Staging!

And suddenly, all eyes were on Alexander again. Darius was startled by the change in Alexander's position, and the surprise unsettled him. He had heard that Alexander was a brilliant tactician, always able to surprise his foes. He felt that would not be the case of him against alexander, the fact that he had taken Alexander by surprise and cut off his supply line a week before proved he was different. But now Alexander had somehow transported himself from one end of the battlefield to the other.

Darius gave the orders to the Persian cavalry to shadow and engage Alexander. Shadow him so that they would not lose sight of him again, so that there would be no more surprises. Period.

From the moment the trumpets had blown, and Alexander had straddled Bucephalus he felt he had set in motion a course that would lead only to one thing, his victory. He began to charge along with Hephaestion and five hundred other cavalry men along the battle lines towards the north. From the corner of his eye, he could see the Persian cavalry shadowing him. Darius has taken his second bait. He galloped with vigor skirting the eastern edge of the river, sometimes almost creating a splash. He passed the Persian left flanked, and still galloped on. So did the Persian cavalry. They were fearful that Alexander would cross the river up north at a distance & attack the Persian formation from behind. So, the Persians kept their pace shadowing Alexander and his swift cavalry, to the point that they were stretched thin, and gaps begin to appear along the Persians cavalry line.

This did not go unnoticed by Alexander.

The night before, Alexander had given one

instruction to his cavalry leaders: every cavalryman would follow the horse in front of him, even if they saw the battle happening elsewhere. Now Alexander would use this tactic to its full potential. He had calculated where and at what location the Persian cavalry would be thinning out once they took his bait of shadowing him. At that very location at the eastside of the river, camouflaged from the Persians was a division of Macedonian light infantry. Only their captain stood exposed holding two pole flags. One blue. The other red. As Alexander galloped past him, he snatched up the red flag. Which meant plan A.

Immediately, the Macedonian light infantry sprang from their hidden positions and darted across the river toward the shadowing Persian cavalry. Alexander and his cavalry veered east as his light infantry rushed past him toward the Persians. Suddenly, the head of the Persian cavalry found itself encircled by the Macedonian light infantry. Battle ensued. Meanwhile, the tail of the Persian cavalry kept watching Alexander's cavalry still moving north, unaware that Alexander had already turned east and was performing a switchback behind his infantry line.

Now, Alexander galloped full speed south toward the center of the Persian army. As he gained speed, so did his following cavalry. Hephaestion, by his side, was hungry as a wolf. There was seldom a greater elation than when these two-rode side by side, sensing a glorious kill. Alexander began to feel his erection.

At the Macedonian left flank, Parmenion's heavy phalanx was taking a pounding from the Persian phalanx. They were outnumbered two to one, yet Parmenion held his ground as best as he could, though the Persians slowly pushed forward. At that location, the Persians sensed victory, but what they hadn't realized that this was all a bluff.

The swing of the knife was elsewhere!

As Alexander and the front of his cavalry galloped past the tail of his cavalry, his troops now understood what Alexander was doing. Alexander kept charging forward while simultaneously urging the tail to follow the body. The sheer brilliance of this tactic gave his troops that extra boost of valor.

The northbound tail of the cavalry had camouflaged the southbound head of the cavalry!

Darius was certain that Alexander was still heading north. There was no reason to doubt it—he had seen him gallop in that direction, and his battlefield pages reported the same. But what he saw next was the face of Death itself!

Just as Alexander cleared his very tail of his cavalry, he veered sharp right. With lightning speed, he and his cavalry crossed the river on to the Persian center infantry, which suddenly found itself at the mercy of Alexander's galloping heavy warhorses. This was the very gap that Alexander had created through his maneuvers. The Persian cavalry had no clue where Alexander was, only a few at the head of the Persian cavalry realized what had just happened. But they were bogged down on all sides by the waiting Plan A infantry.

Alexander was now almost off the saddle, leaning into the battle. This was the glorious charge his father had dreamed of. His infantry at the center brought out their javelins, not pointing them at the Persians but holding them upright so that Alexander and his five hundred cavalrymen could snatch them up as they rode by. All of this happened in mere moments, as the Persians watched, realizing that all of Alexander's maneuvers had been pre-planned and perfectly executed. Alexander now owned the battle, it's every move.

The Persians looked back at Darrius and saw that Darrius had realized the same thing. And Darrius knew his infantry men were watching him, cursing him as he had not foreseen this brilliant move of Alexander.

As Alexander took to his full charge with the javelins in hand, he saw the Persians looking back at Darius, searching for answers. He could sense the Persians' growing sense of defeat. His staging was complete. What ensued was full thrust of the Macedonia cavalry into the arm pit of the Persian formation. Darius's cavalry had overreached its shadowing of Alexander and now it was useless.

The Macedons kept coming through the gap as a torrent of water through a failing dam. Alexander now was off the seat of the saddle. He had now come at striking distance of Darrius and threw his javelin at Darrius chariot. Darrius ducked and the javelin took his charioteer right off his feet, off the chariot to the ground. Such was the force of Alexanders throw. The Macedonian cavalry had Darrius at striking distance. Alexander had him at striking distance. A mere twenty yards. And then it would be all be over.

Darrius lost all courage, the seat of the waning Persian empire crumbled. Darrius took the reign of his chariot, not to charge but to turn and flee the battle.

Alexander knew he first had to clear of the potency of Darrius's army thus he turned south to the rear of the phalanx of the Persian army, where the bulk of the Persian strength lay. By now Alexander had a full erection. When most men's genitals would recede to their groins in the bloody mayhem, Alexander's was livid.

The infantry massacre that ensued bloodied the water downstream. All the jostling and warring made the Persians thirsty, only that they couldn't drink the bloodied thick river water. Cold and exhausted were the Persians. Parmenion and his heavy phalanx company drank their canteens and jostled for round two. News had reached both the armies that Darrius had fled the battlefield. So now the Persians knew the bloodied river was Persian blood flowing. Such a sickening sinking feeling. And sure enough, soon they saw Alexanders parrot feather at their rear. The Persians broke rank and began to flee the battle. The carnage began.

The battle ends. News spread that the Macedonians had captured Darius's mother, wife, and daughter. A bloodied Alexander went to the tent of Statira, Darius's daughter. He looked at the Macedonian guards, who responded, "It's all secured, my lord," with full admiration in their eyes. Only a son of a god could have accomplished what Alexander had done. Alexander enters the tent, and with perfect Persian accents says, "Your father is alive, I let him go ". With saying so he disrobes and without even wiping the stains of war blood or the smell of sweat and horse from his body, he begins to violate and enjoy the great Persian princess.

Thus begins the Greek shaming of the Persians.

Chapter 2

"Kamalaphuli er Biyeta"

326 BCE

They had slipped into the citadel from the main boulevard, through a bronze door that the night before had been closed and barred to the street. Unlike the main gate to the palace, which had been smashed and burned and used for archery in the drunken revel of the orgy, this smaller auxiliary door had been opened from within as it let on to a stair and corridor from the main hall, allowing access for the half-naked Macedonians to relieve themselves on the curb and gutter outside the citadel walls. That is to say, the soldiers used this doorway when they weren't pissing over the upper portico balustrades and down into the river.

As they approached the palace through the ransacked city streets—streets strewn with bodies of civilians and soldiers, rubble, and animals spaced at odd intervals—they heard voices from inside the broken front gates and cautiously entered a doorway to the right instead. It appeared that the enemy forces had commandeered a Pauravas war elephant, driving it down the broad avenue, which bisected the city and terminated here at this intersection with the palace gates.

Aarohan couldn't tell how the Greeks had managed to knock the gates down, but knowing elephant behavior well, he understood that being intelligent creatures, they would not let men run them into a wall of their own volition. As he crossed the street, he noticed that parts of the massive doors were charred and smoking, as were the hindquarters of the pachyderm and several burned-out wagons just behind the beast. He imagined that the interlopers had set the wagons ablaze to terrify the elephant into charging the gates. Although he didn't have time to consider what had transpired here under the cover of darkness, he and his men sprinted across the intersection as quickly as they could to avoid detection.

His Only thought was of Roshan. Aarohan was also unsure where the doorway led, but he needed only to gain entrance to the compound. He would do whatever he needed once inside.

Two curly haired barbarians lay drunk at the threshold as they approached, and he ordered their necks quietly broken and then drag inside the stairwell where his men deposited the bodies in a heap of limp limbs. They then closed the door behind them.

Very little light came to them now from the top of the stairway above as Aarohan considered what to do. He could not know what they would encounter once inside the palace. He pressed on and he and his coterie of a dozen picked men, ascended the stairs with swords drawn. They were almost certainly walking into the teeth of Eskander's (Alexander's) special guard, and they almost certainly would be killed, but he didn't count his life for much now if he could not rescue his daughter.

The wedding of his daughter to the prime minister's son in Kamalaphuli, the capital of the Pauravas kingdom, had been designed to shore up an alliance with the Gangaridai to provide a bulwark against the Macedonian menace. The rampaging Eskander, whose name they had learned years before as he relentlessly campaigned to the west, had made its fearful way thousands of leagues beyond the war front into the Boarder of the Ganges. Ever since he had smashed his eternal Persian foe and burned Persepolis to the ground, he had become known to the whole world, as well as insatiable in his desire for conquest. And yet for all his war lust, he had shrewdly turned the campaign into a business operation capable of extracting the loot and wealth of despoiled peoples and their lands without mercy and depositing them into the Greek kingdom.

But no one considered that the dreaded Eskander could make his way to the capital with such speed. After all, the warrior, King Puru, had assembled his army to march west to shore up the frontier, since their former adversary and neighbor Ambhi had aligned with Eskander. But who could have believed that the Greeks would strike so quickly at the heart of the Middle Kingdom, or travel to the center of the country from the battlefield so swiftly.

Even the night before, as Aarohan sat with the Prime Minister discussing their alliance over a bounty of food and gifts, they talked as if contact with the enemy was still months away. Even the astrologer, present for the evening, had claimed the stars were auspicious. However, Eskander must have decapitated Puru's army within days of his leaving the capital. And the avaricious marauders would quickly have discovered then that Puru had ordered the county's wealth hidden in Kamalaphuli, which precipitated their travels here, for his men could not do without their spoils and booty.

But 'the hows and the whys' of Eskander's advance mattered nothing to Aarohan now.

Last night as the wedding wound down, they heard the warning sound of the konka blast, indicating an enemy. At first the people in the wedding party, among whom were at least fifty newly married couples, continued in their festivities as if they hadn't heard the warning. Soon, however, reports came in of skirmishes along the outer township walls, dampening the celebration. The enemy was looking for a way into the city, but for the moment, the party comforted itself with the news that a large contingent of soldiers, along with heavy cavalry and archers, was stationed there.

As Aarohan had not come with an army but his core troop, he was not prepared to face the Greeks, yet took up rear guard to the east and so at the behest and pleadings of the Prime Minister he had taken up position across the river and to the east of the city. He felt his daughter was safe in the palace. He felt confident that the great Pauravas kingdom , their captital Kamalaphuli could withstand the foe at its gates, and certainly the citadel within the city was built for a siege.

He kissed his daughter then as he went, leaving her in the hands of her new husband and under the protection of his people. But by dawn he saw fires burning near the river, in a location which his spotters believed was within the walls of the citadel, and he knew he had to return to retrieve Roshan. He had been in many battles before as field marshal of the six-thousand strong elephant corps, but he had never felt the concern that he now felt to make his daughter safe.

His men had not yet reached the top of the stairs when they encountered the first guard. They killed him quickly, but killing a man in armor is not a quiet affair, and the sound of his sword and helmet striking the hard limestone floor alerted other guards. They poured down the corridor from the hall, where they had been sleeping off the revelry of the previous night.

What those Greeks faced now, as they ascended the stairs, was a dozen Nanda warriors, each bearing scars from repeated close combat. But this day, these men of the Gangaridai had entered a corridor they would not leave alive. And yet, they would not die quickly, nor would they die quietly. They fought with a fierceness they had never displayed before, spurred on by their general, who had begun to shout his daughter's name as he slaughtered whichever Greek came within his reach.

"Roshan!" He cried out, and the sound echoed in the chamber. "Roshan!" her name on his tongue was a call of a wolf to its cub. And with that sound in their ears his men slaughtered their own number in Greeks and then some, pushing Eskander's soldiers out from the corridor and into the main hall where the aftermath of last night's horror lay bare before them. Women in their torn and bloodied wedding dresses lay sprawled on the banquet tables in among the overturned prepared dishes and fruits, with the wedding gifts open and strewn throughout the room. At a quick glance most of the women seemed to still be alive, but the grooms to women lay dead on the floor. And more still, the mothers and father of the brides and grooms lay dead in heaps, still dressed all in their finery. A single old woman sobbed in the corner of the hall, but he could not hear her.

For the moment he stood in place, he began to notice other victims laying variously about the room, petrified to move from shock or terror. And as he turned his eyes over the carnage he saw several Greek men sit up then, naked on the long tables beside their victims.

He heard the weeping now, but he did not see his daughter.

Fury overtook him. He called her name again.

At that moment a group of archers poured in from the opposite stair and began pelting them with arrows. Aarohan watched an arrow pass by his head the way one would watch a gnat fly by. It spurred him to cry out again, "Roshan!" as he stabbed another Greek who had the audacity to approach him.

At least half a dozen Nanda warriors fell to the arrows before a detachment of armed and well-rested hoplites entered the hall through another door. Aarohan turned to face them with his remaining men but heard the clatter of swords behind him. He looked back in time to see the last of his soldiers fall to the swords of Greeks who had come up from behind, through the stairwell. Without a second thought, he charged toward them, killing several before he was forced to back away, slipping in the blood and gore that covered the floor. Battling down to one knee, the general was knocked unconscious by the butt of a sword from behind.

He awoke, dazed and bleeding, wondering why they had not killed him, to find his hands and feet bound by chains.

"You killed seven of my brothers," called out a voice in Persian.

Aarohan slowly responded, "Where is my daughter?" also in Persian.

"Do you know the penalty for killing a Macedonian?"

"Please, whoever you are, where is my daughter?" Aarohan asked, his voice was steady but filled with desperation.

"You should worry less about your daughter and more about how you're going to die."

"Her name is Roshan," Aarohan said, ignoring the taunt. "She's newly wed to the son of the Prime Minister. Please have mercy and decency for the women and the innocent and the royalty. Do you know where my daughter is?"

At this, Alexander paused. When he had killed the

charging son of the Prime Minister hours earlier, his bride had taken her own life. He didn't want to reveal the details—that he had been about to take her forcefully when she had taken a dagger from nowhere and, instead of attacking him, had chosen to end her own life rather than be violated

Alexander responded abruptly, without remorse, "Your daughter is dead. She took her own life. Pity. She was a beautiful thing."

Aarohan went silent. Numb.

Alexander continued, "I tried to reason with her, but she would not listen. I told her, I am Alexander." With these words he seemed to expect some sort of awe in the prisoner's eye. But if he was seeking a reaction, he would find none from Aarohan.

"Even the great princess of Persia kneeled and accepted me as king, god, and eventually... husband," Alexander added, hoping to provoke a response.

"You killed my daughter," Aarohan replied, his voice without life but filled with pain.

His calmness enraged Alexander. "I, conqueror of the Greek Isles, Pharaoh of Egypt, subduer of the great Persian..." Alexander began to list his many titles, his rage growing as he spoke.

"Aaaaaa!!!" Wailed Aarohan in disgust. Outside had turned twilight hour into night. As if His life had turned night.

But the warlord ignored him, and continued recounting his regent and divine titles, and then, almost on a whim, turned to tell his retinue to carry in the dead body of Aarohan's daughter. He watched closely for his prisoner's reaction as they brought her in.

Seeing her lifeless body Aarohan slumped in silent grief. He made no sound as they lay her before him, but the hall full of men and Nanda princesses could feel his wail reach the very heavens!

"Now you see," Alexander said feeling satisfied that he had crushed the spirit in the seemingly unconquerable man. He walked to the edge of the hall in front of the large balcony looking east toward the Indian plains.

"The son of Zeus . . ." he began saying as he turned to consider Aarohan again, but as he turned, he glimpsed the man whom he thought he had broken completely, take the first of two summersaults toward him.

As Aarohan rolled forward, he managed to pull his arms around to the front—a trick he had learned in his yogi training. He somersaulted again, for he could not walk with the ankle chains, and lunged at Alexander. Catching him around the neck with his wrist chains, Aarohan swung his bound legs out over the balustrade, choking the warlord with his entire weight against the railing. With all his might, Aarohan pulled on the chains around Alexander's neck and yelled out in perfect Greek for the first time, "What does the Greek god have to say now? Speak! Speak!"

The grieving father, Aarohan, wanted to end things right there, right then.

But others responded. Seleucus quickly took a battle axe and rushed at Aarohan. With a swift motion, Aarohan jumped off the balcony, pulling all his weight onto Alexander's neck. Seleucus hammered at Aarohan's chains to save Alexander, and when they finally broke, Aarohan fell fifty feet or more into the river below, disappearing into the depths of the night.

Alexander, the mortal 'God', gasped for breath. When he recovered, he screamed, "Who is that wretched man?!"

One of the Persian generals responded, "My lord, he is the commander of the Gangaridai Elephant Corps. He is Aarohan."

Alexander, still catching his breath, croaked, "Bring him to me! Now!"

Rage filled Alexander's entire being. The sheer dare—the audacity of this man called Aarohan. A dare that mirrored his own!

Chapter 3

Rage / Raga

Fall,326 BCE

Alexander looked up to survey the sky. Harsh late afternoon sun. Clouds hanging in cotton puff formation. A crow caws and flies across his vision field. Pesky crow always caws to mock you. Bad omen.

'How dare this land mock me '. Raged Alexander within. It's been three weeks since the Gangariddi general escaped. Escape he may, but he shall be found, must be found. It is not the escape itself, but the manner of the exit. The prisoner set himself free under the nose of his cohort and himself. In the process making Alexander imprisoned in the audacity of Aarohan's dare. And since the dare made the Great look like the weak, this event was turning into stuff of legend. So, this story has to be changed and changed fast.

Alexander looked at the interrogation master. A Purava captain was strewn spread eagle on the ground. All his limbs tied with rope looped around four stakes driven in the ground in a square area and linked to the harness of two horses at opposite ends. People in these regions have never seen such torture method and for sure Alexander wanted to make a shocking point. He would set precedence to numerous future conflicts where the victor would not only relish being the winning party more so revel in the humiliation of the defeated, not only the army, but specifically the murdering and raping of the population. Followed by enslavement and bondage trade. There were minor examples of such depravity in history prior, but Alexander was the one who would reimagine such cruelty on an industrial scale. Alexander was the progenitor of Kali Yuga.

"Where is your general?". Alexander demanded of the tied up prisoner.

"I do not know", answered the Purava captain. The translator translated.

"Wrong answer " . Alexander gave the signal.

The horses were struck. They galloped. And the purava captain was torn limb to limb, as he screamed his life out of his self.

Alexander turned to Hephaestion. "You! Captain of my bodyguards? Are you? Then let no blade of grass grow until you find the whereabouts of that Gangariddi". Alexander mounted Buchaphelus and rode away.

Hephaestion was furious. Alexander, his lover, never addressed him in such formal way. Hephaestion turned around to the rest expanse of the field, where fifty other Purava citizens where tied spread eagle on the ground. He gave the order to tear up the next three prisoners. The screams. The agony. The Horror!

The rest of the prisoners were tortured by just hearing the screams. Few started to scream, "I know where he is ". "He is Gangariddi. He went east....". Hephaestion went randomly around tearing up the prisoners.

Hephaestion asks for a map that has Gangariddi located. He is handed over a parchment. Hephaestion glosses over it and yell's back at the retinue, "If I throw up on this useless piece of leather, I'd have a more accurate map. Go talk to the locals, kill them, love them, bribe them, fuck their goats if it pleases them, or give your rear end for their pleasure, I need more accurate maps. I will skin you alive if I don't get an accurate map by tomorrow sun rise"

A retinue comes forward with an old fakir. "Lord, this sage has something to say to you..."

The fakir comes forward with piercing eyes, "I can tell you where that scumbag of a Gangariddi went". A translator translated for him.

"What do you want, wise man and why should we believe you?" Hephaestion asked, like wolf sniffing out the air around a lamb.

"I will tell you where to look for him, but what will be my recompense?"

"Your recompense would be that you will have your head on your shoulder and walk out of this tent in one piece ", squared Hephaestion.

The old man gave a crooked look with a raised eyebrow, "Look lad, you can kill me right now. But I saw how your master spoke to you. I'd say you are projecting your situation. It is you who has to keep his head together with his body. Look I am advance in age, I do not care if I live or not. If you give me what I want, I will give you what you need lad."

"What is it that you want? Old man." Hephaestion softened his stance.

"I want my ancestral land to be given back to me, so that my children and grandchildren can have what is rightly theirs. The governor of this land, the bridegroom's father to the escaped General's daughter, confiscated my farms lands through treachery. These thuggish nobles are nothing but dishonorable thieves. I'd see them die for I care more this roach in your tent", with that the old man, with his walking staff pierced a crawling roach on the ground of the tent.

"What is the guarantee that your provided information is worthwhile?" Hephaestion took interest.

"I will travel with your army, search party and if I am wrong, you can kill me", answered the old man in matter of fact way.

" …mmm… fair enough…. ", Hephaestion turned to his retinue. "Give this old man the land he seeks, after he has proven his salt." Hephaestion returned his gaze to the old man. "If you are right and deliver this Aarohan, you will not only get the land that you seek, But we shall double it . We Macedonians are a generous ruler and compensate well our loyal subjects".

"So where is this Aarohan now?"

The old fakir came forward, took his staff to the map that wrapped around a standing frame and pointed. "Your maps are terrible. But this is where the whereabouts of the prisoner that you seek".

Hephaestion stood up, "But you are asking us to go south along this Indus River. We heard Gangariddi is to the east".

"You heard wrong," the old man retorted, "Tell me how large is the nation of Gangariddi? Any large nation needs a river to sustain itself. Tell me, did you not hear that Gangariddi is by a mighty river? This is that mighty river. All major cities here in Bharat are by rivers and so is Pataliputra. It's to the south about two hundred krosh away.

"Look if my back permits, I will ride with your search party to the south to show them the way myself."

Hephaestion signaled his captain, "Take this man to the land he claimed is his, make a decree. Tomorrow, we ride south".

The next day the search party of five hundred men

began their march along the western side of Indus River following the advice of the old man.

"It would be better for your army to be on the protected side of the river, rather than risk exposure to the Riddis on the eastern side."

Alexander with Hephaestion along with the search party moved rapidly south. The old man advised them that the city of Pataliputra was a nine-day march from where they were, and that they should camp from the city three days out and wait for the rest of thirty thousand strong army catch up to them. They could use their base to send out smaller search parties to hunt down the Riddi general. The old man translated all local intelligence to Alexander and his core team. The city of Pataliputra was prepping for war, but not yet certain of the Greeks' whereabouts. The Indians think the Greeks are still in Taxila.

On the sixth day Alexander set up camp and waited for his army's news of the march. He was beside himself with anger that no progress had been made to track down the Riddi general.

He was pacing his tent, expecting news.

"Sire, the scout from the south has arrived"

Alexander waved the retinue to bring in the scout to his tent. The scout bowed and then reported, "My lord, I have gone to the mouth of the river all the way to the south sea. Apart from a few large villages along the way on the bank of the river, there is no city, or any city called 'Palibothra'. We have also extensively asked the locals about Palibothra. They were all dumbfounded, and they laughed at us. Some say we are looking at the wrong river. Such a city does not exist on the Indus!"

Alexander signaled to his retinue, "Summon the old man."

The other retinue came in, "Sire , we have a Page from Kamalapur" . "Show him in" , Alexander barked!

The Page came in, kneeled the custom honors, and handed over a sealed parchment. Alexander teared it open and read the content. He turned red as he was reading it. All within the tent wished that they were not there, as they knew Alexander was about to have an extreme flare up. Alexander yelled out, "Drag that old man here, NOW."

The retinue who was sent to summon the old man came rushing in. Trembling. "Sire, the old man is missing. He is not in his tent. The guards ...."

" Aaagh ..." Alexander wailed out, while taking his sword and pushing aside the retinues. He, along with his entourage walked to the tent where the old man was kept. The guards seeing Alexander kneeled down, "Sire, forgive us, we do not understand how our ward simply has vanished....

Alexander knocked the kneeling guards with the hilt of his swords with force, "Take these fools out of my sight ..."

Alexander went inside the tent. Not a sign of its inhabitant. "Who was the last person, that saw the old man?"

"The meal server"

"Fetch him"

Alexander examined the inside of the tents; he then saw a bag, which he emptied. Certain loose white hair, apparent false skin made of morphed and colored flour, other articles of the facial and skin features of the old man fell off.

The meal server came in, trembling. 'I know nothing sire….' He began to plead. Alexander waved him shut. 'When did you last serve his meal?'

'About an hour ago, I was to take his plates in a moment or so now'

Alexander looked around, there were no dishes or plates or mugs.

The guard then sank even further saying to the meal server, I thought I saw you come out of the tent with the meal tray about half an hour ago. "

Alexander yelled out, 'That old man or whomever he is, he only has half an hour head start. GO find him.! '

Seleucus picked up the parchment that came from Kamalapur, he read the content. He now realizes how they have been duped in the past six days. The parchment stated there was even a mightier river to the east, called 'Ganga' , but of course ! Gangariddi, Duh! And that Palibothra was on the banks of this river.

Everyone radiated out to look for the old man, yet

they could not find him. It is as if he simply vanished.

Chanakkya took out the tilting yoke and harnessed the bull. His aunt said, 'Rama be praised, its providence that you showed up today and you are taking the load of your uncle. You are such a good young lad. '

Chanakkya began to tilt the fields, while the Macedonians foot soldiers searched the villages around him. None of the soldiers came to the young farmer who was tilting the soil . Had they paid attention they would have seen that this young lad of a farmer was very bad at tilting. But that didn't matter, for Chanakkya was master in creating props for disguise and applying it that non could discern his disguises and assumed gaits.

Chanakkya was in fact, the Old Man!

Chapter 4

Fall to Rise

It had been three days since the disappearance of Aarohan. Did he actually survive the fall? Everyone assumed that the general had drowned after falling from the citadel into the dark waters below. The hoplites left no stone unturned in their search for the daring escapee, for the raging warlord Alexander would not—could not— accept the humiliation Aarohan had dealt him. How dare he!

But Chanakkya felt differently about his old mentor. Aarohan couldn't have gone out this way. No one had found his body. Yes, the river's current was strong, and it was highly probable that he had been swept away. But Aarohan was a champion swimmer. Then again, his hands had been tied. But then again, Aarohan had taught Chanakkya how to swim like a dolphin with his hands bound. No. As long as no corpse was found, Aarohan must still be alive.

Where would his mentor seek refuge when the entire Greek army were looking for him. Alexander promised an Olive Garden estate in Macedonia, to whomever could bring him either the body of the general or the general captured alive.

Aarohan would have sought a diversion. Yes, a diversion to lead the trackers off his trail. These Greeks were ruthless, but they had no understanding of the local terrain or geography. It would be a geographical diversion

But where will he seek his diversion?

Where would a grieving father who had lost his daughter seek his diversion?

But of course! He would go back to his daughter. He would take possession of her body, conduct the proper funerary rites. Aarohan would never give up on that!

Chanakkya headed towards the citadel. Who would take care of all the dead bodies. The priests. Then he should go to the temple, that's where Aarohan would go.

Since he had grown up in this region, Chanakkya knew the priestly class at the temple. He made his way through the villages around the citadel, where the hoplites were conducting door-to-door searches. A patrol stopped him, and before the captain could interrogate him, Chanakkya spoke in perfect Persian, "You should proceed and not waste your time with me. I am a commander with Ambhi's army." He produced a leather parchment accordingly. "I am working with my men to find the escapee as well. Good luck."

Once inside the temple, Chanakkya inquired, "I'm looking for someone who might be searching for a relative who recently passed away in the citadel."

The abbot looked up. "There have been so many who've come by. It's been terrible."

"Everyone is in the great hall. Ask one of our eight priests," the abbot added.

Chanakkya entered the great hall, where a few hundred dead bodies lay, being prepared for the final funerary pyre.

He walked through the aisles of the wailing living, and the peaceful dead.

He approached one of the priests but wasn't sure how to ask about the princess's body without attracting attention.

Then Chanakkya noticed something there was actually nine priests in the hall. Chanakkya observed each priest from a distance. They were consoling the grieving, providing the funerary props, and then moving on to the next. Except for one, who took his time processing a particular female corpse. Chanakkya went up to the priest, 'I have come to claim this body, but I would be extremely happy if you would accompany me and help me with the preparation of the ceremony and the pyre for this royal lady' the Priest looked up and bowed his head in agreement.

With the help of volunteers and the priest, Chanakkya moved the body to the designated funerary area, navigating through guards and showing his credentials as necessary.

The pyres were set up along the river where Aarohan had fallen two nights ago. Chanakkya let the priest choose the pyre for the body. The smell of burning bodies and pyres filled the air, mingling with the wails of the grieving

The pyre was lit. The priest went around the pyre with a flame and alighting the tinder that was set. Chanakkya cried. The priest had no expression.

The corpse burned and both men looked on. The pyre structure collapsed, only then the priest let down his stiff shoulder and slumped into resignation.

Chanakkya said softly "I will so dearly miss Roshan. I am so sorry for your loss Guru. But I am so glad to see you again. I was fearful I may have lost you in your fall." The Priest looked up, still a very stoic expression. He did not answer.

Chanakkya continued. "Guru do remain with the temple priest for another week. I will, with my credential claim that you are a priest from Taxila, and that you are here to help with slain bodies. You can take refuge at the temple. I will draw a diversion and lead the Dhoni's to the south. Once that happens you will have a relatively safer passage as a priest travelling east."

For the first time, Aarohan spoke: "Do not attempt to kill Eskander. He is mine to take."

"Yes, my guru," Chanakkya replied.

Chapter 5

Never a Land Conquered without Treachery within

Munshara paced. He looked at the parchment his spy had handed him. "Go on," Munshara demanded, eager to know everything. The news that his long-time rival had been completely defeated by the Dhonies from the west was almost too good to be true. As he paced, he contemplated how best to use this phenomenal news to his advantage. Aarohan would surely be dislodged from his position as chief minister to the Nanda king. All Munshara had to do was play his cards right—ridicule the chief minister into resignation and disgrace. Dhana Nanda was an egotistical king, and all Munshara needed to do was stroke his pride, convincing him to remove Aarohan from the royal court. Once that happened, the rest of the ministers would fall in line and support the rising star—Munshara himself.

But that was only one part of the sutra. The main concern was what to do about the Greek menace approaching from the west. The great Persian Empire had fallen to this young warrior king. Not only had it fallen, but Darius had been chased around Central Asia like a rat in a wheat field, pursued by a rabid fox.

His spies had informed him that, this lad called Eskander was ruthless to the indigenous rulers, but also knew how to forge alliances. He had set up a ruling class in Egypt with the help of local collaborators, he had set up a ruling class in Persia with the help of local collaborators, and it is only natural he would set up a ruling class here in India with would be local collaborator. Now who is going to be this local collaborator?

Munshara had a broad smile on his face.

He called in his retinue. "Go to the palace and request an audience with the king. Tell his chief of staff that it is a matter of urgent national importance. He then turned to his valet. "Bring me my battle gear and prepare my travel cohort with provisions."

With all his pomp and entourage, Munshara rode to the palace in Pataliputra, his banner flying high, the clamor of hoofbeats and sparks flying from beneath the horses' feet. His lead crier shouted for the crowd to disperse. Munshara wanted the denizens to know he was on his way to the palace with important news, something sensational about to transpire. He changed the color atop his banner to signal "Urgent Mission & Declaration." Children in the streets ran after the procession, eager to catch the first scoop of whatever sensation Munshara would bring and be the first to relay the sensational story. Munshara s entourage went through the main gateway of the palace, with an air of urgency. The crier made it a point to throw his weight around the security guards . 'We must see the sovereign now. It is a matter of national security', pushing aside the captain in charge

The chief of staff appeared to respond to the commotion. 'the sovereign is not available right now.'

Munshara stepped forward and motioned to whisper into the chief of staff's ear. The chief nodded and escorted Munshara into the main Darbar. The theatrics ensured that everyone in the procession and its audience could imagine the worst about Eskander and his army.

Munshara began, with only him and chief of staff in audience of Dhana Nanda the king. 'My sources tell me, Aarohan along with his daughter has been killed by the Dhonis. Aarohan's jawan has been decimated. Moreover, the Paurava have fallen, Kamalaphuli is now under Greek rule.'

Dhana Nanda paced. Turning to chief of staff, 'Do fetch Jotayu, we need to mobilize the cavalry , the infantry, and the archers. '

The chief of staff hesitated, clearly reluctant to leave while Munshara was still present and the conversation unfinished. Munshara glared at him, "What are you waiting for? You heard your king!" The chief of staff left, somewhat flustered.

Munshara continued, "My spies tell me, Eskander is already on the march eastward. As your chief of intelligence, I have developed a strategy. But we need to move fast my lord. If you would allow me to explain"

Dhana Nanda, somewhat rattled by the fast-moving events, was looking for an immediate plan of action than wait for his assembly of ministers to convene. Even more so, since his most able minister Aarohan, general of the elephant corps, had been killed.

Dhana Nanda nodded, "Go on."

Munshara proceeded, "I have prepared a draft of document, this will buy us some time. So that we may prepare our forces."

With that, Munshara handed over the document to Dhana Nanda. As the king was reading the parchment, Munshara continued, "Fear not, this is not what we intend to follow through, this is merely a diversional tactic."

The document read so,

" **To the esteemed conqueror of the four horizons, Alexander of Macedonia, Pharaoh of Egypt, King of Persian kings.**

From Dhana Nanda the great lord of Gangaridai, Regent of the Arakans, purveyor of Meghalaya

We congratulate you on your great victories over

the ancient stale civilizations of Egypt and Persia. You bring forth mankind to a new era.

Like you, we have united our lands under a youthful leadership, and we command full control over our territories with an iron fist.

We recognize you have a vast army to feed and support their families. We want to assist in your conquest east and you will find in us a willing partner.

In that regard, I have instructed my minister of revenue to set aside four sixteenths of our taxes at your disposal, provided we come to an agreement and an amenable term of peace between our two great nations! The bearer of this letter has full authority to negotiate on my behalf. "

Dhana Nanda's face flushed red as he finished reading the letter. "One fourth of our revenue? This is treasonous! My subjects would never accept this. We'll have unrest..."

"My lord," Munshara interrupted, "as I said, this is a ruse. It's only a diversionary tactic."

Dhana Nanda paced the room, his thoughts racing. "Leave the document with me. I want to discuss this further with others."

"I'm afraid I cannot do that, my lord," Munshara replied firmly. "Secrecy is crucial if this ruse is to succeed. I fear there may be collaborators within our court who might spy on behalf of Eskander and reveal our strategy. Your most trusted general, Aarohan, is dead. His army, the best among the Riddis and Putris, is decimated. No, we have to move fast. We have to move now!'

Dhana Nanda straightened, realizing the gravity of the situation. "Very well, proceed as you see fit."

Then he paused, then placed a hand on Munshara's shoulder. "You have always had the Nanda's' best interests at heart. If you manage to handle the Dhonies and repel them from our lands, I will grant you one-sixteenth of my territories for your services."

"Sire, you honor me!" Munshara exclaimed, his voice brimming with ceremonial loyalty. "I would assist you even if it were for sixteen paisa. I do it as I hold you as my dearest king. Allow me my leave so that I may accomplish thy bidding'.

Munshara ceremoniously knelt, folding his right arm over his left chest, then stood with purpose. He turned sharply on his heel and left Dhana Nanda's presence with urgency.

Theatrics!

Chapter 6

Double Headed Serpent

Munshara was smiling—a smile of satisfaction at what providence had delivered. This might actually expedite the execution of his grand plan. If there were ever a spymaster who saw opportunity in the face of calamity, Munshara considered himself an avowed disciple of that notion. For him, the path was clear. Why wouldn't Alexander agree to his offer? In essence, he was offering the kingdom on a platter. With the resolute Aarohan out of the way, taming the rest of the ministers would be easy. He would simply use the argument that Aarohan's methods had cost him his life, while Munshara's superior methods would ensure peace. Little did they know that such peace was not peace at all, but a veil for bondage and tyranny.

As long as Munshara had regency through Alexander, he cared nothing for the people of the land. Why should he? Was there ever a tyrant who cared about the land or its people? He had watched the Nandas decimate the wealth of the land through over-taxation. Now it was his turn. And since he was the most able in deception and politics, he thought it only right that he established a dynasty—the Shara dynasty.

By the river of Yamuna, where there would be so many battles and dynasties vying for power. But here was Munshara, setting the precedents of all that was to follow. Kali Yuga begins at the advent of Alexander marching into Asia, setting up the first military industrial complex of constant stream of revenue through warring.

He paced the tent, awaiting the delegation sent by Alexander. He was pensive yet eager for this encounter, like a fox already inside the chicken coop, relishing how much he would gain from his ploy.

The Greeks entered the tent.

It was Seleucus, Ptolemy, and a few other hoplites of centurion status, all with their right hands resting on their belts, ready to draw their swords at the slightest provocation.

Seleucus spoke, 'You are alone?'

Munshara spread his arms wide. "Yes, I am. And I'm the only one you need." He gestured toward the banquet table, lavishly laid out with drinks and roast meats of various games. "Help yourselves, Honorables."

The Greeks hesitated.

Munshara smiled, he went about thrusting his finger in the middle of all dishes and sampling them ceremoniously.

'You need not trust me, and I need not trust you. But that does not mean we can't enjoy finer things in life in each other's company. Come now, treat yourselves. If these are poisoned, I would be joining you in the life after and you can all kill me a second time!'

The Greeks burst into boisterous laughter.

All dug in, as the Greeks were famished after a long ride.

For the next fifteen moments all ate, drank, and eyed each other up.

"So, Indian," Seleucus began, "why have you called for this parley?"

Munshara stood and pulled a sealed parchment from within his robes.

'This is for your master, from our king. But you may read it now, for our king has given me that authority to negotiate at will.'

Seleucus broke the seal and quickly read through the letter. He then handed it to Ptolemy, who also read it.

Ptolemy spoke next. "That's a generous offer your king is making. But why should we settle for a quarter of your revenue when we can have half after we conquer you? We've developed a habit of conquering."

Munshara had a smirky smile, 'you Greeks should be more ambitious. I will give you three fourths of our current revenue for the next ten years.'

The Greeks were taken aback.

"Yes, my lords," Munshara continued, "you heard me right. Three-fourths of our revenue for the next ten years. That will set you, and your future generations, for life. It will also give you the means you need to push eastward—perhaps as far as Siam or even China."

'And your king is going to be alright with that?' Asked Seleucus.

Munshara looked at everyone in the eye, with almost a smile he replied, 'Who said the King will remain the king'. This was said more as a statement then a question, with a chill humor that gave pause and admiration to the Greeks. The statement translated more like, 'You Greeks don't understand politics as I do.'

"The way I see it," Munshara went on, "this is how it will unfold. You will take this generous offer to your young king. He will know that he can have everything without ever needing to wage a war. He will have unfettered access to our military assets, including our elephants and jawans. He will become the Shahen Shah, the King of Kings, in India and Persia."

'In return, you will not interfere with whatever and whomever sits on the Indian throne.'

The Greeks were speechless. They had come to strike a hard bargain with the threat of conquest, only to be handed an offer beyond their wildest dreams.

Munshara stood up. "Carry this parchment from Dhana Nanda to your king, Alexander. And take this unsigned document from me as well."

He paused, gesturing to the table. "Please, rest well. Enjoy our hospitality—food, women, or even boys—whatever pleases you. Stay as long as you like."

"I, on the other hand," he said, his voice dripping with smugness, "Have to leave you to your pleasures, for, I have a king to dispose of."

And with that, Munshara exited the tent, leaving the Greeks astonished.

Chapter 7

Manu

Part 1

Despair

Why does one even breathe… incessantly? What is the point when there is no need?

Why does the heart keep beating… incessantly? What is the point when there is no need?

Why do I have awareness? Even being awake is sorrowful. Can I stop just being to exist?

She didn't have to die like this.

The slumped body lay on the moss bed as it rained.

Subconsciously, he had wandered into this tree cave beneath a great banyan tree, where the moss bed had grown. That had been about a moon ago, deep in the jungles of the Arakan Mountain range. Water trickled down all around him. All the insects had disappeared because of the deluge—the trail of black ants, the millipedes, the beetles, and countless other insects he had played with as a child—memories long forgotten—the critters had vanished when the rain set in. Heavy downpour now. Thunder. The only creatures that had emerged were the slow-moving earthworms and the even slower snails. The chirping of crickets had been replaced by the croaking of forest frogs.

Aarohan awaited. He awaited death.

But Nature has a way of healing even the most despaired soul. The Banyan tree had taken this man creature into its womb. Once, as a fetus, he had been embraced by the warmth of his mother's womb. Now, as a middle-aged man, he lay again, embraced in the womb of this great Banyan tree. Three centuries ago, another guest in a similar state had found solace beneath this tree—a man by the name of Siddhartha. But Aarohan knew nothing of that story. Only a few enlightened monks knew of it, and even fewer knew the legendary Banyan tree's location. The embrace to a grown man, similar to that of a child in the womb, was what the banyan tree felt like to Aarohan. His soul began to recuperate, though he didn't realize it then. The tree was not the only thing that gave some sense of life to Aarohan. A calf elephant would sometime nudge him and leave some ground nuts that the elephant had herself foraged. All his life Aarohan reared and trained elephants, but he never experienced such an act by elephants. More so by a calf. He was taken aback. There are so many mysteries left in this world, if one would only look.

He closed his eyes, not knowing if it would be for the last time.

He remembered his daughter, the day she was born. How he had held her when her mother died, when she was only two. How he had resolved to give her the best. But how he had failed her! The image of her limp body was etched in his memory forever. Why had he put her in that situation? For what end?

Something nudged his cheek. He barely opened his eyes—it was the trunk of the calf elephant, urging him to eat.

It would have been fascinating if his circumstances had been different. He closed his eyes again, hoping death would take him. His mind drifted back to when he had faced the full court of the despotic Nanda king, Dhana Nanda. He had pleaded with the king to take note of the western front. He had begged for the chance to lead an army against Eskander, to meet his martyrdom. But he had been ridiculed, first by his political and military rival Munshara, and then by the king himself.

Munshara had taunted, "Why should we listen to you? Is there anyone here who would second your opinion? Maybe your captain? Oh wait, your captain is dead. Perhaps your lieutenants? Oh no, they're dead too! In fact, all your company of soldiers are dead. Wonder why? Maybe they had too much faith in their commander?" The jeers kept coming.

Aarohan paid no attention to the vile tongue

haranguer. He tried his best to reason with the King. Since the time he had lost his daughter, nuances of politics had begun to escape him. He said, "My lord, please listen to my reasons, even the great Persian king Darius fell to this barbaric Eskander, we should prepare the nation for this coming calamity."

Munshara saw his opening and knew exactly how to stoke the King's ego, "Our king is no Darius, he is far superior, no he is supreme! People thought high of you, they once called you the Bir, the ultimate hero of the armed forces, though I knew better. I say you reek of fear, our Sovereign is far mightier than you ever actually gave him credit for. Why should he cower over the boy Eskander? He commands two hundred thousand infantry, eighty thousand cavalry, eight thousand war chariots, and most importantly six thousand war elephants. And now you say to give you command of the army? On what ground? You, who couldn't even protect his own daughter on her wedding night! What shame!".

To that Aarohan lost control, he took out his dagger in a flash, but Munshara was expecting so, as a matter of fact he was hoping so. He was never Aarohan's match in martial arts. But he was looking for Aarohan to commit.

"There, my lord, you see? What a hot-headed general this is! Bah! Is it not a cardinal sin to draw one's arms in the presence of the sovereign?"

Dhana Nanda needed to show his presence. "Aarohan, your past is light, but your future is night. I decree that, based on the events that has transpired , that you have fallen from my royal favor . Now leave this blessed & gracious court."

The rest of the courtiers began to chant, "long live the King, long live Munshara, Aarohan be gone."

Something nudged Aarohan again—it was the calf elephant. He barely opened his eyes. No, he had not died. He looked down and saw the pile of ground nuts the calf had left him. He still couldn't understand this creature's behavior. Slowly, he ate a few bites. Soon, he heard the trumpeting of an alpha bull elephant, and the calf scurried away.

Aarohan closed his eyes. Is he hallucinating all this?

His mind drifted once more. He relived the moment he left the court. His protégé, Chanakkya, had stood by his side, clearly saddened and disturbed. To soothe his long-time mentor, Chanakkya had said, "Guru, they do not understand... Will you lead us? Your regiment remains loyal to you."

Aarohan stopped. Tired. Exhausted. Drained. He said to Chanakkya, "Will you listen to what I have to say? Our nation is in great peril. We must rise above these petty squabbles. I want to avenge my daughter's murder. But the only thing holding me back is my concern for what's to come."

"Yes, my guru," Chanakkya had responded.

"Then listen. Your first and only job is to search for an alternate king—a true king. Things will get worse before they get better. So do not engage in the matters of the now but set in motion the matters for the king to come. Perhaps the boy Chandragupta, whom you've taken under your wing."

"And remember, never expose yourself the way I did today. You know what I mean."

With those words, Aarohan had parted ways with Chanakkya. He hadn't bothered to return to his home or his estates, knowing they would be confiscated after he fell from the king's favor. The lenders and prospectors were no doubt tearing his property apart by now. But in many ways, it didn't matter. He wanted to leave this wretched place— leave Pataliputra. He needed to go deep within Gangaridai and beyond. He needed to understand... the soul of his country. For nothing else would answer the call to stand against Eskander.

The crickets were back. The moon is shining now through the canopy of the forest. Heavy is the air laden with humidity. Aarohan could hear the deep snorting of the Alpha bull elephant.

He drifted again.

Then it began to rain

Day came. It still rained

Night came. And it rained

The grand hall of the wedding ceremony. Dark and gloomy, with a fire lit in the fireplace at the far end of the hall. Aarohan slowly walked to the shape of a figure lying on the floor. It is so painful, frightfully painful to realize what you will see, even before you see it.

Aarohan wanted to yell, 'No no no, take it back' but he couldn't even open his jaw for, there was a huge lump in the shape of grief within his throat.

Roshan's limp body lay on the cold stone floor in a pool of blood. Her hand visibly red with blood where she pressed it on her side wound before she died. Her face lit by the dancing flame.

Aarohan, crying silent grief, walked towards his daughter, kneeling to pick her body up. And then suddenly, Roshan opened both her eyes, stretched her bloodied hand towards her father.

She uttered the words in whispers without emotion nor pain,

'Save your Daughter!'

Aarohan woke up from his nightmare with a jolt. He woke to a deep vibration. That was a call only a few mahouts knew off. An elephant was in deep distress. The herd was calling out. He then distinguished the call of a calf elephant. Was this the calf elephant that was feeding him all this while? Aarohan for the first time since the day at the court had a sense of intent. He crawled out of his tree cave. It was raining profusely. He walked or rather stumbled along the thickets to the source of the commotion. The ground was muddy, sticky and sludgy. He began to guess what had happened. A calf elephant was trapped in the mud. The moment he realized so, he began to run. Probably the calf had very limited time. It must have stuck into the quicksand and was sinking fast. Aarohan began to run faster. Soon he came upon brooding shapes in the dark. It was an elephant herd. All silent, though all creating that heavy vibration. Aarohan moved past and between the elephants. Then he happened upon it. His baby elephant, the elephant that was feeding him all this time, was stuck in a huge pool of mud. Why did he think it was his baby elephant? Why did he think it was his baby? A sea of emotion welled up within him.

Aarohan knew what to do. He went in search of a palm tree. He found one. Using a wedge-shaped stone, he peeled a stiff bark off it. He went to the muddy pool. Near the calf elephant he began to dig out a ramp with the stiff bark using it as a spade. He had no strength, but he wouldn't stop now. He kept at it.

All the elephants stood silent, watching what Aarohan was doing. They knew what he was doing. And he knew that they knew. The calf elephant stopped its trumpeting, in suspense, hoping Aarohan would free its life from drowning in this mud pool. From the corner of his eye, he picked up an unusually large size of an elephant. He stopped for a moment to look up.

There it was. The alpha bull elephant. Standing twice the height of any of the females of the heard. With his ground hugging white tuskers. Aarohan went back to digging. All the while thinking, so this was "Manu"!

For a decade now he had heard of a legend of an unusually large bull elephant in the Arakan. Many trappers sought to capture it. They spoke of its intelligence, cunning and ferocity. On many occasions the bull had rounded up or charged the trappers even before they could set up their traps. He marveled at Manu's size. The bull was by far & significantly larger than even its African cousins.

Aarohan kept digging the ramp, throwing stones into the mud, which quickly sank. But after he threw enough, the stones began to hold. There was hope. He steadied the foundation of the ramp's slope at the edge of solid ground, then went off to collect vines, weaving them into a sturdy rope. Time was running out. The calf's hind legs and back had disappeared into the pool of mud; only its front legs remained above. Aarohan kept weaving the ropes as fast as he could.

A good portion of the night had passed. Full moon peeping through the forest canopy. Aarohan thought he now had sufficient amount of rope. He lassoed the rope around the front legs of the elephant calf, tightening it. And now he needed to pull. But pull he might, the baby elephant wouldn't budge. This was hopeless. He looked around at the elephant herd was still there, watching. The mother elephant nearby. The bull silent. Aarohan went to the mother elephant. Wild creature it was. It could kill Aarohan with the swing of its tusk. But over his long career as an elephant trainer and elephant rider, he knew never to show fear or tension in front of an elephant. To live as a mahout was to hold your ground with the elephant—his master had taught him that. He wondered. Wasn't that also true for life?

He wrapped the vine rope around the mother's trunk and guided it to pull by his hand. The mother elephant understood. The pull on the rope stiffened. Yet the baby elephant didn't budge. Aarohan pushed his body against the mother elephant in the direction of the pull. The mother elephant gave a jerk of a pull. The baby elephant came half out of the sticky mud pull, but gave out a trumpeting call out of sheer pain it felt around its chest and shoulder. Aarohan flattened the cut of the tug by lassoing the baby elephant many times, but that didn't diminish the pain of the skin cutting vine rope. This is getting hopeless. Then Aarohan witnessed something that he had never seen in his life or ever will thereafter. "Manu" the alpha bull came charging from the opposite direction of the mud pool and jumped into the position right behind the baby elephant. For a moment, the bull was airborne! How could that be? Aarohan never saw an elephant leap like that. There was a big splash, or one should say a big thud. As Manu landed, he ploughed his huge tuskers underneath the baby elephant's hinds and flung the baby out of the mud. The baby landed onto solid ground, bruised and yelping. But it was free of the mud pool. In its place now lay Manu.

Aarohan sat on the grass, exhausted as the sun began to rise. He couldn't believe what he had just witnessed. The Bull had sacrificed its life for the baby elephant.

Manu did not move much. But it kept making its deep rumble noise . The other elephant understood. For hours, they too made those deep noises. Aarohan just sat there witnessing in stupor. Slowly one by one each elephant of the herd came by as close to Manu, trying to reach for him with their trunk and then slowly turning away and leaving. The mother elephant with the baby elephant came by did the same ritual. And then left. Manu did not make much noise. He simply closed his eyes, resigned to his own fate.

Chapter 8

Manu

Part 2

Aarohan wouldn't have it. He could and would do something about Manu. All of a sudden, he had forgotten all his sorrow and the concerns of the world that he had left behind. He had a singular thought now, how to save this crazy elephant. He stood up. First things first—how to stop this behemoth from sinking deeper into the mud? He began to weave more vine rope. By midday, he thought he had as much as he needed. Manu was now chest-deep in the mud, his lower back submerged, his front legs still visible. Aarohan realized the sequence of what needed to happen, his years of elephant experience kicking in. But he needed to move fast.

He started weaving the ropes into a mat-like structure. The sun shone brightly now. It was both good and bad news. The good: the mud pool was drying, slowing Manu's descent. The bad: the drying was turning it into a concrete-like mixture, fixing Manu in place forever. On many expeditions to trap elephants, Aarohan had come across fossilized elephant bones in the earth in peculiar posture. Now, he realized how that could happen

After a couple of hours of labor, he finished making the sorry excuse of a mat. He spread it over the mud pool and slowly crawled over to Manu. Aarohan touched Manu's trunk, and the great elephant opened its eyes. Aarohan whispered in his native tongue, "Easy boy, you're not going to die here today." They peered into each other's eyes. A primordial connection, one could say.

Aarohan began working with the ropes. For the next two hours, he painstakingly lassoed the ropes around the elephant's shoulders and shoulder pits. He only had one chance to do this, and he did it well. Once satisfied, he pulled the ropes together and bridled them into a single strong rope. Finding the biggest and sturdiest banyan tree nearby, Aarohan climbed onto the second tier of branches and pulleyed the rope over to the massive lower branch. He tied the rope securely with the best knots he could manage.

It worked. For now, Manu had stopped sinking.

Now to work out how he could pull Manu out the mud pool. But first feed the elephant. Aarohan went about the forest to pick up banana and banana leaves, and piled it up on the make shift mat in front of Manu. And sure enough the elephant began to pick the edibles with its trunk and feed itself. For the first time in a long time, Aarohan too, felt hunger and appetite . Aarohan began to forage for food. The day turned into night.

For the first time in two moons, Aarohan lit a fire. He placed it near the mud pool, next to Manu. He set up camp there, contemplating how to free the elephant. Manu had stopped sinking, but the tension on the rope was increasing. It wouldn't hold forever. The nearest human settlement was a good twelve-day march through the Arakan range and rainforest. There was no way such a large beast would last twenty four days without him sustaining it. Fetching human help wouldn't work. He himself had to pull Manu out. But how?

He had a thought. It might just work. His timing had to be perfect.

Throughout the night, Aarohan gathered heavy rocks and logs. At daybreak, he placed the rocks and logs to further reinforce the ramp he had previously built for the elephant calf.

By midday on the second day, the rope was growing tighter, still sturdy but clearly under strain. Time was running out for both Aarohan and Manu. Aarohan picked up a large piece of rock and, using a smaller one, began to chip it into the shape of an axe head—something he could hold with both hands, one side blunt and the other sharp.

The day wore on, and as the sun began to set, Aarohan went foraging again, constantly worrying whether the thick vine rope would hold. After ensuring there was enough food piled in front of Manu, Aarohan set to work immediately. There would be no rest for him and no time to waste. With his crude stone axe, he began to cut the vertical root columns supporting the massive branch to which the pulleyed vine rope was tied. Both of Aarohan's hands were bloodied and scared from the bare-knuckle activities of the past two days, but there was no time to nurse them. He carried on through the night.

Deep in the forest, amid the chirping of crickets and the croaking of frogs, came the steady thudding sound of Aarohan's hacking at the banyan tree's supporting root columns. Each stroke was like a blow to Eskander (Alexander) himself, as Aarohan muttered between swings, **"Surji mama er teeyeta"** (The parrot feather of Sun Uncle). Morning of the third day. Aarohan woke, unaware of when he had fallen asleep. There were only a few root columns left holding up the massive lower branch. They were beginning to buckle. He needed to get the balance just right—too much tension, and the rope would snap.

He quickly set another fire and climbed back onto the branch to which the rope was tied. Sitting at the very base of the branch, he resumed his relentless hacking. Thud, thud, thud—the sound echoed through the jungle. He had to cut through three feet of thick wood. For the next six hours, Aarohan chipped away at the branch. He could see the rope tightening, the root columns buckling. All the while, Manu began to stir, feeling the increasing pull of the rope. But the drying mud was still holding him back.

And this is when fate stepped in. Aarohan saw dark clouds up ahead. It will soon rain on the range. Aarohan had to work faster. He was three fourth the diameter of the branch when it began to pour. His hands and fingers were bleeding, washed away by the rain. Water again began to pond the mud pool area. The ground began to soften. Aarohan knew it was now or never. He hacked away, keeping eye on four things. The pull of the rope. The buckling of column roots at the far ends of the branch. How further he had to hack into the branch. Is the rope holding around Manu.

Aarohan sensed it. He jumped down and ran to the last of the two remaining column roots. He hacked it off in the next hour. All the while the rain was pouring. The further side of the massive branch was now barely supported by a single column root.

He climbed back upon the branch. The tension in the rope was reaching its tearing point. For the first time in three days Manu trumpeted. "Yes Yes …. I know I know" yelled back Aarohan to Manu. Aarohan now sat on the portion on the branch that he intended to saw off, or rather hack off.

If there was ever an event that would visually describe the phrase "the straw that broke the camel's back" then this was it. The massive branch along with Aarohan's weight teared away from the tree, the remaining column root fully buckled away at the far end, and as the massive branch went down, it pulled on the rope. The mud pool had turned into wet slurry by now and yanked Manu from the mud pool like a massive tooth from the gum of mother earth. As Manu was being pulled up its front legs got a bit of traction on the makeshift ramp, and now Manu began to pull himself up, even though his hind legs were totally paralyzed from the immobility of the past three days. But the front two legs kept powering on.

Manu was free. The giant limped slowly toward Aarohan. The vine rope, now loose, trailed behind. Aarohan lay on his back on the ground, staring up at the sky as Manu's trunk gently caressed his face. Aarohan began to laugh from the tickle—the first laughter he had known since his daughter's death.

It's been two weeks since the day Aarohan had saved Manu's life. Ever since that time Manu had not left his side. The only time Manu was away when to feed and relieve itself. It had sat like a guard dog by the great banyan tree within which Aarohan had laid. The tree cave was to be Aarohan's final resting place. But Manu wouldn't have it. Just like the calf elephant, it would bring nuts and roots for Aarohan. And make deep vibrating noise. Aarohan knew that as the purring noise of the elephants. Aarohan began to eat and drink.

Then one day Manu simply took him by the trunk and placed Aarohan on his back. He took him for a ride in the forest. It was one of the most elating feelings that Aarohan experienced since the demise of his daughter. He was back from the dead. He never rode an elephant this high. Majestic, graceful yet swift was its movement. Such a large creature would shuffle through the forest effortlessly. And it took queues from Aarohan quite well. Aarohan was the best trainer of elephants in his generation, he could train Manu well. But what was extraordinary that Manu had the willingness to learn and…… Aarohan from Manu. For elephants are highly intelligent and emotional creatures. Aarohan would train Manu.

As they went through the leaves and branches of the forest, the sun shone on Aarohan's back. He has recovered well in the past two weeks. He now knew what it was he had to do. He now knew how to inspire a despairing nation. He now knew how to defeat Alexander. Today Aarohan and Manu descended from the Arakan rain forest, travelling west towards the Gangariddi Plains. His journey to the east had ended.

GANGARIDAI

Chapter 9

Blades of Grass, Blades of Steel

The Pali Pakrit text took Balan a while to decipher. It had been many moons since he had last studied the Franca Lingua of Buddhism, but now, the unfurled leather parchment lay before him. The seal had been tampered with, but that didn't concern him—no one in these lands, or even in the neighboring kingdoms, could decipher the ancient Pakrit. What concerned him was the content: a single cryptic sloka.

"A thousand thunder for a single ring ".

The deputy abbot was standing by, curious to know the

content. He knew the language was foreign, he had taken the liberty to copy down the imagery of the text on a bamboo slat. To be the first person to meditate on the sloka from India is the desire of all rival abbots. It means prestige, privilege above peers and seniority. Balan was, is advanced in his years. Though in good health, the sangha knows he will not be here forever. The one having access to the religious text will always have that claim and the head start in discerning the tantric philosophy. The vicious competition to claim the mantle of morality is in itself immoral, yet it is the best of immoralities.

Balan looked up, contemplating. Is this undertaking even possible? What material even would stand a thousand cycles of a monger's hammer? But more on that later. He now wanted to know how the deputy abbot came into possession of this leather parchment. Anticipating Balan's query, the deputy volunteered a response, "the emissary has been housed in the Bodhi Hall, he has come from the holy lands. He needs rest and nursing; it seems he has had quite a journey. He repeatedly has asked for your audience."

Balan crossed the courtyard into the scripture school and then into another courtyard that separated the structure from the Bodhi Hall. Through the main atria, where the haze of the late morning rays bathed the white pebbles on the ground, mostly used by the students to trace the steps of & while shadowing the Tsi Hing's martial arts motions. As he entered the room he gazed upon the weary eyes of his country man. Balan slowly sat down to impress upon the condition of the traveler from India. 'I am Chanakkya, I am seeking the Indian by the name of Balan. Are you Balan?' Asked Chanakkya in his native tongue.

"I am he, what makes you seek me out this far north? Who has sent you?" , while showing the leather parchment to the traveler. "Who wrote this sloka?"

Chanakkya torso ed up straight. "Your childhood friend Aarohan has sent you the message. He makes a stand against Eskander."

Balan froze. Has Alexander come this far into India?

"Aarohan makes a stand for our people, and he makes a stand in memory and anguish of Roshan."

Now Balan grasped the urgency of the thousand miles journey. He asked the deputy abbot to take care of the traveler.

The fire was rekindled as Balan took his time to process all that Chanakkya had said. It's been a day and half since Chanakkya reached the monastery after a month's long journey, first in the high lands of Tibet to ascertain Balan's whereabouts and then travel deep north into the Tibetan land.

Balan pondered Aarohan's request. He had spent years exploring and perfecting metal forging through alchemy, but what Aarohan was asking seemed nearly impossible. Could such weapons even be forged?

"What weapons are you speaking of—spears, swords? Or does he want to improve the Dhonis' close-quarters battle arms?" Balan asked.

"I do not know," Chanakkya replied. After a brief

pause, he added, "My guess is a forging method to equip fifty thousand Sena."

Chanakkya quizzed, "Can you help us?" .

"My boy, let us go to the armory", Balan replied.

The two along with the abbot went down through the courtyard into the lower levels of the monastery, where they reached a bolted door within the armory. Balan had the key. They entered into a dark hall. The sides of the hall had high apertures which let in day light. Under each day lit floor area was staged a katana, three and three on each side.

Chanakkya was bemused, how different the monasteries here in Tibet were, in comparison to the ones in northern India. "Why would a monastery, an institute of learning and practice of Dharma would house," and with a pause and disapproval "...weapons?"

Balan paused, answered rhetorically, not to Chanakkya but to the Abbot, "Tell me Abbot, what is the purpose of Dharma?"

"Dharma is the vehicle to institute peace". The abbot answered.

Balan continues, "Tell me Abbot, what is the purpose of the temple?"

The Abbot answered, "The temple is the vehicle to institute peace"

Balan continued, "Then, the temple is Dharma?"

The Abbot answered, "No, my Bodhi"

Balan quizzed, "How so?"

"Dharma is the individual peace vehicle, Temple is the societal peace vehicle", the abbot answered.

Balan continued, "what should the temple do for societal peace?"

"Enable society", answered the Abbot

"Even to the point of …." Balan inquired

"…. Even to the point of martial training for and of the righteous against the oppressor"

"There! There you have your answer" said Balan turning to Chanakkya.

"…And who finances the endeavor?" Chanakkya had to ask.

"Same way as the Kshatriya in India, under the patronage of the kings"

The trio approached the first Katana station. Balan glanced at the abbot. "Will you demonstrate?"

The Abbot picked up the katana and, with a delicate motion, turned toward a stand where bamboo stalks grew, supported by iron rigs. With one fluid sweep, he cut through a single bamboo girth at a slant and then replaced the blade on the stand.

Then the abbot moved on to the next station, and went through the same 'Sao' movement, only this time the katana he picked cut through two bamboo stalks.

Chanakkya was impressed, he did not ever witness such smooth motion.

The abbot continued, this time on to the third station. Chanakkya began to feel entertained. Three bamboo stalks in a single stroke

The Abbot stopped at the sixth station. He turned to Balan, and said "The stroke does not yet agree with me for the sixth". Then he turned the hilt towards Balan.

Balan smiled and replied, "How do you know it will agree with me?"

Balan stepped up to the sixth station with the sixth Katana. The abbot took Chanakkya by the elbow and stepped back, to make space for Balan.

For a few moments Balan simply stood there, poised, concentrating. Then with a leap which can almost be compared to the beginning flight of a crane he was airborne. Or was he. He held the katana straight up in the air, his left thigh folded up to his chest in perfect yogi asana, or what the Tibetan would call a 'Sao", all the while balancing his total body weight on the toe of his right straight feet, his only connection to the ground. And then sweep the katana down like a smooth yet devastating tsunami wave. As if all his weight, along with the momentum created by his stance, translated into the one third to two third length of the cutting edge of the steel blade. It went straight in a slant across all the six bamboo stalks, which provided no resistance. As if he sliced , not bamboos but candle sticks. And all this happened at lighting speed.

All three stood there as the bamboo stalks fell onto the cobbled floor.

Chapter 10

To the Lin Forrest of Shao Mountain

The three sat at the heavy timber dining table. Seeping hot thukpa. Chanakkya was anxious to know, if Balan would help. If yes, when would they begin their journey back to India. It seemed Balan did not appreciate the urgency of the mission of Chanakkya. What could he, Chanakkya do to press Balan into either committing to help Aarohan or simply regret to help the master mahout. Either way he needed to know. Time was running out. He needed to head back to India.

Balan slurped on with his thukpa. Chanakkya felt irritated.

The abbot was anxious too. But for totally different reasons. Would Balan leave with this southerner? He cannot leave. Not now, not yet.

"Bodhi" the abbot addressed Balan, "FaMing has arrived, she brings the news that King Xian has fallen."

After a brief silence, Chanakkya too addressed Balan, "King Puru, of the Pauravas has fallen"

The abbot continued, "If Xian's legacy is not protected, the whole of China will fragment into chaos, you know it my Bodhi."

The abbot had hardly finished, when Chanakkya almost interrupted, "Guru Bratha (brother of Guru), Eskander will soon reach the Ganges. Aarohan says if he mobilizes via the river, Eskander will reach the heart of Ganga right onto Pataliputra and beyond. Aarohan needs you now."

"If you leave now our mission to have Buddhism in these lands will be at peril. You have been in these lands for seven years. That would all Be for Not.", countered the abbot.

"....and if you don't return to India, you might as well believe the demise of Buddhism altogether in India and start worshipping the Vergina sun of the Dhoni's (Macedonians). I tell you guru bratha, I haven't travelled unnecessarily these thousand Krosh distance if your presence was not required back in India."

"..... and I haven't come all the way from the Lin valley in the east if China didn't need you now" a new voice interrupted Chanakkya from the doorway of the hall. It was FaMing. She slowly walked towards the center of the hall to the large Himalayan Cedar table. "if we are talking about distances travelled, then I doubt no one has travelled more than I have."

Chanakkya blushed slightly as FaMing brushed his arm while she sat next to him, placing her bow and quiver aside. He was taken aback to see a female warrior, and a very pretty one at that.

Balan sat straight up for the first time as the quartet settled down at the table. "I can pretend to be flattered that three distinguished representations from three great civilization is sitting at this table urging for my involvement in assistance for settling pressing matters for each of these places. But I am not. Why is it that these three great perils is happening at the same time, and for the first time?"

"It seems the prophecies of the Kali Yuga are beginning to manifest," FaMing answered matter-of-factly. Balan raised an eyebrow, seemingly in agreement.

Chanakkya was taken aback by FaMing's candid participation in conversation of state and war. Sensing so, FaMing while sipping on her thukpa, critiqued in Pali, "I am guessing you are a Putri, assessing from your accent and attire. And that your women never speak up on matters of so-called man's business? But you little boys with your fragile royal egos think this is a clash of culture and philosophies of the east and the west that we are facing now with this Eskander character, but if you really want to have peace across the continent you need to understand, your Egos are the reason we have wars. Look at this barbarian Eskander now threatening your lands. Why is he here? So many krosh and so many years away from his homeland. What will he achieve in the end once he is done with what he has come to take from these lands? He will have attained nothing but be a source of misery, bloodshed and death. Your poor fragile little boy egos."

Chanakkya was even more unsettled, being spoken to in this manner by the Chinese woman.

The abbot absentmindedly added, "And that is why Bodhi has insisted on having female monks amongst our ranks. To exorcise our male egos, to Yin our Yang."

Balan was happy with the thread of wisdom bouncing off, at the table and Chanakkya somewhat unsettled trying to pick up on the threads.

"... thus it is not by chance that the four of us, who would have been separated by distance and time , is in fact seating together at this table. We need to correct the things that are going all wrong. Do you understand so Chanakkya? We need to tackle the things of our immediate pressing, but also be mindful of our action or in-action that will fester into something potent like Eskander in a generation or two, if we do not think of the long term that we are simply a part of. So, I choose to entertain our causes in the East for the eventual benefit of the South.

'so be it, then I will go with you to the east and help you finish your planned mission' answered Chanakkya, 'only that, do I have the your word that you will then help with Aarohan's task right after?"

'My boy, the thing that will help Aarohan is not

with me, nor here, but in the valley of Shao Mountain in the Lin Forrest"

To that, the Abbot, FaMing, and Chanakkya looked up from their Thukpa Bowls.

Chapter 11

Ten Thousand Shadows for a Single Step

Part 1

The captain

"I do have new merchandise, never used before," the madame said. To that, the captain thought it might be worthwhile to have a look. The tavern had seen its fair share of drunkards for the night, potential clients for the brothel upstairs. He was selective, indulging in the carnal desires of the flesh only so often, and seldom at that. The campaign had been long and bloody. Though battle-hardened, one could never be certain what the next foray would bring. There were always casualties. It was only a matter of time before it would be his turn. It's all a numbers game, inevitable unless, of course, you outranked the poor men sent to the frontlines—the ones harvested in the fertile grounds of soul reaping. Rank came with better odds, and the bodyguards afforded by his status were no small advantage.

Visiting the brothels was a way to ease out the madness. But to what risk? The captain had seen from his rookie days how so many of his comrades end up with ugly genital diseases, that once contracted one is cursed for life. In exchange for a moment of callous pleasure, one trades in the woes of never having concern-less love making. So yeah, brothels were not the captain's thing.

The madame persisted, "I know you are a man of taste, and I will never give you a merchandise that is sullied. This girl is a virgin, and you will for sure take a liking to all the goodies she carries". The captain looked up. "Ohh no, not the wrong kind of goodies" the madame answered with a smirk. The captain was not interested. "at least come have a look, dear man. Live a little, before you barter your soul away"

Reluctantly, the captain got up from his table and followed the madame up the stairs. Through the thick wooden door into a corridor. The air was laden with perfume to mask the smell of stale sex. He was led across numerous alcoves where his comrades were entertained. And then his eyes fell on the girl. Stunning beauty was an understatement. And he could tell indeed this girl was of decent background. The Madame paused, "Ohh no not that one. That is concubine material, she is princess, family lost in the war, I was thinking of ....". The captain interrupted, ".... That is exactly the one that I want"

"No, you cannot have her, you know the rules. Concubine materials are off limits. You do not want to make this difficult for us. This is a pleasure house, let's keep our dealings 'Pleasant'"

The captain kept staring at the girl. Sensing his gaze, the girl afforded a glance up. Their eyes connected. The captain knew immediately what needed to be done.

He turned to the madame and said, "She is not for me, concubine you say. Concubine it is. The general is on the lookout for such merchandise. I will report back to the general. I presume it will be the regular rate that is afforded for concubines?"

Without waiting for an answer, the captain turned headed out to the doorway.

The General

The intelligence officer to the general, along with his retinue surveyed the killing field. The ambush was absolute. And the execution of the slashes was that of an elite martial troop. That the intelligence officer could tell. He wanted to take his time and reconstruct what actually transpired. It is not every day you have an entire unit decimated. The general would not like this and increase his atrocities over the occupied region and its populace. The best way to limit the gore and blood shed is to discover who were the troops who had ambushed this unit, or better still, curve out a resounding 'pound of flesh' from the resistance or would be resistance who may yet fancy to be loyal to the old dynasty. Make an ugly example of the perpetrators.

His sources had spoken about movements in the western frontiers at various monasteries, that ranks within the monks were eastbound, making their way to a town where they were to meet up. Only if he had intelligence of what township it was. He was seeing some of the validation of such intelligence, more and more there are incidents and growth in intensity. But none of the previous incidents were as egregious as what he was assessing now.

Puncture wounds, deep. Coming in at an angle, meaning arrows lobbed into the group. But what was perplexing is that this was not a random shower of arrows released en mass as commonly deployed in the battle fields. This was precise, take out of individuals but from a greater distance. That did not make sense. These monks, what have they come up with now?

His lieutenant reported, "the field was cleaned up after the ambush, no arrowhead left behind. We are yet to have an artifact to know for certain who are they perpetrators and what region they are coming from, …. for certain …"

The Concubine

'What is your name?' The general queried.

The girl who had been trafficked into the camp after the captain had reported on her to the general's retinue, kept silent.

'I am told your family was on the wrong side of the Han Qin contention,' the general paused. Battle, gore and bloodshed has made all men in the camp numb to the subtlety of feminine interaction. The general was no exception. As a matter of fact, all manners of need by the general would be satisfied the moment he would utter so. However, this time round, he would be a bit more patient. This 'flower' seemed worth the 'gardening' effort.

The girl kept silent

'Listen, lady, the way I see from here, you are in desperate need of allies. Whether you will languish as a sex slave in some brothel in some forgotten region of the country or married off into a respectable house is all up to you. But I would encourage you to open up to me. I know you have been through a lot. I know you have seen your family massacred. But it is best to grow up quickly in this bloody unjust world.'

There was a knock on the cong at the doorway of the tent. The general's tent was in actuality two. The first tent acted as an ante-chamber , where he would hold formal audience with his daily business. Attached to it was the tent that he used as his bathing and sleeping quarters.

He robbed and walked out into the first tent where a couple of ministers were awaiting him. Amongst them the spy master, intelligence officer and the captain.

The group remained silent

The general understood

"So, we have another incident, then? Alright, out with it"

The captain responded, "We lost a full unit, in the valley. It seemed they walked into an ambush that was well executed. It seems the menace of the monks is amongst us."

"How do you know for certain that these are the monks from Tibet?" The general quipped.

The intelligence officer stepped in. "the precision of the cuts, use of arrows, and how the terrain had been used to the advantage of the attackers tells me it is indeed an elite group that had executed the attack. No one is as skilled to what I have assessed"

"How are they receiving their provisions?" asked the general. Not waiting for an answer, the general adds, "burn down all villages within twenty Li's of the incidents and bring in the population of these villages into bondage. Let it be decreed that any village that falls into proximity of such events would be sold into slavery and anyone found to be directly assisting the rebellion would be executed on the spot."

The intelligence officer thought this was a much more lenient response than what he expected. At least the whole population is not put to the sword.

The general made the motion and the ministers, and the trio left the tent. Before the general retreated to his private tent, the spy master handed the general a rolled up parchment. " ...about the girl".

The general took the parchment and headed back to his private tent

The general settled down to have his dinner. He looked at the girl's way and the dish that was served for the girl. It was untouched.

'You gotta eat you know,' while slurping up his soup. 'Without eating, that pretty face of yours would soon turn into a scarecrow look, hah.'

The girl kept silent

After finishing his dinner and while the lads in waiting cleaned up after the general, he tore the seal of the parchment. Read through it. Looked up at the girl once he was through.

'How do I know; you are who this parchment describes you to be? 'The general queried.

Before he could squarely engage the girl, the girl had already risen and prepared the after-dinner dessert that was placed by the lads in waiting. She deft fully re arranged the tray and the tea arrangement, without any clinking noise of the porcelain, set the order of the tea straight.

The general took a sip. A taste that he had only enjoyed at the grand palaces. Hibiscus tea.

This was no ordinary girl. The parchment from the intelligence officer mentioned the girl was royalty, probably a princess. Her preparation of the tea in ceremonial glam says she has been schooled in a royal household.

So, she is concubine material for the emperor.

But more on that later. The general simply needed

to have success in routing out these rebel monks from the west. Intelligence says these rebels are slowly moving east.

'Tongyu' the girl said.

The general slightly startled quizzed the girl, 'Is that your name?

'No, my lord, that is the river the monks are using to move east.'

'How do you know that?

'My lord, my family has been massacred , my father bleed to death right in front of my eyes. I can even now smell the obnoxious scent of the barbarians who did this to my family. I smell the scent flowing east on the Tonyu river.

'I have seen the weaponry used by these rebels. These are full battle weapons. They can be transferred only in two ways. Oxen cart, that can be easily searched by your men on the roads. Too risky, too slow.

'But by boat, it is easy to conceal within the grains and farm tools. On the river, search by your men is less frequent. So yes, I smell their scent moving east by the Tongyu.' The girl finished so with spite in her voice

Definitely concubine material, the general thought, the lass has spice in her tongue. Definitely concubine material.

'Does your nose say where on the Tongyu river will they disembark?' The general played along.

'I will say so if you promise to sell me to the Pinfei house of the emperor.

'Lady, you are in no position to bargain

'I am Princess LaFang of the Qin family, you may choose to harass me or you may choose to listen to me, my lord. Sooner or later, I will be either presented or will be spoken for at the emperor's court. You see, I have made sure your men have seen me, and I am told I am a woman of considerable beauty, which I care of not. But what I care about is that, my scent too , moves east to the emperor's court.

LaFang said so with an air of regency.

The general changed his posture. This could be a useful tool that he could have in the emperor's court.

The general smiled, 'Now now, me lady, do not be upset. You know how it is; one cannot be too careful. And when I deliver you to the emperor, I will not be 'selling' you. One does Not sell to Pinfei house.

'I have grown up in these lands. LaFang answered, 'your rebels will move their cargo under the cover of darkness yet have the full moon light to navigate. Without lighting torches on the boat.

'Mmm... that gives me the time,' the general observed. 'Do you have a thought where the place will be, me lady?"

'The only dock where the moon shines through the mountains on to the valley is ....

'Yangcheng' the general observed. But of course! The girl is right.

The general smiled, "I am sure you will be a good addition to the PinFei, my lady'

Chapter 12

The First Training Spells

This was the most intelligent and willing elephant that Aaron had ever trained in his life. But even then, all is not smooth sailing. Manu seems eager to understand what the master mahout was communicating.

Aarohan scoped a secluded plain by the Lala Khal River coming down the Arakan range into Vanga (Bengal). There was a series of winding paths cleared out within a banana garden. Man, and Elephant walked the range side by side, individually clearly out the stumps. The first few weeks were spent navigating these winding paths, first in slow trot and then in quicker strides. Picking out the juiciest banana stalks that Manu would fancy. Sometimes Aarohan would cut out the stalks and prep the mix with guavas & shatkora in a manner he knew elephants liked. Sometimes Manu would give a guava or two to Aarohan, and Aarohan made it a point to let Manu know of his appreciation.

From the very beginning Aarohan used the thigh pressures to indicate his preference of direction. Though more difficult to train, he wanted his hands free of steering, free to engage with weaponry. Usually, war elephants are a three-person operation. The pilot, who sits at the shoulder. The howdah is placed right behind where two soldiers would take position. First the skilled archer, the second the one with the long spear protecting the side and the rear.

But Aarohan knew probably he would have neither to protect him from projectile or nor his or Manu's hide.

He had to train himself and Manu to perform as a single unit in Combat.

For that, Aarohan set out five phases of training. The first phase is to establish an unbreakable bond between the mount and the rider. He had to establish that as the rider he is Manu's caretaker and protector. He made sure that Manu was well fed and bathed. In the training grounds of Lala Khal, they lay on grass beds prepared by Aarohan during night times. Sometimes the little elephant that Manu had saved would come, seek them out and Aarohan would feed it well too. Aarohan half guessed that bull had sired the little elephant.

The second phase included traversing according to

Aarohan's direction. Just as Aarohan would practice his martial arts steps, he would teach stepping for the elephants that Aarohan developed over his career leading the Gangaridai corps. One two sidestep and then swing the head along with the tusks in the same direction. And then in the opposite direction do the same. They would do the same action over and over again, until it became a neck muscle memory for Manu.

The second phase went on for almost a Moon. This was the basic martial arts training for the pachyderm. It became the foundation for many more moves, strides and sharpened strikes. At specific single commands Manu would learn to charge, or swing to the right, or swing to the left, or stride back to the left, or stride back to the right. Aarohan set up the obstacles in the banana growths, clearing out stumps while keeping certain stamps rooted in geometrical formation. He would use these as the ground to train Manu on all its martial arts moves. Yes, martial arts moves!

The third phase, was essentially second phase but on steroids. The same moves were executed but this time without Aarohan striding Manu. At first Aarohan and Manu would shadow each other on sequences practiced in phase two. Then eventually Manu would learn to shadow all those moves as initiated by Aarohan. Aarohan made sure all his instruction signs & moves were limited to those they had practiced while striding Manu. So that the creature would know what is expected of him in the 'circus' of the battle field. Aarohan always felt he could train elephants to do things as per his signals while he was not specifically striding the elephant. His training with Manu confirmed his career long assumption. Many a trainer in the future centuries would deploy somewhat similar training techniques in the would-be circuses but never perfected to the science as Aarohan had developed. For Aarohan knew elephants to be wild, but not as animals.

Achieving perfection of third phase, essentially made Manu an extension of Aarohan. He would practice his spear moves on the stumps, and similarly Manu would shadow with his tusker on the stumps, only scaled up in might and power. Aarohan felt stronger and younger as he practiced his martial arts. And just looking at how Manu responds to his moves, Aarohan felt assured of his convictions in his future plans.

Then came phase four. Aarohan began to build armament for Manu. Aarohan began to build a Kiln out of clay to prepare an even greater kiln to extract iron from the red soil of the Arakan Mountain range, the same mountain range that was created by the uplifting power of the Gondwana, named after the Gond people, that slammed into the Tibetan plate. Aarohan would work in the mornings heating up the kiln in the manner his friend, and master metallurgist Balan had taught him.

Aarohan had dispatched Chanakkya to Tibet to bring back the Buddhist Bodhi to Gangariddi. It has been many moons, and Balan should have returned by now. Did Chanakkya make it? Why is it taking so much time? At any rate Aarohan realized he needed to push on preparing for what was to come.

As the extraction of the batches of the previous days piled up, Aarohan would, with Manu's help, plough up more red soil. And soon he would begin to have enough smelted iron to cast into half pipes of segmented lengths lined with fibers from the jute plant. Manu's armament for his truck was thus complete. But of course, With the last three ringlets lined with spikes. Now Manu's trunk had turned into a formidable Morning Star weapon. Aarohan blessed the would-be armament set 'Arman'.

Then came the under-belly plates in three segments in two rows. If there was ever the most formidable six pack in world history, then this would be it!

The under-belly Arman was followed by the shoulder and hip plates, segmented similarly in the manner of the Arman armor.

Then came the limb Armans. It took Aarohan about three months to complete the Arman set. There would be many a weapon in war & world history that would be blessed with a name, but only one armament that would be blessed with a name, and never was it made for humans.

Aarohan was apprehensive whether Manu would be as agile with the Armans on. But Manu the giant tusker was made for this kind of heavy gear. Aarohan and Manu took three more moons to practice their battle maneuvers while wearing the Arman armament.

Aarohan thought, both Manu and he were ready for phase five. He now focused on casting two enormous scythe blades, each to be bound to Manu's task. Next, he cast six more scythe-like blades, three of each to be attached to the wooden girders on both sides of Manu. These scythes would be retracted and set within their wooden sleeves running along the body of Manu on each side. Two gears would allow these claw-like scythes to flay out and be locked in place.

Once these armaments were in place, Aarohan and

Manu again went into battle maneuvers but this time with the scythes flayed out. Manu would slice though stumps of banana trees and stacks like hot knife through butter. But of course, after a certain while Manu would grow tired. Aarohan learned the limits of Manu's strength and stamina, both crucial to know and exploit in actual battle.

It's been almost a year since Manu and Aarohan began to prepare & train at the foothills of the Arakan. They would time and again visit the elephant herd where Aarohan first met Manu. Under the moonlit nights, as moon rays would filter through the tree canopies, Aarohan would light a fire to rest by, and yet meditate on his life, his daughter and fundamental structures of society or rather its failings that had led to such tragedy.

It was time, Aarohan decided.

It was time to return to Pataliputra

It was time to prepare the Putris and all of Gangaridai for the menace named Eskander.

Chapter 13

Ten Thousand shadows for a single Step

Part 2

"You may come forward and take your Ashana at the Jade station," the prime minister to the throne decreed, his voice carrying the weight of imperial authority. General Ming's expression remained composed, though a muscle twitched briefly on his brow. None of the other generals in the new empire had ever been granted such an honor.

'You honor me, oh lord of the seven realms.' The general, with ceremonial stride took up his position on the left hand row of the Empire hall. He gave a quick glance at the company of general in the audience. He wanted to know how many of his colleagues were comfortable with his progression of the station. Instead of being marked, he wanted to be the one who would do all the marking. His glance was answered by all his colleagues in the manner he would expect. It seems for the time being he would have his colleagues as his lieutenants. He now would have the title of supreme commander of the imperial army.

The prime minster continued, "The emperor, recognizes the valor of general Ming for subjugating the rebels at Yangchen. "

The ceremonial drum and cong rings out.

"General Ming will, now hold the insignia of the Supreme commander of the Grand Imperial Army, as decreed by the heavens and the Divine sovereign of theses seven realms, the Emperor."

Another sound of cong rang out, and court retinues decorated the general with regalia of the supreme commander. The title of Supreme Commander of the Imperial Army now rested on his shoulders; heavier than any armor he had ever worn.

After the court feasting, the Emperor asked the general to accompany him for a stroll in the imperial garden.

The garden was well lit with torches. In between the stations of the torches, there were the gleams of pulsating lights from thousands of fireflies. And in the background peeking through the nights sky the disc of the full moon. The reflection of the moon light bouncing of the stream that meandered through the garden. At the center of the garden over the stream laid the pavilion structure. The pavilion jutted out from the brilliant hues of plants and orchids in the garden. It seemed the royal landscaper is a spatial painter.

A few of the palace retinues had prepared the ceremonial tea and a musician played the Guzheng. One wouldn't think a bloody coup had occurred only six moons ago. Empires come and go, but the talent that creates the aesthetics of life seldom perishes.

The emperor spoke, "You have done well, General Ming. You single handily captured the rebel forces at Yangcheng. You have done, where so many others have failed. Tell me supreme commander, what is the current read of affairs of the rebels?"

The general felt he was finally getting into the inner circle.

The general paused, with an air of prudence, proceeded. "My lord, we have made significant progress since our triumphant intelligence coup with the rebels. All of the crack team of the rebels have been taken prisoners, and they are proving to be great source of critical information. The remaining resistance will be dealt with in due course."

'I have also been provided information there is a political delegation with a martial entourage, that has arrived from way south, from the holy land of India. They are seeking to take back the rebels back to India and try them under their laws. It seems these Buddhist rebels has been stirring up problems both in India and Tibet and are wanted by authorities of both these regions.

The usurper Emperor spoke, "Have the Indian delegation pay me a visit. I want to see and judge these people myself. And see if we can return them the favor and send a delegation of ours to India. Perhaps there is an opportunity here for more than just an exchange of prisoners."

'Yes, my sire, consider it done 'replied the general.

The General continued, "I do have a very delicate nature, or I should say a 'orchid' to present to you. The most beautiful 'orchid' I have set eyes upon. And I believe such an exquisite orchid should be possessed by the most esteemed. As a matter of fact, this delicate orchid was the one who helped yours truly in assessing the information and determining where the rebels would congregate. I have never witnessed any woman with such intelligence and acumen. She is royalty, but all her family members were killed in the recent rebirth of the nation led by you . She was about to be interned into a brothel when the ladies of the high society let us know to rescue her."

The Emperor turned to Ming, now fully interested. "Where is this woman?"

Ming gestured toward the far end of the garden. "I have arranged for her to meet you this evening, my Emperor."

And with that the General motion the retinue, who were observing them from afar from one of the high platforms within the garden. The platform had an ornate

Chinese kiosk with a Cong within. The retinue rang the Cong. The door at the far end of the Garden slowly opened. It had a processional path leading from it to the location where the Usurper Emperor and the General were strolling. Out came a lady in an exquisite silk white and indigo cheongsam. As she proceeded, landtoms was played by several musician hidden away in various chambers along the perimeter of the Garden. The lady gracefully yet slowly walked towards the emperor. She had a partial veil draped down from her head gear. Though she was walking, she seemed to sway to the rhythm of the music played. The moonlit night, the fragrance of all the flowers in the garden, the music all wove into the perfect fabric of romanticism that the lady wore as a sensual effect. From the opposite side a whole entourage of courtiers approached the king, the lead being a eunuch, who carried a wide circular dish filled with a thin film of mercury. The lady approached the emperor but stopped at the customary five yards away from the Emperor, and provided an exceptionally elegant courtesy. The General looked at the Emperor for approval, would he grant the lady a proper audience.

The Emperor, unfurled his cross arms and gave a gesture of welcome.

She rose and walked towards the emperor in the ritualistic 'bride to be' stride.

She stopped right in front of the Emperor, not within his personal space but enough that the Emperor could entertain a whiff of the lady's fragrance. Subtle, peaceful, yet romantic, arousing.

The Eunuch with his circular dish, which was in fact a reflective tray used in matrimonial ceremonies, came forward. The lady guided the tray with her ceremonial stick and positioned it in the manner that the emperor could gaze upon her from underneath the veil. The moon was there, the garden was there, the mood was there. There would be many a poet and playwright who would compare the beauty of the lead female character in romantic plot lines, be it the likes of Rumi, or Shakespeare, to the beauty and aura of the moon. But few men in their life time are lucky enough to experience this moment the Emperor would, for lack of a better phrase, live within that moment.

He saw an extremely gorgeous feature of a radiant face.

But what gave it that allure, was her smile. A willing smile, a smile with no inhibition, but of a friend who had known you as her childhood friend, grown up with you and selected you to be her mate. The trust. The love. The maya, a word that captures these feelings only in the Pali Pakrit.

The Emperor was taken aback. "And what is your name, my lady?" the Emperor asked, his voice soft, though his curiosity was palpable.

The woman met his gaze with quiet dignity.

"I am LaFang, daughter of the Qin family," she said.

In that moment, as the moon hung overhead and the garden seemed to shimmer around them, the Emperor realized he was in the presence of someone extraordinary.

Chapter 14

LaFang

'Will the emperor deprive me the pleasure of his esteemed company?' La Fang asked the emperor, with a slight hint of tease.

The Emperor actually blushed, at least internally. And he did his best not to betray his blush that he was feeling well up to his chick.

'Tell me a bit about yourself,' the Emperor took charge. He looked at the general and the rest of the retinue to excuse themselves, which they were already in the process of doing so.

'Ahh, I don't want to bore the Emperor, with my insignificant life story. Besides it may upset your palate.'

The emperor wanted to disarm the conversation, 'I sense you may have suffered in this last unnecessary but unavoidable conflict. I can sense you are royalty. You can be at ease with me.'

'Thank you my lord' La Fang responded softly, 'You are not only astute of martial affairs that saved our nation, but understand matters of the condition of the human heart' . LaFang said it in a manner that made the Emperor drop his formal guard.

LaFang noticed the slight change in the emperor's posture.

LaFang continued,

"I was born into the Shijin family, the youngest of seven siblings. My father was the civil state treasurer. Though he was employed by the defeated emperor, he did not endorse the fiscal policy of the old establishment to prop up whims of the emperor, that had no benefit to the people.

"That did not sit well with your predecessor. Though the emperor did not dare to depose my father publicly, for my father was a righteous man and as you may have heard, enjoyed immense popularity with the people.

"So, the Emperor did the thing he knew best, send his black guards. One evening we were a loving peaceful family, the next morning I was the only soul alive in that household. The color of our house name was aquamarine , which was the dominant theme in the interior decoration of my home. But that morning the house took a dark red hue ...with spilling of blood of my...."

La Fang choked up and went quiet, for she could no longer finish her sentence.

The Emperor , too, stood there in silence . Then he gave his hand, the regal frame that a king would offer to his queen in ceremonial processions.

They walked together ceremoniously to the focal point of the expansive garden, the pagoda.

When they both settled down on one of the reclining couches, the emperor asked the curious bit, "Why did you help the general?"

"My lord, we just want peace in the lands. We want these endless killings to stop. The rebels from the west from the highlands, was again disturbing the peace you have set out to establish"

"I am glad that you see things that others seem not to see. They would say I am ruthless in killing the populous, but I do say, I do it out of necessity. You see, fear is the great establisher of peace"

"My lord, I am of the faintest of hearts, not able to digest the visions of warring men. Will the lord excuse me so that I may collect myself?'. La Fang was clearly trembling at the moment. The emperor thought the lady next to him would faint. He had been responsible for the murderous rampage and scourge for the region, summarily killing all who were members of the old establishment, be they civilians, bureaucrats, tax collectors, or law enforcers. But the clear grief melt down of the lady, evoked a soft response within him. He signaled his retinue to come forward. 'Please escort the lady to the palace ladies quarters. See to it that she is treated like an empress and given all of the royal provisions. She is to be taken absolute the best of care. Is that understood?"

The retinue bowed, and gestured LaFang to follow him.

"I am sorry my lord, for ....." LaFang bowed as she began to ask permission to be excused.

"Don't mention it .... Please take rest. Once you have recovered, we can continue our conversation tomorrow." The Emperor looked on as LaFang departed the court.

The general took note from afar. This has indeed been a good investment.

Chapter 15

Lady of the Court

Next morning the Emperor asked LaFang's audience and to have breakfast with him. La Fang presented herself in a white gown with blue peacock motifs, highlighting her dawn blue eyes. Though the Emperor couldn't quite put his finger on it, she had done her eyelashes in a way that mimicked the peacock motif eye pattern.

"Ahh, my princess, happy to have your company. I pray you found your accommodation to your comfort?" The Emperor played his cordial self.

"My lord embarrasses me. I had the most exquisite

accommodation that any lady of a high name could hope, or even dream of."

LaFang immediately took charge and began to serve the emperor in the manner that a concubine or queen consort would, instruct the servers on the sequence, mix, and flavor of the dish and liquor to be served and in the right amount. She executed the serving in the manner a true connoisseur of royal banquet and felicitous occasion would demand. The servers, fifteen in total, were well orchestrated by LaFang, even though she had known none of them. The servers themselves were in total awe at the knowledge and skill of how LaFang instructed them. They had sprite in their feet for the way LaFang guided them was like a well-choreographed dance. They too played along with a certain cheer in their delivery. There was festivity in the air, all because LaFang knitted the mood.

As the delicacies were served, LaFang went to the corner of musicians and picked up landtom , the Chinese four string instrument. The first notes that came out were not from the instrument but from LaFang's vocal cords. It permeated as if at the lower floor level and then ascended to the ceiling level. She manipulated her voice to produce reverberations that echoed off the walls, giving the illusion of new notes forming from the sound waves themselves— a technique not found in Western classical music.

The timbre of the timber wood was perfect to LaFang's tone. Her ballad came out in waves, washing across the hall. Some of the servers would pause in their work and simply gaze upon LaFang, and so would the Emperor stop in his eating. Yet LaFang nodded to all, individually to carry on , even as she sang and played. She was the mistress of the moment, drawing in the emotions of everyone present.

While she played and sang along, a peasant song about simple joy of food and family, she guided the servers to present dishes according to her delivery of the lyrics.

Never was there a war lord who understood music or nuances of joy of simple life. For if they did, wars would never scar the earth. And LaFang with her beauty and her fine arts slowly demonstrated to the Usurper Emperor, blade is not the answer to all life's problems.

The singing, the dancing, the music ended. And everyone cheered, even the Emperor raised his cup and broke a smile.

After breakfast, the Emperor proceeded to his audience hall and asked LaFang to join him.

"That was quite the performance," the Emperor remarked. "Who taught you to sing?"

"My mother did. She was a singer at court once," LaFang replied.

"...And she is no longer with us?" the Emperor asked, without much tact.

LaFang answered softly, "...since the events of the night of the black guards"

"I'm sorry that I made you sad," the Emperor said, sounding genuinely remorseful.

"I too lost my family, my parents, my siblings to

war, to the old kingdom. I vowed to avenge their deaths ever since the day I lost them. ...and now that I have vanquished my enemies, I thought I would have peace, but low, nothing takes away the pain."

"Tell me me-lady, how do you lessen your pain, or have you even tried?"

"I do not try to lessen my pain, instead I channel it. Towards others. So that they may not face the same fate that I have experienced, and mitigate that source that has caused me that pain. Then my bearing and experience of that pain has meaning." LaFang opined.

"What if the cause of your pain is your enemy?" The Emperor challenged her.

"Especially if they are my enemies! If I can break the cycle of violence through empathy, then of course!"

".... And what if that enemy does not desist? It comes to exterminate your family as the black guards did ? Then your empathy would protect them?" Cold was the Emperor's query

LaFang stiffened her lips, "No they should be stopped. But only they. Not the whole village or villages punished for the wrongs perpetuated by the few. I would only get rid of the prick and not the whole arm."

The Emperor sensed that he might have lost some emotional connection with LaFang.

He tried to salvage the moment. "I heard you singing last evening. You have a melodious voice. Do you sing to lessen your pain?"

LaFang responded without betraying any emotion, "The Emperor is generous with his compliments. I was singing to a very sad boy, who was crying unconsolably. "

"Ahh, you have met the imposter emperor to be, eh?". The Emperor was visibly upset that the boy king and LaFang had met.

"I sought him out, my lord. I heard him cry. So, I went to him. And since there was none to take care of his grief, I sang to pacify him" Answered LaFang

"You are not to meet the boy again". The Emperor snapped sternly.

"Yes, my lord." LaFang answered while bowing her head.

At that moment, a retinue entered, requesting an audience. "My lord, the Indian delegation awaits you."

LaFang stood up to have her leave with the Emperor. But the Emperor motioned her to sit.

"Call in my minsters" the Emperor commanded.

A contingent of twelve ministers filed into the audience hall. The general was amongst them as well. He was surprised & somewhat elated to see LaFang by the Emperor and seated so close by him. Surprised that the lady had, obviously had the attention of the Emperor, and elated that it is his introductions that has allowed the lady to have confident audience with the Emperor. He nodded to LaFang and LaFang in return acknowledged his presence. Emperor noticed this exchange, then motioned the general to come and take his seat at the station of prime minister. The general betrayed no emotion, but one could see his steps having that extra sprite, more dignified.

As the station with the status of the prime minister, the General presided over the session. He signals the cong to be struck. With that the usher arrived.

"The grand hall is graced with the presence of the sovereign! The day's session shall begin "declared general Ming.

"Let in the Indian delegates" the general began the day's proceedings with the most important agenda

The Indian delegate entered, with their bows, as is customary for Indians to appear as when in audience with any foreign power. All cultures had their primary potent martial piece of weapon, for the Indians it was their recurve bows. And they were impressive to behold, for some would be six feet in length. And they were never discharged in regular stand-up positions. Instead, they would be knocked while kneeling, the front leg anchoring the bottom tip of the bow to the ground while the archer would pull back on the string with all his might. And it would be an impressive and fearful sight to behold. The recurve technology was solely known to the Indians at this period of history, and they guarded this zealously. The part where the recurve members would connect, they would cover it up with either sheep's skin or leather holsters. Furthermore, the Construction of the bow geometry would be kept an absolute "until death do us part" secret. So, it was a great shock when the Indian delegate came in their full battle gear including with their prized bows. The war general had an urge to confiscate all the weapons with the objective of having the bow.

Balan gave a stare at the general that a warrior would give before he would scalp his victim. He led the Indian delegate into the main hall of audience. There were fifteen of the Indian delegates.

"Greetings, O fist of the true kings of China "Balan addressed the Emperor, which clearly pleased the Emperor, though he did his best to not betray his elation.

"Ohh great emperor," began Balan after bowing his head to the emperor in the Indian style. "We come from the holy lands to the south of the abode of the gods, the Himalayas. We came to you in peace and further the cause of peace between the lands. We are grateful for your hospitality. We have been provided provisions and given restful abodes, and we thank you for that." Balan quickly went through the royal greetings protocols.

"Great, but you have not traveled great distances just for our hospitality, have you?" The Emperor cut straight to the point.

"No, we are not here for your hospitality, though that can easily become the highlight of our travels. We are here for some urgent matters of our state security. And your state security. With your permission we would like to discuss these matters great secrecy at the earliest opportunity"

"Yes, you may do so now and here. "

"As your intelligence have known and reacted to for some time now, you are aware that there are a great many rebels who have arrived from the western highlands. What you may not know is that these Tibetans monks are also causing havoc and in greater force in India. They have this crazy idea that all men are created equal and that monarchs don't have divine rights. You, the sovereign that sits on that throne, do not have that right...as a matter of fact that throne does not need to be there to begin with! "

To that the whole court gave out a gasp ......

Balan raised his hand to indicate appeasement to the crowd .... "This is not our opinion. We consider such thoughts blasphemy. But we are simply setting the argument of these demented monks.

"Our kings in India are facing more agitation from the monks within the peasant society. As a matter of fact, these monks have a more potent presence in the south. If these heretic Hinayana Buddhists have their way, it will drastically alter our religion.

"So, we are here to take back these rebels that you have captured in your river operation."

General Ming interrupted ..." We do not give away our prisoners Willy nilly, they will be questioned, set an example for, and executed by torture. Why would we want to give away our prized prisoners? "

Balan continued, "For the mere fact that if they succeed in India, the birthplace of Buddhism, guess who is going to follow next."

Balan paced the hall, going in circle, making eye contact with all ministers and those who were present there. Then he stopped in front of the general, "These criminals possess vital information about their operations. We would advise you to not torture them so that you, we can extract untainted information. As you know, torture only produces false information." Balan addressed the general

"If you will not give us the prisoners, at least allow us to interrogate them. We have Ayurvedic compounds that compel the individual under the influence to speak the truth. Allow us to have our way and then you may dispose them off as you may, tear them limb from limb and scatter them to the four horizons, we don't care."

The general spoke "why should we simply give access to our prisoners to you? What is it in for us?"

Balan turned on his heel and faced the general squarely. The way he moved caused the general's shoulders to stiffen ever so slightly. Balan took two steps toward the general, his expression stern, and then he removed his bow. The atmosphere grew tense.

"I noticed how you were eyeing my bow when we entered the hall. You like our Indian bows, don't you? You know how fiercely we guard the secret of their construction? Tell you what—you can have mine." With that, Balan's stern expression transformed into a smile. He held the bow out toward the general. The general was taken aback.

"What, you folks don't accept gifts from your guests? What kind of culture doesn't accept gifts from guests!" Balan retorted in an offended tone. The atmosphere again began to turn tense.

"We are honored to receive your gift Ohh leader of the Indians", a soft but firm female voice rang out within the hall. It was LaFang who spoke those words. Everyone paused. LaFang continued, "our emperor would honor your such magnificent gift, isn't it Ohh lord?", while turning to the Emperor. The emperor smiled at the graciousness of LaFang,

"My Consort speaks my mind; we will gladly accept your very generous and precious gift. Furthermore, you may interrogate the prisoners as you wish.'

For the third time that day, everyone in the hall was stunned—not because the Emperor had granted access to the prized prisoners, but because he had referred to LaFang as his consort!

LaFang also turned to the general and smiled at him, allowing him to be soothed by her charm.

Balan turned to LaFang, "Apologies me lady, we were not civil enough to recognize regent consort in our presence. I assure you someone in our camp will be standing out in the cold tonight for not letting us know the Emperor is with Consort.'

"Ahh lord Indian, you flatter and embarrass me in front of the Emperor. Besides, I would host your unfortunate colleague who would be standing out in the cold night in our royal ladies quarters . We can't have an Indian go cold, can we?' replied LaFang in zest.

Balan burst into laughter, "Now I am sure everyone in our company would claim to have made the mistake of not being aware of your presence!"

Balan turned to the Emperor with a zesty smile, "you have the most pleasant company of advisors and consort! We must take leave now; I am sure you have your citizens waiting for your audience."

The Emperor replied with a smile, "Go in peace Indian, and do not have too much fun with our prisoners, for we do not want to be deprived of our own fun!"

With that the Indian delegates turn and leave with a bit of cheer.

The Emperor looked back at LaFang with a twinkle and bemusement in his eyes. One would even think that he felt there was a bit of chemistry developing.

The general looked at the bow in his hand with a twinkle and bemusement in his eyes. One would even think that there was a bit of 'chemistry' developing between the general and his new toy. Men are such simple creatures.

Unbeknownst to the general, however, Balan had intentionally brought a flawed bow, ensuring that the Chinese would not gain access to the true recurve technology.

Then the general stood up to proceed with the rest of the listed audience to be had. But before he could announce the next agenda item, LaFang gestured to the General, "May I offer up an audience that might be equally entertaining how these Indians were to the Emperor?"

While she said it she glanced at the emperor for an approving gesture.

The Emperor just smiled and gave the gesture to 'take it away'. LaFang clapped her hand, and the minister of culture stepped into the audience hall. He strode up to the front of the assembly and then addressed the emperor, "Ohh great connoisseur of the fine arts & taste, purveyor of delicate aesthetics …." …

'Ahem….' LaFang subtly cleared her throat, with a smile, indicating to go directly to point

'…Err… my lord we have amongst us the world-renowned drama troupe from India. They seek audience with you'. With that the minister bowed and gestured his arms in the manner of the theatrical Performers. LaFang thought, the minister of culture had a penchant for the stage.

'Sure, let them in!'

Looking at LaFang the Emperor continued, 'This should be fun, more Indians! '

The Cong was struck.

The processional doors flung open, and in came an entourage of dancing troops and yogis with their colorful antiques. They were supported and followed by musicians. And then people in colorful garb with graceful strides came in as the main body of the procession.

Chanakkya led this group. He stood in front of the Emperor and spoke in Sanskrit, with another person translating into Chinese

"Namaste, Ohh king of kings! I present to you the great performance Gharana of the Gangetic Plain, KalaKoushalla. We have been traveling for three monsoons and have arrived at your seven kingdoms a monsoon back. We have performed in many of your major townships with great fanfare, and now we have finally made our way to your capital within Lin mountains. With your permission, we would like to invite you to our play and grace the inaugural occasion that will premiere a fortnight from now!"

"The Emperor does not leave the palace but only for state affairs or in front of a mighty army to vanquish an enemy!" The general declared ceremoniously.

"Then are we to be deprived of the auspicious Emperor's presence from our Inauguration Day?' Chanakkya protested, 'we wanted to forward all our proceeds of the first play to the royal coffers as gratuity. Will the Emperor deprive us of that honor?" Chanakkya inquired with a pretense innocence.

The Emperor now amused, looked at the general. That's a lot of revenue. How will the general now bend the rule to and at the same time assure security for the Emperor.

The general was in a pickle. 'We appreciate your offers, but the sovereign's safety & security is paramount.'

LaFang changed her posture. The emperor sensed she wanted to contribute to the conversation.

"Perhaps our lady of the court may dispense wisdom that might help out our general here?"

"My lord places to much faith in me' LaFang bashfully protested, 'but if the general would allow;' turning to the Emperor, "I hear we have an magnificent arena large enough to hold Five thousand people. Why not have the inauguration play in the Arena. The Emperor does not have to leave the palace. We can charge the audience for the tour of the grand palace. You can charge the audience for your play. Apart from your first day royalty, you can continue the use of the arena in exchange for a reasonable royalty. I mean what better venue would you get anywhere in the region, forget the region but the country?"

Everyone blinked.

This was indeed a great solution to the problem, everyone came out not only as a winner, but in a handsome manner.

The Emperor looked at the general with a raised eyebrow and a candid expression,' well?'

The general replied with a smile while bowing his head, "The lady of the court is indeed wise!"

'Then so be it. Sort out the details with my ministers here. I look forward to watching this famous play of yours'

'Do we have more Indians to entertain today? 'the Emperor asked amused

'I think we have had more than the fair share of Indians today' LaFang quipped, ' Can we excuse ourselves for the day ?'

'Yes, I too am tired with all these foreigners popping up. Perhaps the lady would accompany me to the royal lakes to enjoy some cool afternoon breeze?"

Chapter 16

Proposal for Life

"My lord, I am flattered. Right now, I am not in a state to judge my emotions for romantic matters. I lost all my family members only recently. Will the sovereign give me four moons to grief and allow me to mend my heart? The sovereign has the right & privilege to have any maiden lady of the realm. Will those be more amenable to the emperor than a broken person such as myself? I hope I have not offended my emperor with my condition. "LaFang said softly.

The emperor looked on to the shimmering light reflection from the late afternoon sun. 'Yes, I am the emperor, and I am entitled to choose any dame from the realm. But I have been intrigued by you, your presence, and how you carry yourself. And I'd rather have you at my side as a willing consort. So, I will give you the time you have requested.'

"My lord, I am tired of all the cycle of killings and bloodshed. It is very personal to me. I have lost everything in this endless, sense less cycle of violence . I would beseech that you allow for all ethnicity and of all political strife be integrated into the royal court. Let the deposed boy live, under your protection & supervision. Come forward as the benefactor of the nation. You can set up an example that may set off a precedence that influence not only this society and region , but across all civilization and across time." LaFang added.

The mood of the Emperor changed, his jaw line stiffened. "You are sounding off the propaganda of the rebels. Had I not known your recent tragic story, I would have thought you were one of them."

'Apologies my lord, it is not my intention to vex you. I thought the rebels were in support of the boy king and not universal peace representation of all. I mean what do I know of the affairs of learned men. I am simply expressing my feeling & tiredness about all perpetual killing and bloodshed. Excuse my emotional soapiness '

'The boy king cannot live," the Emperor stated as a firm regal edict. 'Who is to say he is going to grow up to be my assailant, the rallying figure for the rebels? No, he will have to forfeit his life'

'Ohh my lord, no, please' LaFang pleaded with tears welling up in her eyes, 'He is just a boy! Why not teach him the way of civility, protect him as you would as your own son, and then how can he kill his own guardian father figure?"

The Emperor kept silent.

Then uttered the words that would seal his fate, "The boy has to go."

LaFang was mortified.

The Emperor motioned the captain of the barge to take them ashore.

LaFang couldn't hold back her tears, and kept saying, "He is just a boy, my lord. You could have been that boy."

Next morning LaFang stayed within her quarters, spending the whole night holding close the deposed boy king. The boy said nothing, only before sunrise took LaFang's hand and rested his chin on it. "I know my time is near. And I am okay with it. I am ready……but you should go have some sleep. You remind me of my mother."

LaFang couldn't bear the pain. Her being in the presence of the deposed boy king, felt like she was fending off his impending death. But hearing those words by the young boy made her stern and resolute. Something needs to be done to avert this needless killing.

Chapter 17

The Play

Part 1

Chanakkya, along with his performance troupe, stood impatiently at the service gates of the palace. "Let us in, you sleepyheads," he called out. It was early morning, with the sun just a twelfth gradient high above the horizon.

"Show us your papers, coalface," one of the guards grumbled.

'Here are your papers, or should I say royal edict! Slit eye" taunted Chanakkya, "Now that we have traded insults, let us in, I don't have all day to smell your ass fruit breath."

"Ass-fruit?" The first guard was perplexed. "What kind of swear phrase is that?"

"The kind that comes out of the ass of the chicken". And with that one of the performing troop members brought forward a large weave basket with layers of hay within, nestling hundreds of chicken eggs.

"For your buddies" Chanakkya added. "Also come by our kitchen in the afternoon, and we'll show you how real food taste like." Chanakkya made a gesture of kiss as he said so.

"Now I need to move these lazy retard fuckers into the grand hall so that we can began our rehearsal for the play. We needed to start like yesterday."

"Hold on, we need to check all your cargo, before we Let you in." The second guard said sternly.

"What, you guys are afraid of colorful cloths and props? We are too gay for you?" Chanakkya bemused.

"We have to check all your goods, royal decree" the second guard now stepped forward, "I am the captain, and I decide what goes in and out of this place."

"And I'm the captain of this troupe, and I have a royal decree too," Chanakkya replied, his sarcasm edging into irritation.

"Let us a do a random sample search and let our esteemed artist get back to their art making" the first guard interjecting between the two interlockers

The first guard signals some of his comrades and all went through the third, ninth and second last cart.

The third had costumes, props, wooden weaponry and a whole lot of protest and yelling from the caretaker of the play.

The ninth had frames and painted screens for the play background and more protest from the caretaker when one of the frames broke during the guards' search.

Chanakkya was showing impatience. 'At this rate, you will wreck all my props, and we will never start our rehearsals.' He said so while striding up to the troublesome second guard. The second guard grew belligerent. 'You will pass only when I say so, else you'll have a taste of real blades then your flimsy wooden tooth picks.'

Chanakkya's face flushed with anger. "Alright, that's it! Everyone, pack up. We're leaving. I'm not dealing with threats from some stray dog. I'll go straight to the emperor and tell him the play season is off. He can kiss his twenty thousand liang goodbye because some braying donkey felt threatened by our toothpicks. Maybe we should put on a play about a low-life captain who lost the Emperor's revenue and got his head stuck on a pike. Smart!" Chanakkya waved his hands dramatically, signaling his troupe to pack up.

Before things could escalate further, the legion's high commander descended from the watchtower. With a burly, hairy hand, he delivered a resounding slap to the second guard, knocking him off balance.

'You illiterate?' The commander thundered over the second guard, who was totally taken aback by the smack down from his superior. 'These guests of the Emperor have the royal pass, and you are playing the tough bully? You are dismissed here. You will do latrine duty today! Now go shovel some human shit. '

The Commander came forward to Chanakkya, "These idiots don't recognize honorable people when we are graced by them. Please accept our hospitality." Turning to the rest of the searching party, "You heard me, let these foreign guests of ours through".

Chanakkya reached into the inner pocket of his vest and brought out a colorful parchment. 'This is for you and your family. Premium seats right next to the royal booths. They are worth fifty Liangs, half a year worth of salary of this arrogant guard" gesturing at the second guard who was now slowly finding his feet, "and gods know how much it would be on the black market ", Chanakkya winked on the commander.

Chanakkya then yelled out to the rest of the troop, "C'mon you pretty ladies, on with the show. Pass along."

Chanakkya said "Good day to you commander", then as he was passing the second guard, he made the mule that he was leading, kick dirt with its hind leg, "that's what happens if you are rude. From the possibility of sitting next to the royals, to shoveling human doo, while eating dust of a mule's hind! "

Chapter 18

Prisoners

[This portion contains torture descriptions]

Balan and his compatriots paced the area before the prison cells. The warden, came up to them, "we would like to show you our facilities that allows to tease out confessions from the prisoners."

'Show us the way'. Balan concurred.

The warden took the visiting company through a thick oak door to a hall. A circular skylight in the center would let in the light from the roof. The elements would pour through this oculus. Sun, rain, wind, dust, haze. Right below this oculus lay a blood-stained flat oak table with contraptions attached. On of which was the spread-eagle mechanism and the other was the vise that would elongate the tabletop with its unfortunate guest tied to it.

The warden continued, "usually just looking into these contraptions makes the prisoner sing. "

"However occasionally we get a tough guy, laden with faith bullshit or ideological chickenshit, then we start turning the screws.

"We usually start with pulling fingernails. That finishes the interrogation pretty quick, though there is a lot of screaming involved.

"If that doesn't work, we use the hammer to break all the knuckles. That gets everyone talking. But these times less screaming but more whimpering.

"And then we place them slowly into the table, strap them in. When they look up, they see the contrast between freedom and health above and their tortured fate below. Those blue skies, or cloudy grey sky, the wind and the rain always have a profound impact upon the prisoners. It seems these are the best torture tools. Just like an un bequeathed love is a torture for the lover, a thousand-fold more is the torture of a prisoner who has a glimpse of freedom. So, I have come to realize, a lover without his love is the same as the prisoner without his freedom. Funny is human psyche. Tell me Indian, does your compatriots' drama play cover any love and torture story?"

"I have no idea what story or drama they will perform. We

have nothing to do with them" answered Balan.

'So, what happens when the threat of blue skies and rainbows fail to break the prisoners?" Balan continued.

'Ahh now comes the best part. You see Indian, we first have to have approval from the Emperor. If we are given the go ahead for 'torture to death', then we bed our prisoners. We tie their limbs here and here... 'the Warden showed the straps at the four corners of the table 'and then pull them or sheer them apart. Of course, there is a lot of screaming and as the ligaments give in, they pass out. Then we have to revive them again and continue the process. Usually by now they all give in."

"Gruesome" Balan observed, "is that your worse torture contraption?"

"There is one, been only used twice if I know my history well. The first one was when I witnessed my predecessor execute the torture scheme. Instead of using straps he used these hooks into the limbs and then pulled. Boy the screaming and the scene...ugh...bad for my palate. And then when the hooked flesh was torn, he'd do it again. "

Balan was taken aback by the matter-of-fact way the warden described all this. 'Where is your predecessor now? Retired?"

'Ohh, I killed him" the warden said nonchalantly." ...when he supported the previous king, betrayed the current Emperor. I got a lot of names out of him, using his own technique on him. You see..." with a pause and pride the Warden continued, ".... that was the second time!"

Balan paused, "you enjoy what you do…. Then you would be interested in one of our own novel techniques. We use the spores of certain mushrooms to induce hallucination and mental horror to the prisoner. You now induce pain without actually maiming them."

'Where is the fun in that?" The warden pondered. "I mean, I do want to see your mushroom methods, but I'd rather see 'em permanently maimed."

Balan forced a smile, "you can have your fun. But do not do anything to the rebel prisoners until we have our way. I want them unharmed and in one piece for our methods to be successful. Prestress doesn't work well with Mushrooms. They will lose their minds completely, then they will be useless to me, and to you. So be patient. Once we are done, you can feed them to rabid dogs.'

'That's a good idea, Rabid dogs. I haven't thought of that yet! 'Answered the Warden with an innocent smile.

Balan replied, "I'll leave you to your sick devices , but we want our subjects to be unharmed until we are done with them"

With that Balan turned and left.

With that the warden felt quite happy, that his methods were ascribed as 'sick' by the foreigner.

Chapter 19

The Play

Part 2

Balan & Chanakkya were in the great hall enjoying the feast with their companions, the feast thrown in honor of the Indians by the Emperor. They sat next to each other, with the emperor in close quarters but by his own side, staged on a grand table.

'It's quite a coincidence that we have two groups of Indians amongst us. Have you met each other before?' The Emperor queried.

'No, we have not. Like China, India is a large country. I come from the eastern part of the country. From

Palibothra.' Answered Chanakkya. Whereas my elder here…. 'Chanakkya paused and looked at Balan to complete his sentence.

"We hail from the northern part of India," Balan began. "But we arrived here via Tibet, in pursuit of the rebels. They have caused chaos... though now is not the time or place to delve into such grim matters, Your Highness."

'No complete your thoughts," the emperor insisted.

Balan hesitated but continued. "Well, these Tibetan rebels first stirred up unrest in Tibet and then fanned out to India, wreaking havoc within the Nanda Empire. I was tasked by the Nanda king to pursue them in Tibet. Once we quelled them there, we followed them east. Little did we know they had made such inroads within your kingdom as well."

'It is great that you now have most of them in custody, but I need names to carry back to India to once and for all, squash the rebellion in my country."

The Emperor nodded, then shifted topics. "What do you know of this Eskander, who defeated the Persians and the Egyptians?"

"I know nothing, Your Highness, or as much as your intelligence chief might," Balan said, looking pointedly at the general.

The general remained silent.

"Perhaps we need to unite our forces, from China to India, to counter this warlord menace from the west," the Emperor mused aloud, though it sounded more like a statement than a question.

'Maybe we can pose it to the Indian Ambassador due to arrive in two days' time' the Emperor continued.

Both Balan & Chanakkya paused for a fraction of a moment. Balan observed, 'maybe he will have further instructions for me and my troops."

Chanakkya, after a pause, not looking at Balan, addressed the Emperor, "maybe we can bring forward the opening of the play in honor of the Indian Ambassador? we can have our inaugural three days from now. Two days from now Would be our last *rehearsal*.'

The Emperor thought for a while, "Sure that would be a grand welcome to our royal guest. Tell me, is he a big fan of your plays?"

"I'm not personally acquainted with the Ambassador, my lord," Chanakkya replied.

'I think it's a swell idea my lord, I will organize the diner for our esteemed guest, if my lord so wishes' . It was LaFang who entered the hallway. The Emperor gave the motion, so that she would sit next to him.

"Then it's settled. We shall have the inaugural play on the day of the Ambassador's arrival," the Emperor concluded.

Everyone continued with the feast.

The General nodded too, in a manner that seemed to reflect his thought. 'Something does not sit right'.

Later that Evening: In the Royal Ladies' Quarters Chanakkya paced the antechamber of the Royal Ladies' Quarters.

"The Lady LaFang will see you now," announced the usher, showing him the way.

Chanakkya followed the Usher into a grand ornate hall lined with Gold and Burgundy motif.

"The lady will join you in a moment". Then the usher left him.

The double swing door on the other side opened, and in walked Lady LaFang. Dressed in white, aquamarine, & blue silk stripes, for she was, is if a light contrast & the pearl to the Burgundy hall. Or one could see her as an orchid within an ornate vase. And that's how Chanakkya beheld Lady LaFang at the moment. Simply mesmerized by her beauty and her setting.

Lady LaFang sensed what Chanakkya was feeling.

"You shouldn't be taken aback by all the pomp of this place. Tell me, O actor, how are you finding our accommodations for you and your troupe ?" LaFang said so with an expression of formality.

Chanakkya snapped out of it. He too took a formal

pose, 'Thank you for your hospitality, we find your accommodations and food quite agreeable.'

"Excellent," LaFang replied, "what can I do for you?"

Chanakkya came forward unfurling a parchment. 'Me lady, since we have the play couple of days earlier than planned, to honor the Indian Embassy soon to arrive. We wanted to run the sitting by you and the way we want….' With a pause Chanakkya continued, 'the staging of the play to happen, so that the royals would have the best vantage point '

With that Chanakkya began to go over the play arrangement and seat layout with lady LaFang. 'May I make some suggestions?' LaFang continued and drew out a couple of alternatives to her layout. 'All of your play focus should be on this area'. **But her finger was not on the stage.**

And at that moment the service door opened, and a couple of retinues came in with refreshments. They served the Lady and the guest. With the main usher standing by.

LaFang flipped the parchment to the layout of the stage, 'Tell me, where are the royal servants seated?"

Chanakkya answered with a pause, 'We haven't had a specific designated area me lady'

LaFang made a comical horror expression,' what no seating for our lovely ladies and the gentleman here! There….' She started to scribble on the parchment. 'There, do you approve of this layout?" LaFang handing over the Parchment to the Usher.

The Usher looked at it, and with a stoic expression answered, ' It all looks good to me , my lady. But the lady knows best.'

'You never have an opinion, do you? One would say you'd make the perfect husband!' LaFang teased.

Then she flipped the parchment, and made some marks, "Here, these are my thoughts and suggestions."

"Consider it under advisement. Me lady" Chanakkya folded in the parchment inside his pouch.

"Ohh I almost forgot!" Chanakkya continued, "The troupe have a gift for you, me lady." He waved and a chest full of fancy play costume were brought forward, "for your retinues to have fun".

Lady LaFang smiled, "We shall have a look sometimes then".

"Please my lady if you have any other thoughts, do not hesitate to call for me. I will now bid goodbye; I already have taken so much of your time"

Lady LaFang nodded and left with her retinue to the inner chambers.

With that Chanakkya turned around and left the way he came in. As the door was opened for him, he found himself face to face with the General standing in the doorway.

'Ahh the Indian, master storyteller. How are you today?" The General bemused. "What plot are you preparing for us in your play?" The general quizzed.

'We shall tell a great story. It will bring tears in your eyes' Chanakkya smiled and bowed his way out.

Once Chanakkya had left, the general gave the Usher the look. The Usher came by. The general raised an eyebrow, "Well?"

The Usher replied, "he came to ask the lady for her opinion on the royals' seating arrangement"

"…mmm…" the general continued, "something does not seem to sit well." Looking at the Usher, "you know the drill, you report to me any cough, sneeze and glance that seems out of place. Something up with these Indians that I feel does not sit right."

Chapter 20

Curtains

It was mid-afternoon on the following day, a moment in history where competing events would dictate not only the course of the future but the very manifestation of fate itself.

From the outskirts of the city a rider came riding in full gallop. His attire, all black. His face was wrapped around a black cloth. But he brought out a yellow flag exhibiting extreme emergency. He was interrupted by the guards at the gate. He showed them the security medallion, and then yelled at their captain, "You! Ride with me, for I cannot afford to be stopped at each security post. This is of outmost security concern; your fucking life depends on it!"

The two galloped towards the palace.

An observer on top of a pavilion noted the incomer. He immediately raised a large flag of his own, this was purple, green in color. It was observed by one of the Indian performer troupes at the rehearsal hall high tower. He in turn waved a flag of his own to various observers below.

Chanakkya, said out loud, "The alarm is being sounded, we have to act NOW!"

All of the troupes ran to the prop boxes and took out all the wooden swords and spears. Only that those were not of wood but had a sheathing of wood. Once splintered a ribbon like long blade was exposed, what would in later centuries called the 'Urumi' of Sangam. For it was Balan, who first figured out the alloy that would allow for such high tensile yet thin iron ribbon blades. This flexible ribbon blade would become the clandestine weapon for the Indians.

Chanakkya's messenger reached the quarters of Balan and his troops. Balan already knew that a spy had returned from his expedition that would probably expose their ruse of being in the palace. Balan gave the instructions, Chanakkya's troupe, fully armed is to meet him at the prisoner cells and wait for his command.

Two competing sets of events now raced against each other.

The General received the news from the spy, and his expression immediately changed. "Follow me", he commanded everyone present. He then yelled out to his lieutenant, "confine all our foreign guests to their quarters under armed supervision, both the actors and the delegate from India. There should be no change to my orders until you see me. Let us find out what actually is going on here."

A contingent of palace guards were rallied up and they went directly to the grand hall where the Indian drama troupes were supposed to be rehearsing. They found the hall almost empty, except for a few young lads. They came upon them and the captain of the guards asked them with menacing tone, and drawn swords, "where are all you Indians?"

The lad, but answered as he was instructed to answer, "they all went to the grand pond for taking a bath, they should be back soon."

The captain left a few guards at the grand hall and took the rest of his palatial guards to the pond.

In the meantime, the General rushed to the Emperor's audience hall and asked for a security detail with the Emperor immediately.

'Your highness we have grave concern about the security of the palace and the true intention of our Indian guests.'

'What do you mean?'

'I had my messenger sent out to the Indian embassy. The Indians were surprised to learn that an embassy had also arrived from Tibet. They mentioned they never had representation in Tibet, nor there was any Buddhist rebellion in India. Our Indian guest are pretenders. '

The Emperor stood up, 'Sound the city wide alarm , Now !'

Balan shoved the general's issued paper to the prison warden, 'we want to interrogate the rebel prisoners.'

The warden opened the heavy iron bar double swing door. And moved aside for the eight or so Indians to step in. Four of them went forward, while four stayed behind the warden and the two of the guards at the gate.

'So where do you keep your keys?' Balan asked in the manner of an enthusiastic tourist coming to the prison for a day visit.

'Ohh, I have them personally on me all the time. They all have to come by me to either get in or get out.

'What happens if you are indisposed?' Carried on Balan

'Tough luck, all have to wait' said the warden with an air of indispensability.

'Surely, have you lost your keys sometime?' Balan mused.

'In my thirty years being with this prison, I have never misplaced a key, never had a jail break , that is why they made me the warden. And if there was ever a need of a second set of key, then the general has spares in his Safe.' The warden paused. He felt he was giving away too much information to the foreigner in his enthusiasm.

Just then the city-wide alarm, the ringing of central

cathedral bell rang out.

'Wait hang on, now what we have here', the warden disengaged in conversation with Balan. Then slowly regained his official composure, 'Sorry that is the security alarm, we will have to pause and secure all facilities until....'

As the warden turned to Balan, he and two of his guards fell to the assaults of the Indians.

'Well, there is always a first time....' Balan said with sarcasm as a he took the keys from the warden as he lay on the floor. Balan gave the signal to Indian 'actor' troupes who were now in complete battle gear, that they had smuggled in as prop for the Play earlier. Chanakkya, appeared along with them. '

'Where is your armor?' Balan asked Chanakkya. Chanakkya answered,' I will never have use of them'.

Balan smiled and quipped, 'scholars' .

Balan leads them through the inner chambers, finally arriving at the 'rebel' cells, twelve large cells in number. He unlocked them and let the rebels out, who were in fact his men all along!

The Indian 'actor' troupes supplied the armor and weaponry to the freed 'rebel' prisoners. With forty of Balan's own men, and sixty of the 'Actor' jawans, and about two hundred of 'Rebel' soldiers, Balan now commanded three hundred warriors, well inside the palace walls.

Now History never heard of these 'three hundred' men but would surely feel their impact.

The Emperor commanded the General, 'find me those wretched Indians, wherever they are, and have them in chains, Go!'

The Emperor himself took his palace guards and went to his residential quarters. He quickly put on his armor. His retinue brought a set of weapons for him, and as he was adjusting his attire, a whole lot of clamor and clashing of weapon noise broke out.

'They are inside the palace! The darn Indians! You take your men and re-enforce the guards. Eight of you follow me. '

The Emperor made his way with long strides to the ladies chamber. He was concerned about LaFang. And he also wanted to eliminate the boy king. He began to put two and two together, and realized that the rebels were here to free the boy king.

He came upon the guards who were guarding the main entrance door and nodded at them. The guards opened the main chamber door, or rather they tried to. It seems it was locked or blocked from the inside. They tried again. failed.

They looked at the Emperor. The Emperor yelled at them, 'What are you waiting for! Break it down!'

The guards brought the battering ram and had a couple of swings at it. Apart from the splinters on the ornate panels, the doors held sturdy as ever, for they were designed to withstand external assault of this very nature.

The Emperor feared for LaFang's safety. "Burn it down if you have to".

A couple of the guards applied oil to the doorway, and lit it, while the battering ram kept on ramming it.

It took a good twenty minutes before one of the door panels gave halfway.

One of the eager guards tried to shimmy in and was met with a single powerful arrow in the shoulder. That made the rest of the guards cower.

'Break that fucking door down', the Emperor yelled.

In the meantime, the noise of clamor and fighting intensified and it was getting close. Where was his general? Surely the whole of the Emperor's army needs to be here, right now.

The door finally gave away, with smoke and amber all over the place. The few who were first to venture in, even with their shield held up, fell to the ground either with arrows in their thighs or shoulders.

The soldiers finally consolidated and formed the Wall barrier with their shields. They went into the ladies' main chamber, lounging area. They found a few of the eunuchs who were stationed within the chamber Lying wounded on the floor.

The Emperor yelled out, 'show yourselves you filthy coward Indians!'

Then behind one of the columns a female warrior in full battle regalia with bow drawn replied with stern authority, "There is no Indian here. Only a Chinese woman to set things right."

"Reveal yourself" replied the Emperor, somewhat taken aback.

The woman warrior came forward in a white and peacock blue armament attire. It was in fact LaFang!

She was wearing the armors that was hidden away in the chest supplied by Chanakkya.

Balan pushed forward, with his three hundred prepared and ready jawans. His flare and grace of martial arts are unparalleled. He would infiltrate the resistance in front of him, create a gap, and then his jawans would follow him in. He was fearless, crafty with his spear 'sang' which also had a side blade. He yelled out to his jawans, 'Men! Stay, Stay, Stay with me ', all the while he was forging, or rather, sprinting forward.

The three hundred Indians made mincemeat of the palace guards. They kept moving fast and forward. For they knew if they allowed the palace guards and the regulars to regroup, they would not have a chance, for they would be vastly outnumbered.

The three hundred spanned out to various halls and simply took any guards but spared any civilians or palace personnel.

Balan knew where he needed to go, for Lady LaFang had provided the location on the parchment when she discussed the sitting arrangement for the Play with Chanakkya!

The vast majority of the guards were at the grand pond. Soon the captain realized they were misled. And then word came to them, the palace was under attack by the Indians. They galloped on their horses towards the royal palace in full earnest.

Balan faced General Ming.

He took three steps forward, as if to present himself to the General, so that the general may have Balan in his striking swing of his sword. The General committed and Balan took the fourth as a sidestep, it seemed more like choreography rather than an evading stance. As he did, he had the hilt of his spear between the leg of the General. In one motion Balan, using both his momentum of his sidestep and the imbalanced General because of his missed swing, he flipped the spear so that both the hilt & the General was airborne. The General fell on his back. And the spear point was now facing the General's neck.

Balan unceremoniously killed the general in the following move. Fast and skillful was the maneuver that left the palace guards in fear, and in shock.

Balan glanced back at the guards for a brief while, with his menacing eye piercing through his protective helmet. He looked back to his jawans, and said, "protect my back" and began to sprint towards the inner sanctum of the palace. Balan wasn't sure if the objectives of their mission were still alive.

Haven seen their general dead; the palace guards

were demoralized. They pulled up a passive resistance with the front line of the Jawans, while the rest of the Indian Jawans followed Balan to the inner sanctum.

Chanakkya, in the meantime with a group headed towards the main gate of the palace, with the intention of closing off the gate. Securing the palace premises against the Regulars who were now being organized, was the paramount objective for him.

A severe battle ensued between the guards at the gate and the Jawans. As the Jawans were superior in number, the guards at the gates were eventually neutralized. The gates were then closed & secured.

The Emperor was in total shock, to see LaFang in battle gear, and apparently a skilled warrior, had taken him by surprise. The Lady of the Palace, steeped in aesthetics, music, culinary & entertainment traditions, is in fact a very capable warrior! The Emperor's mind was racing. What else did he miss!

'Where is the Boy?' The Emperor hissed.

'Safe!' Answered LaFang, '....and as long as I am alive, he will remain that way'

'We can change that pretty soon, seize her!' The Emperor yelled.

A few of the palace guard's broke formation from the shield wall and rushed LaFang. But they were met with highly precise arrows piercing their thighs and shoulders. The remaining guards maintained their formation and slowly moved towards LaFang. LaFang, realizing her situation untenable preemptively rushed the formation. The palace guards did not expect such skillful martial maneuvers from a woman, and LaFang took full advantage of their bias expectations. A few more guards fell, but LaFang was overwhelmed. Three long spears were now being leveled at her, and LaFang knew not if she would outmaneuver these guards. By the corner of her eye, she noticed that the Emperor moved away from the lounge area. A chill ran down her spine, for she knew the boy king was now in mortal danger.

The guards moved onto LaFang for the first strikes. But just then a yell rang out across the hallway. As the guards turned, they saw Balan airborne with bloodied Spear in angle of attack. He was followed by his Jawans. The palace guards were now severely outnumbered, and all fell within moments. LaFang recovered and had no time to acknowledge Balan's interception. She sprang into action in search of the Emperor.

The Emperor in the meantime moved from room to room and eventually found the boy king in the servants quarter. He did not hesitate a moment but went in for the kill. But all of a sudden, he felt he had no strength left in his arm, and he was passing out. And then he felt the pain in his back, but the most debilitating and sharp pain was in his liver and lung. He did not realize but he had six knives piercing his back, all unleashed by LaFang. The Emperor turned to see LaFang with six more knives in her two hands. 'Step away from the boy!' LaFang said in a deep tone even for a woman. The Emperor slowly moved towards LaFang, blood oozing out of his mouth, he fell on LaFang. LaFang put away her knives and then held him tight, as they both sat on the floor.

'You betrayed me," the Emperor uttered feebly, more blood oozing out more from his mouth.

"No," LaFang replied softly, tears streaming down her face. "You betrayed yourself the moment you chose to kill an innocent child."

'I loved you', the Emperor said breathing towards his last counts of breathe allotted to his life.

'….and I could have loved you, if you would only listen, and stopped all your blood shed…." LaFang answered while stroking the Emperor's temple.

' …maybe it's better this way….' With a feeble smile the Emperor exhaled his last breath.

LaFang stood up, folded the arms of the Emperor in a regal pose over his chest. She undid her cape and covered the Emperor with it.

She walked into the main hall, with her blood-soaked attire, and walked past Balan. Balan looked at her and called out to her, 'Are you alright?'

She did not answer and walked towards the balcony. 'Are you alright!', Balan asked again.

'No, I am not Alright' answered LaFang.

'You men, when will you ever learn.' She lamented, while a streak of tears ran down her cheek.

LaFang was in fact FaMing!

Chapter 21

The Foundation of Lin at Shao Mountain

The Abbot looked at the high priests of the temple. 'The Emperor has been eliminated; the old dynasty will be reinstated. But for lasting peace we need to …. you need to have your say to the denizens.'

The high priest acknowledged, "My old mentor, you will find my courage matching the Jawans, Buddha willing. I know what needs to be done. I will mediate peace"

Chanakkya looked down over the battlements to the outside grounds. The grounds were teeming with the regulars, and in the distance the siege towers were being brought in.

'What do you suggest? ohh priest'

'Open the gates for us, let us talk to the captain.' The high priest began to formulate his plan.

'What! We would just simply let them in. They want us dead, in case if you haven't noticed they are building a siege tower.'

'No, they do not want you dead, they are simply afraid of the Emperor. Now that he is gone, they will listen to reason, and most of them are sympathetic to the old kingdom. Let me now talk to them. You can go back to your militant ways if my approach does not work.' The high priest reasoned.

Balan came in, hearing what the high priest had to say. "You may proceed with what you want to do. Chanakkya will ensure the gates will close behind us if they walk away from peace."

Chanakkya turned to Balan, concern in his voice. "How... how is FaMing? Is she unharmed?"

Balan paused, "She is unhurt.... But she is not doing well emotionally. It seems she had developed a rapport with the deceased Emperor, and she taking the final measure is not sitting well with her."

"Let me talk to her," Chanakkya started on his way. Balan held Chanakkya back by the arm, 'not now, she needs space to recenter her emotion.'

Chanakkya was unsure how he could console her. He decided he would talk to her, just be there for her. But now he needed to focus on the threat at hand, the siege of the palace that was developing outside the battlements. He, Balan, the high priest, and the abbot agreed upon the strategy on which they would attempt a parlay with the regulars.

The Jawans raised the Flag of Parley over the battlement. The portico gate of the main Palace gates opened and, the high priest and his council of priests stepped out. Balan also joined them.

The council of Priests and Balan with a parlay flag approached the regulars and stopped mid-way. The captain of the regulars and a few of his lieutenants approached from the other side.

'We will accept your surrender, and you and your men would be justly judged in the royal court', the captain stated.

Balan answered, 'Shouldn't you start with profound gratitude and a thank you?'

The captain was taken back. 'What do you mean?'

'We have rid you, your tyrant Emperor, and secured the Life of the right full heir to the throne, the boy king, the father of whom was the one to receive allegiance of all of you. So yes, I think a 'thank you' is in order. '

The captain regained his composure. "We can dispense with niceties once we determine whose heads stay in place and whose roll."

'No head is going to roll' the High Priest said firmly,

'Enough of this bloodshed, this country now needs stability. We recognize the boy king as sovereign. And the way the community of priests sees it, this does not need to escalate any further. As long as you all give allegiance to the living king, we see no reason for any prosecution of ...Any One!

The Captain laughed, 'until, of course, another of you groups come and kill this boy. And then we have to worry about our heads, who keeps it, who doesn't.'

'That is why, we are changing the role of the monastery...' Interjected Balan, 'your allegiance will lay with the office of the Emperor, not the person...while the monasteries allegiance lies with the person. They will ensure the security and continuity of the royal line. The monks of the Lin Forrest of the Shao Mountain maintain the order of things.'

'So, these monks, these 'Shao Lin' monks decide who gets to be the emperor?'

'No, they do not. They are monks, limited in number, not like the numbers in your army. They will be there to hold the Honor of the Throne, & its Security only, if they step out of bounds, you will take them out. And they will be highly skilled in the martial arts, so if any of your future errant generals want to usurp the throne, well that would take significant effort, for they will have to take out these monks first, the guardians of the empire.'

The captain pondered for a while. 'Let me confer with my peers, the captain thoughtfully laid those words out.

Balan and the high priest bowed their heads in

response.

The captain along with some within the rank walked back to his peers. They discussed, they paced, they had a lot of hand waving too. A dog scratched the back of his head with his hind leg. A flock of pigeons flew around in swarming formation. The mundane actions in the surrounding carries on, and yet in these mundane moments sometimes the momentous occur.

The captain and his peers came back. He raised his hands and then paused. 'We are listening, tell us how this thing plays out?'

This time Balan spoke, 'You all, the army, the palace guards, the monks & the priests will take oath of allegiance to the boy king. Then the high priest will auger the boy king into ascension. Then the rest of the civil servants, judges, and the citizens will pronounce their oath of allegiance to the new emperor. There would be a council of advisors, that would have representation from all segments of life, which would include the high priest of how you term it,,' Shaolin Monks' , and yourselves. And there shall be no prosecution of the deposed emperor's followers, nor of the people who helped rescue the boy king. Simple, yet this will ensure peace

The Captain looked around at his peers. They were all slowly but firmly nodded in approval.

The Captain turned to Balan, "I want to first know if the lady of the court, LaFang is alive and well. If any harm has come to her, then you can kiss all this peace initiative goodbye, for I for one would not rest to put the head on a pike of anyone who may have caused her harm."

Balan looked at the captain with thoughts. He was feeling encouraged. FaMing has indeed made an impression on all, and her words will carry weight to establish peace.

'She is fine, O captain. She was the one who took the life of the Emperor when he sought to kill the boy king. She is my mentee. Know that Captain, she was one of the key members who put this plot together to bring about peace and save the boy king….so you decide, if you want to be on the right side of history.'

The Captain was dumbfounded. His mind was racing.

Then the Captain took his right hand to his left chest and clicked his heels. 'We accept your vision and terms. Will this all be written down?'

"Yes," the high priest said, stepping forward. "We will convene to set up a constitution that everyone can recognize and abide by."

The High Priest bowed his head while taking both his hand cusped into each other and raising it to both Balan and the Captain.

'I am doing Fine!' FaMing snapped, responding to Chanakkya's query of how she was doing. The three of them were sitting in the large dining hall adjacent to the audience hall in the grand palace. Food, fruits and drinks from the royal kitchen had been served. The ascension ceremony occurred a day ago.

The Indian embassy had arrived three days ago and were taken completely aback on what had transpired just before their arrival. But they didn't realize that it was their anticipated arrival that had triggered all of the events.

Everyone was present at the ascension of the new emperor to shore up support for peace in its infancy to take root. FaMing too, was present, loud and center of the ascension stage, only playing second fiddle to the new emperor. The boy understood, that it was only because of FaMing that he lived.

FaMing mentored the boy, teaching him the basics of governance and the immutable tenets of justice. Her maternal love for the boy grew with each passing day, but she couldn't help but wonder if she could have changed the Emperor's course. Could one of these warlords, perhaps just one, have been cured of their madness?

"Yes, I am fine," she again said, but this time more moderately. No point hurting Chanakkya's feelings.

Balan now looked up, "my dear, you should accept the outcome. You did as much as you could have done for the war lord. Yes, you did use emotion to infiltrate the inner sanctums of the palace, but only because of that ploy does the boy live! Remember, you were the one who brought us here, accept the outcome. "

Chanakkya's expression grew firm. "I believe I've done my part in achieving your goals. Now it's time for you to help me with Aarohan. This tyrant was a despot, but compared to Dhoni Eskander, he was nothing. We need to return to India. O Guru Bhratha, you said what would help

Aarohan is here."

'Yes, it is', answered Balan. 'Finish up, we will seek out the thing that we came here to look for.'

Balan led the two to the library of the palace. 'People say I am the greatest alchemist and metallurgist alive, but you see, I too had a mentor. And before me, he too traveled both to Tibet and China. He ended up making his final days here in the Shao Forest. And he wrote his treatise, called 'Dhatu Shastra' here. Before passing away he sent me a parchment saying, his book was in fact ...... here in this library! Aarohan too was aware of this book, and my interest in it. And that is why he sent you to fetch me,

The chief librarian approached them. "Take me to where you've stored all of Sadhu Indrajit's works and parchments," Balan instructed.

They were led into a remote section of the library, by the courtyard. Balan went through a litany of stored wooden slats. He started to set aside a few of the slats. Chanakkya looked at Balan, if he should go through them.

'By all means, go ahead.' Balan continued to pull some of the slats.

Chanakkya looked into the slats for some time. 'These are written in the Pali Prakrit; However, they don't make any sense. There seems to be large segments missing'. Chanakkya observed, crest fallen.

Balan finished pulling the bounded slats, he looked satisfied. 'The numbers match' Balan seemed relieved.

"The reason they don't make sense is that they need to be placed in the right order." As he spoke, Balan began ripping open the bindings.

The chief librarian gasped. "Please, sir! Be careful with those—they are priceless! They were authored by Indrajit himself!"

Balan paid little attention to the librarian's protests as he mixed and matched the slats. Once the others understood what he was doing, they remained silent, watching intently.

"The instruction he sent me was 'a drop that creates ripples in the pond,' meaning the arrangement must be concentric. Twenty-seven bounds split into three give us eighty-one segments, which must be arranged so... one becomes nine, two becomes eight, but only for the inner circle. For the outer... if my pattern is correct... the thirteenth becomes thirty-nine, the twelfth is thirty-six, and the eleventh..."

"Thirty-three!" FaMing and Chanakkya said in unison.

Balan smiled. "Good! Now that you understand, help me sequence them."

Chapter 22

Forge Recipe

The following day Chanakkya and FaMing came in after their breakfast. They had helped assemble the slats in the right sequence, but it was Balan who was up all-night deciphering what was written.

'Do you have what you are looking for?' Chanakkya asked apprehensively. He was concerned that they had spent too much time in China, and that it was high time that they needed to head back to India. For it may already be too late for Aarohan.

"No, I understand what is written, but I don't understand what it means," Balan replied, frustration heavy in his voice. He hadn't slept the previous night, and the bags under his eyes told the story.

'May I have a look?' Chanakkya queried, desperate to move things forward. Balan handed him the re-bounded slats, study this portion, this is where nothing makes sense'.

Chanakkya poured over the slates, back and forth, several times.

'It does not make sense, apply the 'Nirjash' , essence of the environment. How is that even possible?' Chanakkya said, feeling dejected.

Balan got up, and strolled into the courtyard, there was a board walk through the slender young bamboo garden. He traversed the pathway. Then he began to appreciate the architecture of the place. The various motifs, ornamentation, patterns, craft, materiality. Then it struck him!

Balan yelled out to Chanakkya, 'I think I have got it! The chief librarian, where is he? Bring him to me, Now!'

Chanakkya got up, hurried, and fetched the Chief Librarian, or more so forced him into the audience of Balan.

'Sire, how can I be of help?' The librarian said, somewhat perplexed.

'Speak to me, O librarian' Balan gave him full attention, 'Tell me of this place'.

'This place?' The Librarian queried with a tone of confusion.

'Yes, this place, this courtyard, this garden, what do you know about this place? Tell me whatever you know, do not leave out anything', Balan's tone became authoritative.

'Well, it was designed and maintained by the great sage, IndraJeet.' The librarian began, 'he designed all the motif and cast them himself....'

Balan interrupted the librarian, which was very unlike Balan; Chanakkya was surprised by Balan's impatient, 'Everything here is done by IndraJeet? When did he build this place?'

'...About ten years ago. He set the stones, within them the metal motifs, and he was also very particular about the species of the bamboo to be planted here, and how often to plant them, and when to remove them.

'......Remove them?' Balan again interjected.

'Yes, they would be kept only for the rainy season, and early autumn. Then he would harvest them.'

"And after the harvest, what did he do?" Balan pressed, as if the answer held the key to the entire puzzle.

The librarian seemed lost for words. "I—I don't know..."

Balan stiffened up. Most men are callous. And Balan didn't care for that much. But when callousness derails history in crucial moments, then those callous men simply should not have been there. For they had hindered, by their presence, the progress of history. And Balan detested such kind of men. Not only are they useless, but they actually are harmful.

Balan turned his attention to the bamboo grove. The growth was sparse at the front, moderate in the middle, and dense at the back. Similarly, the patina on the metalwork attached to the wall varied between these areas. Balan ran his hand over the metal motifs, tracing the differences in the formation of rust. He followed the motifs to the back, bent down, and examined a relief on the wall that seemed to hold significance. One keystone had notches, almost like grips. Instinctively, he placed his fingers in the notches and turned the motif—it came loose.

Inside was a block, a metal block, free of stain or blemish. If IndraJeet placed this here, it would be at least ten years old, yet no stain or rust had formed on the metal block. Balan smiled. He stood up. Turned.

He now looked back to the group standing on the other side of the bamboo growth. He looked at the world in a very different light now. For he now understood what IndraJeet's slats contained.

[There are Iron Columns located all around India. None of these iron columns ever accumulate rust. Even to this day metallurgist haven't figured out the constituents of these iron columns. It baffles the scientists, the chemist, and the metallurgist. Some claim they have figured it out, yet when it is time to replicate the process, they have always failed.

IndraJeet was the progenitor of that cast iron alloy, and Balan had just figured out how to cast them from IndraJeet's treaties!]

It's been a fortnight since Balan, FaMing & Chanakkya had packed up their Oxen carts for the treacherous journey to the south. All the monks and interns had lined up the steps of the monastery to bid their master goodbye. The Abbot & the High Priest had pleaded with Balan to stay the previous evening. "Bodhi, your presence is needed here. The clans in the north need you. Your work is not done yet."

"You will carry on. Right now, I'm needed in the south to stand with my friend against the Greek barbarian, Eskander. You will take each of the katanas in the sacred hall to the five holy mountains in the north, where our patron clans reside. These stations will act as Walls of Will for those who seek to preserve peace. Show them and let them practice the ways of the monks who liberated the Shao Mountains."

[History would bear out, within a thousand years in the Lin Forest of 'Shao' mountain to the north, Balan's vision would pan out. But then again that is another story.]

Chanakkya had noted the large katana shaped bundle on the oxen cart. He was curious to know which of the six Katana was Balan carrying back to India. He also wanted to study it, to know what it is that made this blade so special.

So, as they were settling down on the eve of their journey back, he took the opportunity to examine the katana. He unbridled the bundle, and for sure this did not feel like the steel of the Katana.

Chanakkya was anxious. 'Bodhi, we have been tricked, there is no blade in the bundle. Someone has replaced the katana with these bamboo stalks', revealing some samplings to Balan.

Balan was not perturbed. He packed the bamboo shoots in a way that they would remain moist.

"No Chanakkya, we have not been tricked. I packed those stalks here. If you know your tantra you will know these bamboos are more valuable than the Katana that I sent to the five monasteries."

"This makes no sense. Aarohan sent me across a thousand krosh to bring you back, thinking you would arm his army. And now, you're taking bamboo stalks to Gangaridai? What kind of tantra is this?" Chanakkya was exasperated.

Balan smiled and replied, "Don't get riled up, my boy. You will see soon enough. And we are not going to Gangaridai, not just yet."

GANGARIDAI

Chapter 23

Convergence

'Wake up lads', FaMing called to Chanakkya, and Balan who were taking a nap under the arch awning of bullock cart. 'We are here, Balan'.

Ever since the incident of her hands being forced to kill the usurper Emperor, FaMing had become a different version of herself. Silently, she had come to realize the unjustified killing of human beings, any human being. Even the evil ones, the amoral men, they too were reared into becoming what they become or what they do. All of it is driven by ego, mostly of men, and jealousy, mostly of women.

And she wanted none of this.

Balan sensed what FaMing was going through, and he could sense that she was maturing as a complete sage warrior in her own right. He could see she didn't consider him as her mentor anymore. And that was alright.

Chanakkya, too sensed that FaMing was a different person after her time in the Palace. Did she fall in love with the murderous emperor? How can that be? Or did she simply develop a sympathy for the wayward warlord? But all that can wait. He was now concerned that they had taken too much time in their Chinese expedition and time may have very well ran out for Aarohan. He needed Balan at Aarohan's side. And that too yesterday. He was anxious that they now had to travel way south beyond Pataliputra. This would extend his mission by another six weeks at the least. This time lost was not boding well with him.

Balan jumped off the cart. They were at the confluence of the river Tel and Mahanadi. He looked around. And then pointed to an encampment by the shore. 'That's where we need to go'.

'Careful Guru Bhratha, they may be river pirates, I advise caution' an apprehensive Chanakkya warned.

'Fear not my lad, look at the banner' Balan smiled. 'But we can always use caution. FaMing, you want to take vantage point ? '

FaMing took her long bow & quiver, jumped off the cart, and traversed to a high point in the vicinity.

The banner that was flown over the shanty settlement was Tibetan, but more so, that everyone recognized, it was Balan's coat of honor insignia!

'You have your men this far south! Guru Bhratha?'

Balan smiled, 'I still have some tricks up my sleeve, eh lad? Come let's see what they have in store for us.'

As Balan approached, there was activity in the encampment. A man came forward to greet them, 'Sire, it's so nice to see you again. We have been here waiting for almost a moon now, but we would have waited two more moons as instructed.'

'Nice to see you junior abbot! I hope your mission was successful?' Balan enquired.

'Yes master, it was. We have what you have asked us to retrieve. Was your trip to the Shao mountains fruitful?'

'Yes Manasha, we have our fruit 'Balan bemused.

Balan turned to the direction of where FaMing would have taken station and waved. It was okay for FaMing to join then.

Manasha gave out a long laugh, 'I was wondering where Lady FaMing was. I am glad my neck was not pierced by her arrow! Trust me sire, we are not compromised'

'Come you all must be famished, our retinues will prepare your meals, resting quarters. And your baths will be ready soon.'

Chanakkya bemused, 'Royal service in the middle of nowhere! How on earth....'

After the trio had been well rested after their

afternoon meal, they all gathered at an enclosure where two bullock carts were stored.

Manasha addressed Balan, with the gold that you had given me, I was able to obtain two cart loads of iron ore, from the Deccan. I believe they are of high grade.'

Balan went to the carts and looked under the coverings, picked up a piece of rock and examined it. 'You have picked well Manasha, all those years apprenticing with me has paid off' . Balan was pleased.

Balan turned to Chanakkya, 'We have what we needed. Now you will lead the way to Aarohan, it's your show now!'

Chanakkya was ecstatic. 'We will head to the outskirts of Pataliputra, I will plan the route.'

Chanakkya still had questions, how was this all arranged. And in such short period of time ! FaMing too, was perplexed.

Balan was enjoying the moment. 'You see when we decided that we were to travel to Lin Forest, I had dispatched Manasha along with eleven others of his cohort to southern India. Regardless of what I wanted to retrieve from China, whether we would be successful or not, this ore was needed for forging of the weaponry. Of course, the element we have brought from China will make our weaponry far superior to the Greeks, but even if we failed, there would be enough ore for Aarohan's army. So why wait until our expedition to China was complete? Manasha had instructions to wait here until the end of monsoon, and of we did not return , to proceed to Pataliputra and sell the

Ore in the market. Regardless, it would have been accessible to Aarohan. I just saved you eight weeks of labor!'

Chanakkya was simply ecstatic, 'What are we waiting for!'. And in his joy, he hugged Balan, he hugged Manasha and was about to hug FaMing. But she had her arm crossed. And so Chanakkya stopped his awkward embraces. But he didn't care, he was happy. Relieved!

Chapter 24

The Forge: Part 1

Chanakkya looked up into the knotted beads within the hanging sutra of the branches of the great Banyan tree at the eastern outskirts of Pataliputra. The record keeper was standing beside him, with the expectations whatever information he could provide would be supplemented with a handsome 'baksheesh' tip, for the keeper did have information, he thought would be valuable to Chanakkya.

Before the record keeper could speak up, Chanakkya picked up the threads of certain colors and bead combinations.

"Let me guess, these are the ones that the grand general Aarohan had placed in perpetuity with you? "

"Yes sire," answered the record keeper, but the confused expression of how Chanakkya knew these were indeed the ones made Chanakkya chuckle.

Chanakkya kept studying the knots in the beads, about three hundred or more in total. Slowly gleaming out the information embedded within frequency and spacing of the knots and the gaps in between, the code that only he and Aarohan could read. The information is from two months ago. The beast is ready. The meeting point is the way to the east towards the Arakans. A foundry has been constructed.

So, before the record keeper could speak up again, Chanakkya gave him a pouch of coins, that would be a considerably generous amount of Bakshish.

'You will provide no information of these beads to anyone , when it was placed and that I have read it.'

Saying so Chanakkya, tore down the hanging sutras and placed it within his carrying pouch.

Both Balan and FaMing was looking at Chanakkya from their Oxen drawn carts.

'So?' FaMing had the inquisitor expression.

'We go east to Pundra; he has stationed a foundry at the confluence of the river' answered Chanakkya

'...and you know all this by simply reading the threaded beads?" Wondered Balan.

'You guys are not the only ones with skills here' retorted Chanakkya, feeling a bit more spunk in his voice, as he climbed onto the cart next to FaMing. "Ouuu, look at my man go" FaMing teased Chanakkya while locking her arm to his and giving it a zesty squeeze. Chanakkya visibly blushed, to which Balan gave out a hearty laugh.

The Trio with their bullock carts of iron ore cargo slowly headed out of the outskirts of Pataliputra towards the cardinal point in the horizon where the sun rose over the Arakan.

They traversed through western plains of Ganga which took a moon. As they travelled Balan and FaMing took in the beauty of the landscape. And the abundance of resources these lands provided. Chanakkya acted as the trios' guide. And took pleasure in describing the culture and nature of the land. Eventually they reached the Ganges where it runs south and Balan surveyed the area.

"I hope your master succeeds in repelling this Eskander from the west," Balan observed with concern. "If the Greeks are victorious, they'll never leave this land of plenty. I will forge the blades that Aarohan needs, but I believe there's a better way to defeat the Greeks than an all-out battlefield engagement. Will your people rise when the time comes?"

Chanakkya remained silent.

"Tell me this much: is the land ruled by a tyrant or a just leader?"

Again, Chanakkya remained silent.

"That tells me enough," Balan sighed. "The people aren't warriors. They've allowed a tyrant to rule over them."

'Are you thinking of what you did at the Lin Forrest of the Shao Mountain?" FaMing finally spoke. 'The Greeks are mobile, and they are on the conquering campaign, unlike the despot ruler whom we took out. Will a similar strategy work?"

Balan contemplated. 'They do not have a castle to consolidate behind, but at the same time they are not anchored to the trappings of governance.' Balan paused. 'Do you know the way of the Hassasins ?'

Both Chanakkya and FaMing kept silent.

FaMing said, " that means we will have to go in with a small force. If the mission fails, then its game over. And the Dhoni's like to make an example of their captives. Death will be slow"

'It won't be a 'we" Balan said. 'I will go in alone.'

'Master, you are no longer young anymore. These Dhonies know their business. They have been at it for the past twelve years.

'Twelve years of doing certain things in a certain way. It is their strength, but it is also their weakness." Balan answered

Chanakkya arranged for seven boats to carry the ore across the mighty Ganges. Slowly they made their way to the south and then reached the confluence of the river that had been indicated in the sutras.

Chanakkya told the duo, "Let me forge ahead and see if I

can identify any sign, or beads on any prominent trees to know where abouts of my Master."

"How can you be sure?" FaMing asked, 'The information he has left behind has to withstand weather and chance destruction."

"If I know my old comrade well. He will look for something permanent, a rock formation, something like that. "

Chanakkya tried to recall all his trainings with Aarohan. What and how would Aarohan have his information set in nature for them to track.

'The are no Kotthin Shila _ rock formation in this part of the country, it has to be something else...'

'Why are there those periodic gaps in the tree line ...?' Balan asked, pointing to the eastern horizon with superficial voids within the dense forest. 'Is this one of your bead codes laid out? "

Chanakkya stood up over the bullock carts carrying the ore, and surveyed the tree line, excited and all. 'Guru Bratha, you are right! It is indeed a code. Let me decipher it, 'Chanakkya gazed across the eastern horizon, as if the very land spoke up to him.

Aarohan spoke to the trio through the very land they stood on.

'It is through that gap, half a day journey. We will find him by a brook there after."

The trio along with their bullock carts plied through the forest path that had been cleared through only a few months before. As they brushed through the growth, leeches would tag on to them. They would cut one off, and two would end up in its place. Annoying.

"I do not believe my master alone has created this path, obviously he has had help." Chanakkya said.

"One would think at least a few hundred of them, looks like your master is busy recruiting people." FaMing quipped.

The trio with the bullock carts traversed the trail that had been cut through the forest for them. Dense were the growth as only a few beams of sunlight reached the forest floor.

"How do we know we are indeed on the right path? And it is indeed Aarohan who leads us through this path?" FaMing contemplated.

Balan veered the Bullock cart to the side of a large tree, stood up on the cart and picked up a woven pouch hanging halfway up to the height of the tree.

Balan took the pouch and handed it over to Chanakkya, who was busy de leeching himself.

'What is inside?', cautioned Chanakkya.

'My guess is you will find salt inside'   Balan answered

Chanakkya opened up the pouch, and indeed there

was salt inside the pouch.

'Use it to get rid of your leeches. Sprinkle the salt on top of it and see what happens.'

'And yes, we are on the right track, for only Aarohan would place it there, knowing whoever is tracking him, would need it.' Observed Chanakkya.

After relieving himself of the leeches, Chanakkya handed it over to the other two.

By late afternoon, they reached a clearance in the forest. A brook ran on the farther side of the clearance. Indeed, there was a mud stupa forge right next to it. There was also a large wooden lodge on the opposite side of the forge.

They have found Aarohan! Or rather his base camp.

'Where is your master? 'Balan said, once they surveyed the area and saw no sign of Aarohan.

Chanakkya went up to the door post of the lodge and found couple of thin jute ropes with beads hanging from it. Another message.

"My master says, we should make ourselves at home. There is nourishment wrapped in Banana leaves in the pantry. And bathing water in the large wooden barrel in the 'Snan Khana'

"We need to find some fodder for the oxen and unburden their yokes. I'll go look for some ox edibles."

"No need, you will find dried hay underneath the jute spread over there", answered a voice entering the clearing.

It was Aarohan!

He slowly walked into the center of the clearing, where the sun rays had a robust play. He stood firm, tall, straight. He was carrying a bundle of sticks on his back. Chanakkya thought his master looked taller, of a stronger built.

It is as if History had come and took center stage for the Eon!

"Master, it is so nice to see you again."

"It is nice to see you, my friend." Answered Aarohan addressing Chanakkya not as his student.

"Speaking off friends, I have brought along ...." Chanakkya paused and gestured towards Balan.

Balan had tears in his eyes. FaMing never saw Balan emotional. And was in awe of Aarohan.

"I am so sorry my friend, about Roshan." Balan said.

"It is alright my friend." Aarohan answered, his tone measured. Extending his arm for the arm long shake. Balan took it with gusto.

"Come inside, you all must be famished. Let us get some of your energy back." Aarohan continued.

The four went into the lodge.

The three travelers sat at the center wood table, while Aarohan did a quick table spread. Both Chanakkya and FaMing rose to assist Aarohan. Aarohan simply made the palm motion to sit. His gesture was not a command but a polite compelling gesture. Both sat down.

"You all have travelled far, regain your strength and rest. I will go settle the oxen." Aarohan said

When Aarohan came back in, the three had settled down to drink Chai and Moa, that they found in the pantry.

"Will you not introduce the lady to me?" Aarohan sat down opposite FaMing.

"She is my apprentice. Has attained the thirty stages of your Martial Tantra".

Aarohan raised his eyebrows, "all thirty? ...mmm..."

Aarohan turned to his old friend, Balan, "Have you attained what you were seeking my old Shagred ?"

"I have helped establish a kingdom the size of the Nanda's. We have set in motion the Tarika that will ensure continuity of Dharma & Justice through martial monasteries."

"Impressive" Aarohan said

"I am sorry to hear that you have been sent into exile. You have set up quite a base here. But where are your people? I have journeyed a thousand krosh to bring the ore you had requested. So where is the army?". Balan sounded a bit disappointed.

"They will come when I call them" Aarohan replied

"What makes you sure they will do so? I should be prepping to craft weapons for how many? Five thousand, ten thousand? You do know the numbers of the Dhonis."

"For now, I need to build weapon and armor only for one" Aarohan replied, with no expression on his face

"I needn't bring cart loads of ore for you" Balan visibly getting agitated. FaMing never saw Balan lose his temper. This is not looking good.

"What makes you think it's for me?" Aarohan replied, still without any expression on his face.

Balan paused. He took control of his temper. "Tell me who then? "

Aarohan stood up, went to the side wall to pick up a flame. "Come with me ". He led the three outside on the lawn. It was a full moon now, but the dense growth almost had the moon beams blocked. Aarohan led the trio through a path in the undergrowth. They walked by the brook cascading down a hill. He guided them to the top. Then he threw the flame torch into a pile of prepared bon fire. The fire blazed up.

Aarohan then gave out an echoing howler that resonated across the valley.

The four stood within the dark forest. Aarohan at the front, while the rest observing.

Soon the forest began to rumble. Sounds of Leaves and brunches rustling. Balan and FaMing intuited Aarohan's call had attracted a pack of Wild dogs, and so they took out their sword and spears. Focusing on the undergrowth in the direction of the rustling.

Balan expecting something soon to emerge from the bushes. He steadied himself, looking intently at the bushes. But what came next, they were not expecting. The moonlight was covered by a huge shape that emerged from the trees. A good twenty-two-foot-tall behemoth. All fell back instead of Aarohan.

"This is what we need to armor up" Aarohan brought the light closer to the creature that had emerged from the forest"

It was Manu!

Chapter 25

The Forge: Part 2

Balan prepared the mud bath by the side of the brook. It was early fall. He had embedded a wooden framework within a portion of the mud bath. Aarohan led Manu to the mud bath and slowly made him lie on his side, with his huge head, ear, and, most importantly, his tusks making an impression into the leveled mud bed within the frame. He did the same for the other tusk as well. Aarohan then took Manu for a dip in the brook and scrubbed off the mud. Balan and Chanakkya carefully removed the frames with Manu's tusk impressions and brought them to the casting hut, where FaMing had prepared a hot white plaster paste. Balan immediately poured the paste into the two tusk impressions, ensuring the form was captured for forging work. All were impressed by the humongous size of the tusks, and they wouldn't have been surprised if someone told them that Manu possessed a rare gene once active in the woolly mammoths of ten eons ago.

A day later, the alchemist Balan began to melt the ores he had brought from the Deccan. FaMing, Chanakkya, and Aarohan took turns stomping the bellowing fan to raise the temperature of the furnace. It devoured the charcoal wood that Aarohan and Manu had gathered over the past three moons. When the cauldron was at the right temperature, the ores were added to extract the iron. The charcoal mix provided the carbon needed to turn the iron into steel, a technique Balan had perfected from his knowledge of Indian metallurgy and Tibetan practices he had observed during his seven years teaching the Bodhi Dharma to the monks.

Aarohan was a brilliant military tactician and a veteran trainer of war elephants. Everyone considered him the authority in such matters. But when it came to weapon casting, no one came close to Balan's skill. Aarohan, Chanakkya, and FaMing watched in awe as Balan demonstrated the process of casting and forging the blades for Manu. All four hammered under Balan's direction. Hammer layer one, fold. Hammer layer two, fold. Hammer layer three, fold. The process continued through nine cycles.

"Is it ready for the final pour?" Aarohan asked, hopefully.

Balan smiled. "We're just beginning. You wanted a wonder weapon, and you shall have it."

"Bring me the bamboo shoot beds," Balan instructed FaMing. Along with the ores, Balan had nurtured bamboo saplings from the ones he collected from the Lin Monastery in the Shao Mountains. He battered the bamboo shoots into a pulp and extracted the juice. Slowly and in very minute measures, he dripped the juice into the molten ore.

None had ever seen a technique like this, not even in the present day, for it is similar to the technique used to form the Ashoka Iron Pillars, which never rust and have baffled scientists even to this day.

Balan repeated the procedure nine more times, completing eighty-one folds and nine bamboo drip interludes.

The entire process took about a fortnight.

While the four of them toiled, hammering each of the six-foot blades, they discussed the best possible strategy to defeat the barbarian Eskander, playing out various war game tactics and strategies.

"How much do we know about his tactics?" Balan asked.

"He moves fast, leads his cavalry, and never takes the center. He usually starts with the right flank but will quickly shift to the left and then to the center. He plays to the fluidity of the battlefield," Aarohan replied, his gaze fixed on the far horizon.

"From what I've gathered, he's been on a war rampage for more than a decade. His troops are battle-hardened, and armies from the lands he's conquered have joined him. It seems foolish to engage him in an all-out war. What is your strategy, Aarohan?", Balan quizzed.

"Mobilize the whole populace," Aarohan answered.

"You don't have a single following, if you discount Chanakkya. You're banished from Pataliputra. How do you intend to build up an army of at least forty thousand if you're going to stand a chance against this Eskander barbarian?"

"It's true we don't have any followers at the moment, but there's a path I see. I need you to forge me the blades for Manu."

"And then what? Manu is extraordinary, but you and it charging at the Dhonis' army won't make much of a difference."

"He's not an 'it.' He's a 'him,'" Aarohan corrected.

"Whether it or him, there's still an entire army to contend with," Balan retorted.

"Just give me the blades. That's all I ask, my dear friend. Then you can walk away from our efforts to counter the Dhonis," Aarohan insisted.

FaMing and Chanakkya felt uneasy as they witnessed these two strong personalities at odds.

"On the contrary, I propose something completely different," Balan continued. "We do what we did with the Chinese usurper. We established dharma in Tibet and the Yangtze plains by setting up monasteries and taking out the pretender—not with an army but by using Hassasins."

"You suggest we do the same with the Dhonis?" Aarohan asked.

"Yes. That way, the operation remains less dependent on chance, and we can handpick our team."

"That strategy worked because the Chinese Emperor was static behind walls. The Dhonis are mobile, and they don't anchor themselves to any castle or fortress. It might seem easier, but it's a tougher target," Aarohan argued.

"Who would lead such a suicidal mission?" Aarohan asked warily.

"I'm actively considering it," Balan replied. "What about you? Will you join the operation?"

"I avoid risky ventures these days. I only take on what I'm certain of. If your operation fails, Gangaridai will be totally exposed. I can't take that chance. I'll focus on training my army."

Balan glanced around. "And where, pray tell, is this army?"

Aarohan was clearly offended but continued hammering the red-hot blade. 'let us then take two separate initiative my Sagred, 'Aarohan addressed all, 'I will , with Chanakkya soon head towards Pataliputra, to rally the denizens . FaMing and you can regroup with your crack team of Hassasins , and a have go at your plan. '

The other three joined Aarohan in hammering as the conversation faded, focusing on the arduous task.

Chapter 26

The Third Way

A stray dog lay at the side of the ceremonial courtyard.

Munshara was feeling pretty good. Today was the day. After years of bureaucratic and political maneuvering, he had his prize within his grasp—the seat to the Nanda throne. He thought he had skillfully manipulated the king into secretly negotiating with Eskander, the Greek warlord, only to insert himself in the middle. The scheme was as old as the Vedas themselves: set the terms to show the king in a compromising light, offer better terms to the marauding Eskander so that Eskander found him a willing collaborator, and negotiate titles and land for the ministers of the court. When the time was right, make public the king's secret terms and accuse him of treason. Deniability was key, but a few repositioned titles, deeds for fellow ministers, and the promise of peace to the citizenry could go a long way. Just create enough discontent among the subjects—a feat easily achieved through crippling taxes and draconian laws, which, of course, he himself did not "approve" of but reluctantly "executed" on behalf of the tyrant king of the Nanda dynasty. When enough was enough, he would step in to save the nation from this tyrant king. So typical.

But how Munshara executed such a ploy was anything but typical. He knew timing and staging were everything. Give the accusations a story comparable to the canonical and theatrical *'Jatra'*, and it would become a tale for the ages. Deliver it in the manner of a classical conspiracy of a sold-out monarch and a folk hero saving the day, and a new dynasty would be born. Yes, Munshara was feeling pretty good. All of this took time—first, getting rid of Aarohan, the thorn in his side with his lofty, obnoxious ideals, and then removing his protégé, Chanakkya.

But today was his day.

Jotayu could not believe what he was witnessing. He knew this day would come—that Munshara would one day claim the throne—but to see it happen, or about to happen, was something else entirely. Seeing this dishonorable, amoral man about to take the throne filled Jotayu with disgust. Yet again, the country would see corruption in its lands, as if the Nanda dynasty wasn't bad enough. Jotayu, with his company of captains, proceeded to the area marked for dignitaries—or rather, for those who needed to be watched.

A lot had been done in haste, yet it felt as though things were orchestrated, despite the haste. That meant it was planned, and that meant no rash action should be taken, for lives were at stake. Lives had already been taken. The captain of the royal guards had arrested the regent, Dhana Nanda, on the orders of Prime Minister Munshara. The details were unknown, as were the number of lives lost in recent nighttime raids in the city of Pataliputra. The past nights had been chaotic and uncertain. Summons had been sent to Jotayu to return to the capital from the western borders, where the might of the army had stood vigil against the threat of Eskander. Porus had been defeated. Aarohan, who had been the first to raise the alarm against Eskander, had vanished. Some said to the east, some said to the Lankas, while others surmised that he had gone to the northern Himalayan lands, to China. At any rate, it was unbecoming of Aarohan to leave when his country needed him. Then again, fathers are never the same when they lose their daughters, and Aarohan was only human.

But he, Aarohan, should have been here, now, in Pataliputra. Now. And things could have been and would have been different.

For the moment, Jotayu chose to wait and see, ensuring his military strength and personal security were intact. He had divided his troops into four divisions—two remained at the borderlands while two accompanied him back to Pataliputra. Of those, one division was stationed at his ancestral village to protect his family and the families of his men, while the second stayed with him to witness the day's events. This division contained the best of his personnel—the crack teams, including select members from the archers, the phalanx, the cavalry, the charioteers, and a good number from Aarohan's legendary elephant corps, now under his command.

Jotayu was a military man, to the bone. Coming from the Kshatriya caste honor, martial arts and loyalty was beaten into him ever since he was a child. These were the characters essential for the warrior class. It is expected that the Kshatriya would be imbued with such notions. But on the flip side, one was also discouraged from engaging in certain things. Such as politics. To swear allegiance to the king and refrain from all politics is the creed of the Kshatriya. Such notions do liberate the warrior, but it also handicaps him from taking the rightful action in times of dynastic changes. And today will be the day when dynasties will change hands.

"Remember your linage, remember that you are a Kshatriya "Munshara had told Jotayu the evening before, when Jotayu returned from the front. "Remember that your oath, nay, your very being, is beholden to the throne. Not the person, but the throne. Remember that."

"We the ministers have found Dhana Nanda guilty of treason for conspiring with Eskander, we ....."

"Treason? When negotiations by the king termed as treason ", Jotayu retorted.

"Since Eskander has been promised this land, and Dhana Nanda as his satrap. Since you and all your Jawans are supposed to fall in line under the barbarian's command! Yes, you look surprised. Dhana has sold this land to Eskander."

Jotayu remained silent, realizing that much had transpired in his absence from the capital. How he wished he had his intelligence officer, Chanakkya, to advise him and make sense of the situation. He did not trust Munshara at all.

Munshara continued," you may not like what is going on, you may not want to hear what I have to say , but listen to the Rajya Sabha . As a Kshatriya that is your duty "

Jotayu kept silent.

"Look would I have called you into the capital with your men if indeed we were in the wrong? We know your men is encamped outside your ancestral village; we know you have a contingent of jawans here in the very capital.

"All my ministers were opposed to you being here. But I told them, you being in the capital is the best thing the citizenry can hope for. People know you to be a patriot, I know you to be a patriot. Will you then prove us to be wrong? Nay, I told the ministers, Jotayu being here would prevent bloodshed."

Munshara paused, gauging Jotayu's reaction. Then he leaned in, lowering his voice slightly, "You don't have to support me, the person, but support the will of the Rajya Sabha."

That did the trick. Munshara knew exactly how to play Jotayu's sense of duty and Kshatriya honor. The political ploy and Kshatriya code of conduct had, in many ways, hamstrung Jotayu, and Munshara knew it.

So this morning, Jotayu's and his forces does not only ensure the whereabouts of the only potent force that could upend Munshara's plans but also give credence to the proceedings to the denizens of Pataliputra . Munshara had become the Master of Ceremonies and Fate on this day. Munshara was feeling pretty good for this day.

The procession of Brahmin Monks came from the banks of the Holy Ganges, preceded by two columns of drummers setting up a solemn hymn and beat. This theatrical procession was only reserved for the extraordinary event of coronation of a king. The Putris of Pataliputra have been tensed for the past couple of nights. After the regent guards changed their allegiance to the Rajya Sabha and Munshara the Prime Minister, a daily dose of midnight raids occurred. Terror reigned over the nights. The drumbeats announced the events of the day to commence soon, and that the Putris are expected to be at the town square. So, it has begun, the transition of the throne from one dynasty to a new king. The denizen Putris of Pataliputra are resigned to whatever may happen on this day. For at last the nightly raids of terror would stop, and things needed to simply stop.

The procession ends in the town central square, where the public court 'Gono Adalat 'has been set up. The hilly terrain slopes down to the square, where tiers of steps form a stadia of seats in front of the square. The square then opens to the 'Ghats', docks formed by the brick paved steps receding into the water line. The western end is reserved for regent pavilion, where today awnings of royal regalia have been set up, only this time it's the insignia of the 'Rajya Shabha' that takes prominence. No royal insignia is to be seen.

The middle center of the square is given to usually performance, political and religious festivities. This is where the trial of the disposed king is to occur, with the whole township encouraged, nay, rather compelled to witness the proceedings from the tiered galleries.

The trumpets associated with the Call sign of 'Rajya Shabha' is blown. The 'Gono Adalat' is brought to order.

"My dear folks, Putris of this great city of Pataliputra," began Munshara. "Today with a heavy heart, and on behalf of your Rajya Shabha, I call these proceedings. We, the ministers, your ministers, have been observing closely the events of the past moon, with anguish and concern.

"In the borderland kingdom to the west, the Dhonis have subdued Puru and taken Takkhashila." A murmur rippled through the crowd. "The vile barbarian Eskander now makes his way to our lands. Our land—our motherland—has never been in greater peril. This is when you would expect your king to defend the motherland. This is when you would expect assurance from your regent that your children are safe, your elderly protected, your women secure.

"Your king is obligated by Dharma to do so. But you all have your questions: What has the king done in these past moons to fulfill his duties toward you? Toward this great city? I have heard your queries—where is the king? I ask the same: Where is the king? Where is the king, in this hour of peril? Hasn't he raised your taxes to build a vast army for moments like these? Hasn't he raised taxes on your harvest threefold, promising safety, security, and protection? Shouldn't he be arming our glorious Jawans? But we know the answer. He has only been busy leading his decadent life at the palace. The Rajya Sabha would not have arrested this king for his callous lifestyle or his dereliction of Dharma-bound duties. But things have come to light in recent days that compel us to take immediate and necessary action against a treasonous man—one who is not worthy of being called king. Yes, today, we will, through the proceedings of this Gono Adalat, in broad daylight, before all of you, present evidence of treason by this king. Let your eyes and ears be the judges of what has transpired and what the verdict should be, as per our laws and Dharma."

Munshara paused dramatically before continuing, "Let the Adalat be in session. Bring forth the accused king."

At the sound of trumpets in unison, and drums beating, a vary frail Dhana Nanda is taken out from a make shift pavilion erected as the holding pen for all the political prisoners , taken into custody in the past weeks .

The stray dog remained where it was, nonchalant about the proceedings.

The crowd remained silent. Knowing very well that the outcome of the proceedings is a foregone conclusion, that they should simply be present and witness the change of governance from one tyrant king to another in the making. Just sit it out, show allegiance to the new power, who or whatever that may be, and to not lose title, property, or one's life in the process. In many ways no one was vested in the trial but to be present only to cover their hides.

Dhana Nanda stood on the accused podium. Now realizing his most trusted minister of decades is actually the architect of his downfall; scheming, plotting all this while. The Court Crier walked onto the center of the courtyard , unfurling the official scroll, began to yell out loud the charges against the Nanda King to the subject audience.

'the court, in the presence & authority of the Rajya Shabha, bring the Gono Adalat into session, and place the disgraced Dhana Nanda on the accused square." Once again, the trumpets rang out.

"The charges against the disgraced are as follows, that Dhana Nanda the disgraced king of the Putris, knowingly and secretly, without the knowledge of the Rajya Shabha negotiated with the Barbarian King Eskander of the Dhonis, to give away the city of Pataliputra as a satrapy. That Dhana Nanda, the disgraced king of the Putris, with malice towards the Putris & nobles of this great city, increase the taxation threefold and committing the increase portion to the Dhonis, this he negotiated without any knowledge or consultation of the Rajya Shabha."

The court crier then turned to the Five Punchayek Judges, "What are the court sanction charges for such heinous action by the disgraced king?"

The five Brahmin judges who were part of the morning procession look towards their spokesperson. "The charge for such action is High Treason".

The town crier then ceremonially marched to the pavilion of the ministers, and declared, "the charges of high treason has been leveled at the disgraced king, is there any one to act as Rajya prosecutor?"

Munshara rises from his seat, "as per law of the Putris, I , Munshara , the prime minister of Pataliputra will be the state prosecutor to try the disgraced king".

Munshara moves to the prosecutor's podium, first looks upon the denizens, then to the assembly of generals, and then slowly and finally, with an air of reluctance upon Dhana Nanda. The 'Yatra 'play has begun.

"My former lord, you have been accused of high treason. I have in my hand the treaty that you have signed with Eskander, the barbarian king, it bears your seal. Do you deny the authenticity of this seal". Munshara raises his hand and shows a scroll of paper. Even though no one can have a look at the content of the scroll, the theatrics is good.

Dhana Nanda remained silent.

"The content of this executed treaty is as described in the charges against you, do you deny the charges?"

Dhana Nanda remained silent.

Unbeknown to anyone, the whole family of Dhana Nanda is held hostage by Munshara, imprisoned in the last couple of nightly raids. Munshara had said when he visited the cell of the deposed king, "Whether your family lives is up to you. You know the law that has been newly instated by your own decree, if a high official admits to his crimes , he , his family and retinue can be banished to ' Vrindavan' , but if you deny the charges, your family will be at the mercy of the court".

Munshara slowly walks down to the accused pavilion, again 'theatrics 'is what he is seeking. He slowly but resolutely raises his voice, "O king, you must plead your case, do you or do you not agree to these charges?"

Dhana Nanda, opting for the best outcome for him and his family, yet knowing very well that they may well be gone 'missing' i.e. assassinated while in exile to Vrindavan, looked to his personal retinue, and nodded.

The retinue stood up, and announced, 'The king is aware of the charges made against him and is ashamed to admit guilt of his charges.'

To this, there was a huge murmur within the crowd witnessing the proceedings.

The king retinue continues, "The Nanda will opt for exile as has been offered by the court for admission of guilt"

The murmur in the crowd grows even louder.

Then suddenly from the eastern hill a conch bellows. As loud as one would hear during battle formation. From the eastern steps a figure slowly walks down in a white chador.

Most of the audience turned their heads, a few recognized the figure, while others squinted their eyes to see who this person was.

Munshara immediately recognized the man walking down the steps. This was completely unexpected. His intelligence had assured him the man was a thousand krosh away, in the north. But there he was, walking into the square.

Slowly in the crowd the murmur begins with the name of the individual audible,

'Aarohan, That's Aarohan!' . Aarohan had returned

after being absent for thirteen moons since his daughter's death.

Gasps and murmurs spread as Aarohan made his way to the center of the field, stopping ten paces from the town's crier. He first looked into the crier's eyes, then slowly turned toward the crowd, deliberately ignoring the ministers and the accused.

'I am Aarohan , Once the commander of the elephant corps of the Gangareed army, and today I have something to tell you that will expose the plot concocted by the very people who has organized this sham trial' . Aloud and clear his declaration rang out.

'Enough' Munshara shouted out, 'under what authority do you interrupt these hallowed proceedings? You are exiled Aarohan, and yet you have appeared here today breaking the cardinal rule of exile. Guards cease him!'

Jotayu and his captains leap up from their seats in protest and the moment they do, parliamentarian guards holds them , surrounds them at spear point. Chanakkya, who had been asked to stay back & observe things from a distance by Aarohan, slowly recedes into the crowd who are almost standing on their feet on the higher tiers of the gallery. Chanakkya rushes back into the back streets to make has way to the outskirts. He had been given specific instructions to bring in the remainder of the Jotayu's force into the town square if there was any sign of apprehension of Aarohan.

Ignoring Munshara's command Aarohan addresses the crowd 'Today I come to thee, my country man , not under the Rajya Shabha laws, who has no authority over me , nor that of the king, whose decrees are invalidated by this very Rajya Shabha, but I came to thee as a citizen of Palibothra , and I have something of grave importance to tell you. '

Even before Aarohan could begin his address, a contingent of twelve soldiers surrounded him at fifteen spaces.

Aarohan stopped. He let his chador fall, to reveal a full battle gear.

Seeing this, Munshara was elated, 'this is going to be a full-blooded drama indeed,' he thought to himself, 'this is too good to be true', he mused.

"I have no quarrel against you, my jawans, but today is not about you or me . If you try to arrest me you will do so at your own peril", saying so Aarohan revealed his Jaghnal , the spear with a hook blade at one side.

A couple of Aarohan's lieutenants, seated with the generals, rush forward to Aarohan's aid , only to be held back by the Parliamentarian guards , one being wounded at spear point. Two eager guards surrounding Aarohan step forward to disarm him only to be menaced & wounded by Aarohan.

"Arrest him", yells out Munshara.

And all remaining ten soldiers lunge at him, only to realize that even though the general is a generation older, he could better them not only in one-to-one combat but his style, swinging with momentum of spear hook would wound significant number of the guards. The crowd watches with intensity, witnessing a gladiatorial fight that ever was, holding their breaths.

But Aarohan is only one man. Though his martial arts were far superior he couldn't hold back a whole contingent. He darted up the steps to be met with another guard whom he strikes down. He veers right and takes to the alley that led to the eastern cliff over the Ganges.

The guards followed him, and so did the crowd's anxious gaze. A few amongst the crowd began to chant Aarohan's name, they began to say, 'Aarohan is our general. Long live Aarohan! '

Seeing the crowd's reaction, Munshara raged. "Find him, and this time, kill that bastard!"

Aarohan runs through the alley way up the steps on to the cliff looking down at the town square . The eyes of the crowd are on him, realizing that this probably is his last moments, being pursued by the menacing guards.

At the top of the cliff in the opening, Aarohan makes his last stand. With nowhere to go he turns around. He addresses the guards, "you know this is an unjust Rajya Shabha, do not ally yourselves with such treachery, lay down your weapons". A few of eager guards laugh at him, "you are bold old man, lay down your spear or we will kill you . This is your end, grandpa."

A couple of archers come up the steps and take position, awaiting their captains' instructions. The captain of guards breaks through the siege of guards, slowly taking a few steps, hands raised to give the signal to dislodge the arrows.

Aarohan looks over his shoulder and sees the drop of the cliff some seventy feet below into the river Ganges. He looks down at the crowd, complete utter silence from them in fear of witnessing what is about to happen. He looks back to the guards, the thuggish looks in their eyes, the same kind that you see when a man has decided to kill.

Aarohan rushes the siege guards, they step back. The captain gives the signal, and the archers release their arrows. Aarohan summersaults down to avoid the volley of arrows that flies a hair width above. All misses him, except one. A point finds its way between his chest armor and the left shoulder plate.

The crowd grasps.

Aarohan turns on his heel and sprints his mightiest strides to the edge of the cliff. For the second time in a year & a half, Aarohan jumps into the void.

The crowd gasps a second time.

Aarohan splashes into the Ganges.

The guard on the cliff looks down to see any sign of life. The crowds rush to the ghats to see if there is any sign of Aarohan.

Munshara is livid with anger and beside himself. Chaos has descended on proceeding that he had meticulously planned. He wanted a drama, but not of this kind.

For the third time the trumpets rang out. If the morning affairs were to be described as tense, this Moment would make it look serene. Soldiers and Guards stood in formation in-front of the crowd with the spears drawn. Jotayu & the generals are also held back.

Munshara came down. He needed to conclude this affair of the public court as soon as possible, without further derailment. He yelled out to the Punchayak Judges, "you have heard how the disgraced king responded to the charges leveled at him, before we were rudely interrupted by that treasonous man Aarohan. What is your verdict ohh wise ones?"

On the other side of the court Jotayu had had enough, he stood up & began to leave the proceedings. Munshara immediately yells back, "No one leaves the court until I say so!"

"I do not recognize the legitimacy of this proceedings, I will not bear witness or give credence to such mockery of justice", replied out loud Jotayu.

The crowd listened in silence, not knowing how things would be unfolding.

Munshara, commanded the general of the parliamentary guards, "you have the order of the Rajya Shabha to arrest anyone who leaves these proceedings until these proceedings are declared over"

Jotayu, moved by what he has seen happen to Aarohan, replies back, "Do your worse, kill me if you must, but my men will avenge my death. So careful when you draw your weapons against me."

Munshara, thus gives the command to his general, "So be it , kill any one that leaves this proceedings without my permission". Jotayu, and the generals have to be killed either way.

A few amongst the crowd started to yell, "So will you be killing us too? For we have witnessed enough of a mockery of justice today. This is 'Matsonnay '! This is anarchy!"

It seemed both the crowd and the generals are simply getting out of control, Munshara realized . This day may end up in bloodshed well beyond what has already transpired.

Munshara turned towards the judges, "O wise amongst us, do you have a judgement "

The chief of the punchayak rose, "We have heard of the admission of guilt by the king. We were ready to give our verdict. But the unusual interruption by General Aarohan has given us pause'.

Munshara replied, "So, the court does recognize the unusual nature of the interruption, I would thus beseech the court to fulfill its duty and land us a verdict then?"

The chief judge held up a hand. "My lord, you misunderstand our position. We wanted to hear what the general had to say before your men unceremoniously pushed him to his death."

Before Munshara, could remind the judges that

Aarohan had Broken the law by violating the terms of his exile, a second judge stood up pointing towards the river ghats, "It seems we might actually hear what the General had to say after all. Look its Aarohan!"

Aarohan's Conch rang out again. The crowd paused; the guards paused; the generals paused.

From the water Aarohan simply rose, walking on the steps of the ghat, while the arrow still lodged into the shoulder plate. Imposing. If his morning entrance had presence, this second appearance after his dramatic death-defying dive was even more theatrical. But that is not what held the crowd. What held the crowd was what followed Aarohan.

Something large breaks the wave, and then steps on to the Ghats, making a deep rumbling sound.

A giant Tusker of an elephant standing twenty-two feet high at his shoulder emerged from the water behind Aarohan. In full metal armor, with a battle howdah on its back. But what was mind boggling was the size of its task, and pair of gigantic six feet long blades attached to it, glistening in the sun. As the elephant swung its head the blades swayed side to side. No one would want to be within the swinging radius of those tusks. Belted to the body of the elephant were three additional blades on each side, flayed out. If there were large blades attached to the wheels of a chariot, those would seem like toothpicks compared to ones flaying out from the sides of this giant tusker. The crowd simply gasped at ....

The soldiers simply gasped at....

The stray dog simply jumped up and darted out of the courtyard, at the sight of……

Manu! In full battle gear!

Aarohan walked in war strides. He blew on his conch as he walked, which was followed by the most deafening trumpeting of an elephant, Manu, the crowd has ever heard. The buildings and the walls around the Central Court simply echoed the trumpeting, amplifying the pitch. The theatrics of such a display is simply un paralleled.

Aarohan, with the arrow still stuck to his left shoulder plate armor walks towards the center of square, within the vicinity of Munshara. Munshara trying to keep a good pace distance away from Aarohan simply steps back, but trips and falls on his back. Aarohan approached him, all the while Munshara tries to scamper away while on his back. Aarohan does not look at Munshara, but only once he does look down. And while he does so he pulls out the arrow from his shoulder plate with Gusto.

He looked back at the parliamentary guards. "Stand down my Jawans, or if you fancy, be cut down". The guards lowered their weapons.

The blades of Manu are not far behind. Munshara was at his wit's end, as the swinging blades of Manu pass by him.

Jotayu with his retinue comes forward. The events have been moving fast. By this time, his elephant corpse made its way to the town central square led by Chanakkya. They faced the parliamentary forces elephant corps. Aarohan turned. Numerous commanders on both sides of the standoff were his pupils. He had been their mentor. He proceeds in the middle. Manu follows him closely. First, he turns to Jotayu, who himself was mentored by Aarohan. Jotayu promptly states, with authority, "What is your command? O Commander & Master. Your corps awaits. "Jotayu made sure the whole crowd heard and now knows where his allegiance lay.

Aarohan nods.

Aarohan then gives the call and signs for the trained elephants to sit. And they do so. He turns to Manu. And gives the command and sign. And the behemoth bellows out a thunderous trumpet and simply sat down like a trained canine, on its hind leg, but all his scythe blade still flayed out. Ready to jump into action at Aarohan's mahout commands.

Aarohan then turns to the Elephant Corps of the parliamentarian forces and walks over to them in his battle gear. He addresses their commander directly, "We are standing down, you will stand down. There will be no more bloodshed today. Do you understand? "

The commander of the parliamentarian forces steps aside. He nodes. "We will comply "

Aarohan gives the call and sign to the elephants in the parliamentary brigade. All the elephants sat down.

The crowd, which had been watching with bated breath, erupted in cheers. Apprehension at the beginning of the day had turned into suspense, and now into elation and soon to be Jubilation. By nightfall, the people would feel an overwhelming sense of relief, perhaps even hope that the government had finally transferred into good hands.

Aarohan moves and stands squarely facing the crowd. As he sheathes his blade, the blade of Manu's task comes to his sides, as if he is protected by the two of the largest blades in the history of Mankind.

Aarohan began, "...As I was saying my dear country men …."

The chief of the Punchayak turns to his colleagues and says, "We are going to know what Aarohan has to say, after all!"

Chapter 27

The First Encounter According to Coenus

The Macedonian page stood at the entrance to the tent shaking between two heavily armored hoplite guards, both of whom stood ready to seize him at any moment if the word came from their sleeping master.

"My lord, General Coenus has returned," he managed to utter.

Alexander lay on his fur-laden bed, eyes closed, but now aware that the news from the expedition could not be good. Had the news been good, the general himself would have shown up at his tent.

"So why is he not here?" asked Alexander, still from bed.

The page hesitated and responded, "My lord, he may not last the night."

"Have his second or whoever's fit, speak to me."

"My lord," the page's voice now trembled audibly, "the general was the only one who returned."

Alexander stood up without another thought and robbed himself to venture out from his tent. As he left, the page added, "Six horses returned with the general, laden with bloody sacks."

Alexander paused at that and understood the beardless youth. "A war message," he thought to himself, feeling a burning anger now. "And a war message to me?!"

"Take me to the sacks," he demanded, needing to see for himself, but he looked at the two guards with hatred before leaving the tent. Neither returned the glance.

A fortnight ago, Alexander had dispatched Coenus, his most successful general and the commander of the cavalry of his massive right phalanx, as an advance party to seek-out, route-out, spy on, and/or engage the fabled Gangaridai Army at his discretion.

For the past one and a half years, ever since the incident at the Kamalaphuli (Chakdara) Palace, and the subsequent slaughter of the entire population in retaliation for the attempt on his life by that wretched Aarohan, Alexander had only received poor intelligence on what he faced with the Gangaridai. Furthermore, all attempts to locate Aarohan at that time had proved futile. The Greek army had, upon flawed reports, moved south along the mighty Indus and never engaged the Gangaridai once. They were told the city lay on the bank of the river Indus. Which made sense at the time. Then Alexander and his generals realized that the Gangaridai were actually located further east of the Purava across the Indus River, where ran another watercourse, mightier than the Indus, called the Ganga, where the empire lay, the distance to which was unknown. Rumors of the land beyond the Ganga had already percolated into the minds of his men, who now believed it to be a place of mythical beasts harnessed for the martial use of the kingdom. Such had once been the talk of the Persians, and of the same Indians whom he had already crushed, so he was used to dispelling such nonsense, and shedding light on the errors of these corners of the world.

He had, however, already wasted a year and a half, and forward momentum wondering around this massive land chasing phantoms. While he should have followed his own instincts but had been misinformed by that cunning Chanakkya. Alexander now regretted not sending out his own Macedonian scouts immediately after what transpired at Kamalaphuli, but he had relied on local information then. This meant it was late when he finally sent out Coenus with three hundred of his best cavalries further east. Now, he thought he was paying for his hesitation. Ares did not reward the hesitant.

They arrived at the stables. The stable men made

way when they recognized Alexander's guards coming toward them. They then showed Alexander where the sacks lay beside the recently returned horses.   But something about those mounts struck him at first sight, and so he approached them. As he got closer, he realized what it was about them that seemed different. He stroked one of the beast's long snouts, but the creature would not look up at him, only down, and the animal further could not stop trembling. The horses were terrified. As these steeds had been habituated to blood and gore for their entire lives their current alarmed state was remarkable. He quickly turned from the horses then to the bloody sacks. A few of his soldiers from the intelligence corps stood ready with him to inspect them.

"This will not be mentioned beyond these walls," the God King said, and everyone looked down, knowing that it was a death sentence to violate this word. "Open that sack!" Commanded Alexander.

As they did so, the men present anticipated that they would find the severed heads of the Macedonian cavalry men. They were wrong, however. What they saw instead were the severed male members of the regiment lying together in a carnal heap. The veterans gasped. For the first time since Alexander had nearly had his head bashed in by the Persian Satrap, Spithridates, and saved by Cleitus the Black, he felt a shiver in his spine. Not that he was worried about his own life, but for the very nature of the message itself. This was no ordinary sign — it was personal. And Alexander knew instinctively that it could only be a warning of vengeance and that it must have come from Aarohan.

Alexander moved away from the vile sacks and

their repugnant contents, and back to the horses to inspect the wounds and to settle a question in his own mind. He typically could visualize the cause of wounds with close to certain accuracy which often gave him an uncanny insight into what had occurred: the nature of the weapon, the force behind the instrument, the angle of attack and precision of the strike, and thus the nature and skill of the attacker himself.

But what Alexander found here did not make sense, or none that he could deduce. The wounds were fresh but had been attended to in the past days. The obvious arrow wounds had been treated with ointments and stitches indicating that the Gangaridai had patched up the Macedonian horses after the battle for the journey back. Strange as it was for an enemy to have patched up Macedonian Horse, this was not the aspect of the wounds that bewildered him. He pulled a torch closer to one of the horses to better inspect it. To begin with, it was the claw marks he found that perplexed him. He had been told of a large cat in the area, the Bengal Tiger, but how would a man use a tiger as a weapon? Making matters worse, running perpendicular to the claw marks were long incisions, also stitched and medicated, but what weapon, sabre or sword, could make such consistent and long slices down the length of a horse? The Macedonian had seen all the engines and weapons of war, if not in person, then in pictures shown to him by Aristotle, and yet what could have made these?

Alexander had seen enough. He needed to talk to his general, Coenus. Army decorum dictated the battle-wounded individual would be taken, by stretcher, if necessary, to Alexander's tent, for all to see, but Alexander wanted to prevent the army at large from learning of his failed expedition. He therefore went straight to the infirmary tent instead. There he found Coenus pale from loss of blood. Alexander thought he was viewing a corpse, but the general's eyes fluttered as he entered without ceremony, and suddenly the grievously wounded man awoke.

When he saw Alexander, he grew perturbed. Alexander tried calming him, but Coenus demanded the nurse sit him up. He was bleeding through his sheets, but the nurse did as he was told and helped the defeated man to sit before his king.

Alexander did not say a word but waited for Coenus to be repositioned in his soiled litter, and then listened as he spoke.

Coenus began by saying: "Surji mama er Teeyeta!" He repeated the phrase again. Alexander said nothing.

He knew what it meant. Of the limited, accurate intelligence he had received regarding the Gangaridai, certain of his spies had informed him that "Surji mama er Teeyeta!" was part of a battle cry that called every warrior to take the king of the Macedonians' Parrot feathered helmet, which, for all intents and purposes, meant to take his bloody head.

"Alexander!" Coenus suddenly said breaking his chain of thought. Not addressing Alexander as "my lord" meant he had broken from all form, but Alexander pretended not to notice the breach.

"I do not have much time," the general said. "I have failed you, but in many ways in this defeat I have also experienced freedom. Freedom from war and conflict. I wish such a realization would have come to me under different circumstances. Now I know I will not see my beloved Macedonia again. I do not have the strength to report on the full expedition, but I leave you what matters most." He continued with his eyes fixed on Phillip's son, "On the evening of the fourth day we descended on a large clearing in the forest. Soon my scouts reported Gangaridai ahead. I knew we had a better chance in the open maneuvering with our horses, knowing what happened with Puru in the forest battle of Hydespas, and we assumed defensive position on all sides.

"Night fell. And soon the Riddis torched up our fronts, sides, and rear. for the first time we realized the enemy's true scope. We were surrounded in a circle of about eight hundred stadia wide. Their flames burned throughout the perimeter and yet they did not move any closer to us. After some consideration, we decided to conduct a night charge. I chose to attack our rear, for we already knew the ground there. Our goal was to break through their lines in darkness, but as we gathered speed toward the flaming line it seemed with every stride the torches themselves elevated off the ground. They lifted higher and higher until I realized the line was not comprised of infantry nor cavalry at all, but of elephants! Can you imagine how many elephants are required to form such a long perimeter ring? Maybe fifteen-hundred, or more!

We continued the charge, hoping to have our momentum carry us through. But when the flames were still at distance, I heard a deep rumbling followed by the most thunderous of elephant' trumpeting, and then the entire ring of elephants followed in with their noise. It was as if the heavens cracked open. In the face of that sound the horses would no longer charge. They seemed confused, and all the while, the elephants continued their deafening trumpeting.

At that point a volley of flaming arrows shot toward us in arcs through the night sky. A few of our soldiers fell, but we soon realized that we had not been the intended targets, for the arrows dropped to the ground where pools of oil lay at random intervals. The ground was ablaze. The ground was prepared beforehand for us to walk into it.

We fell to disarray, and while they could see us, we could not see them.

"Then, Alexander," and he gripped his king's hand at this point, smearing it with blood, "I tell you . . . out of nowhere, charged hundreds of Bengal tigers! Tigers larger than lions! Our horses panicked. They bucked us off and tried to run from what was coming. But where? The tigers were everywhere and pounced on anything and everyone that moved and began eating the horses and the soldiers alike, ripping and tearing hunks of flesh and bone. They were ravenous as if they hadn't eaten in days. The sound of it...

"These tigers were their war dogs! But how can you train tigers? We fought the tigers. But as we killed several a greater number of our soldiers fell to another volley of arrows." Croenus then coughed blood.

"I rallied the troops to form the tortoise formation, for the tigers were better dealt with in this way, besides many were now feasting on their kills – no way for a soldier to die in that manner – but in our formation we became as sitting ducks and soon the flaming perimeter began to close round us, and we heard the chant, "Surji mama er

Teeyeta!" coming louder and louder still, from all sides. It seemed like a colosseum, and we were the sport. We steadied ourselves, but what came next was worse than what came before – a giant elephant of a size I have never seen – larger than the African bull, with colossal tusks grazing the ground; only the tusks were strapped with immense blades. The armored elephant simply smashed through our formation, like we were bamboo shoots, slicing its massive head left and right through our men, with arrows and spears raining from its top. Our phalanx could neither hook nor tear its under belly or leg pit. The beast was armored head to foot. And then . . . Then the creature reared on its hind legs like Bucephalus, and crushed us like we were ants.

"I will say no more of the slaughter. Next morning, we were bound. I was taken inside their commander's tent. About forty-three of our men had survived the carnage, a remarkable number from what we had faced. The Gangaridai were well marshalled too. They did not abuse nor torture us. They gave water to the wounded. And after a time, they read out our crimes (as they called it) against India. But we were not charged if we had killed soldiers in battle, we were charged as looters, murderers, and rapists. "They knew us well. They even knew what regiments and formation we belonged to, and of our battle history and crimes. Their leader, Aarohan, spelled out each prisoner's crime, and then had those men executed unceremoniously. A few stood to claim innocence. Bloody cowards, those, for when they proved it, they were given the option of leaving India or resettling amongst them and abide by their laws. Some chose to stay; some to go. Their commander's argument, who spoke perfect Greek, was that it was no case of desertion for the Greek who left India, for India had never waged war on Macedonia.

"Aarohan further proclaimed we had no right in India, and that you, YOU, Alexander had no right over them as sovereign, and thus they had a claim on you, for your war was illegal, and you were a trespasser first of all, before whatever other crimes you committed next; as they claimed, your rape, murder, and pillaging. If you come into their hands, you cannot hide behind the title, 'God King.'

"The men who had charges of rape against them were first castrated then killed, and their members were loaded into sacks and returned with me to remind you of your crimes." Saying so, Coenus feebly removed the white sheet covering his body and exposed the ghastly wound which had been crudely stitched with dark thread and drenched in ointment to retard infection. Alexander, the God King, recoiled then. Gauging his lord's response, Coenus said: "I too was charged with rape, dear Alexander." Speaking thus, he looked to his right hand where he gripped his own severed organ.

"I know you will have my tongue cut out if I talk in such manner, but my hour is here. I plead you, Alexander, listen! Go back to Macedonia! The army will not survive these people, they have a different philosophy about life and this war, and they are numbered as the blades of grass on the savannah."

Coenus tried to straighten himself on his death bed then, but he had difficulty raising himself any further. He gave up the attempt and added, "After the executions, Aarohan turned to his troops. He said, 'Those of you who have fulfilled your covenant with me by killing one Macedonian, you may retire in life now, you may leave my company.' But not one of them took the offer. They all answered, 'We choose to stay!" We choose to fight.' Not one left him. Alexander, you have met your match!"

Having discharged his duty, Coenus slumped back to his bed. Looking up to the roof of the tent he said, "For me, I choose to leave this wretched place, I choose to be in Macedonia. My Alexander, enough is enough, follow me back."

With those words, Coenus went limp and released his last breath. The pound of muscle that had been beating ever since he was a fetus stopped – as it will for all being. Regardless of ego or legacy.

The next morning, the general's death was announced. He died of a sudden illness, and his men, some three hundred troops, had returned to Macedonia in retirement. Many men did not believe this story, and their belief like a cancer spread fear among the ranks for those things which lay beyond the Ganga.

Chapter 28

First Encounter According to Ratan

Early morning rays hit the wooden door before him. Ratan pauses a moment at the threshold, realizing now all that he might have lost while he was away. He opens the door and watches his silhouette drape across the floor as the rest of the house lightens with the soft light. Entering, he feels as though this was truly his home for the first time; he feels like a lord, no, the caretaker of his homestead.

The sound of the latch alerts his wife to some presence in her home, and she comes into the entryway from the opposite internal courtyard feeling anxious, frightened, and excited all at once. Might it be her husband, or something else? She nearly faints when she sees him.

"Is my Karta (caretaker) okay? Are you hurt?" She utters with great apprehension when she regains herself. "We won," he responds, "We bettered the Dhoni's (Macedonians)."

She screams for joy at that, and embraced him for the victory, but mostly for his return. After some moments she releases him, and he takes a chair overlooking the verdant courtyard and sits.

"We won," he says again, triumphantly and with pride, "and we can win," he adds now fully realizing what it means that they have won in the safety of his home.

The rest of his family now enters the room and seeing their father for the first time in six months, they run to him. His daughters cry. His eldest son stands off some distance at first, but then comes to him and hugs his father, wiping a tear from his eye as he does. Like their mother they have long since taken him for dead. After they have embraced him, they are all eager to hear his story.

"Where have you been?"

"We fought the Macedonians." His sons are most happy to learn how their people have fared against the now fabled Dhoni.

Ratan's mind is clear, nirvana-clear, as he begins telling the story. His words begin flowing with both pride and gravity, for the war he knows will come.

"I saw him. I have seen Aarohan!" he begins, knowing that his children will love to hear of the great hero.

"Do you remember the day, Moti, your uncle came to me, and I left suddenly? Now I can tell you what I have been up to. And, yes, you have guessed right that I was recruited for the war effort. They knew that I was a trapper, and that I had certain knowledge of the routes within the great Sundarbans. I travelled to the appointed place, and when I reached the outskirts of the mangroves, as I had been instructed, I found my trapper company waiting for me. They too had been summoned for the task of trapping for Arohan. Along with my trapper company, I met Chanakkya. It was he who gave us the mission. We were to trap as many tigers as possible in three months, for which we were paid up front and ordered to maintain zero contact with the outside world, not even our families. He further told us that if we wanted to leave our duties, we could, but that our country needed us and that we would be paid handsomely for our expertise, which we were.

"We set to work. Digging tiger pits, preparing cages, camouflaging the pits, and preparing the bamboo lattice cover to cage the pit-fallen tigers. I was given all the resources I could use. At first, we were slow, but soon we began to trap a tiger every three days, sometimes two per day. In that time, we trapped eighty seven tigers, keeping them in their pits and feeding them wild pigs all the while.

"Then one day Aarohan arrived on an elephant the size of which I have never seen followed by a hundred and fifty or so elephants with their warrior riders. They came in total silence through the forest – amazing to see a hundred elephants and their retinues moving as one company in silence. Such force, such discipline. We were inspired. All the warriors were lean in thought and fierce in purpose. They had a singular emotion; they had a vision. Each day was a step forward to that vision.

"Aarohan asked us to confine the trapped tigers in cages that we placed down in their pits for the purpose. At first, we needed to get them into the cages and so we placed raw meet inside. Once the tigers were in, we dropped the gates and imprisoned them. At that we removed the bamboo latticework off the top of the pits so that we could pull the caged beasts out. The elephants did the rest, pulling the cages up and out from the pits. As they lifted them, the tigers made tremendous racket, but lo, Aarohan's elephant, they call it 'Manu', approached the troublesome tigers and trumpeted the soul out of them. And then, by Buddha, all the cats would go silent. Each of the cages was covered with cow hide and lifted onto the elephants, one on each side.

"Once all the tigers were packed in their cages alongside an elephant, we were asked to join the march north. We travelled for twenty days, avoiding townships, meandering through villages. People there would notice us, and make way, knowing this was Aarohan's brigade. Our movements never preceded us, however, for the villagers themselves were as an extension of our army. Each village further welcomed us with the call: "Aakdoom bakdoom, ghora doom shajey" I have heard it so many times that I can never forget it, just the sound of those words readies me for battle. Even the elephants would rise from their resting positions when they heard that chant!

"Soon we reached advanced territory, within striking distance of the enemy. Aarohan came to us then. I've never seen a calmer man in my life. He was the Buddha incarnate. The only difference was that this was a warrior Buddha. He had come to find out when the tigers would be at the peak of hunger if they had not been fed.

"We answered, 'Twelve days.' And he responded after some reflection, 'Stop feeding the tigers.'

"On the ninth day of not feeding the tigers, we mobilized again in the early evening, by next morning we had reached a valley plain. When we arrived, we saw other men in the field, digging shallow pits into which great quantities of oils were poured, as per Aarohan's precise instruction. After the pits were dug, another group of men came out of the tree line pushing forth a great number of at least fifty wild pigs, which they slaughtered in the center of the field. They then drained their blood so that the ground turned crimson and took the carcasses away. The smell of blood drove the tigers crazy, who were already mad with hunger. Those animals then began to focus on the location where the slaughter occurred with a maniacal attention.

"We also saw the gathering of some two thousand war elephants from the east along with their warrior riders. By Buddha, how impressive the great armored elephants appeared along with the splendid war howdah on their backs. And you should have seen the massive outer blades attached to Manu's tusks, measured to the tusk size, and gleaming in the sun, honed that a man could shave with.

"In the afternoon we took up camouflaged positions, and waited in silence, watching the field. As evening fell, we heard noise on the far side. We watched the forest edge with intensity. Soon men appeared at the tree line. When I saw them moving out of the foliage, I had the same feeling as when a tiger appears silently from the mangrove stalking its prey.

"After lingering at the field edge for a time, the pompous Dhoni's strode out into the valley as if it were their very own Greece. Knowing what lay ahead of them, I almost felt bad for what I knew would come.

"Once they had marched about a thousand yards beyond us, the silent order came through the ranks, and we slowly closed the circle at their back. My company, with our tiger cages, had been placed in front of the elephants, and as it turned out, Aarohan and his elephant Manu stood directly behind me. You should have seen Aarohan in his battle gear, his armor covered by the white Dhoti & Chador.

"By now it was full dark, and there in front of us, a pair of Aarohan's riders came out of the night. 'Jadrel (general), ' they said, addressing Aarohan, the ring has been closed.'

"In response, Aarohan silently lit a torch. Suddenly the ring of torches lit up around us. I realized only then how massive the ring of elephants actually was. For the first time, I felt no fear whatsoever of the Dhonis. I felt I could eat them up, come what may.

"We waited, then for the Dhoni's to react, which they soon did. They panicked and charged our line. What happened next stole the heart from their horses. Manu began to make a deep vibrating noise. It seemed to emanate from his forehead. It was a sound that was picked up by all the elephants as they began to follow him. We could feel the vibration even though we were standing on top of the cages. As the vibration reached an almost intolerable pitch, Manu let out the most deafening elephant call I've ever heard, all the while standing on his hind legs. Everything stopped for a moment, even the wind, and then the rest of the elephants joined in, all 2000 of them. It was as if the heavens had cleaved asunder.

"It was not long before we realized the Dhoni's had stopped their charge. The trumpeting had its effect: their horses would charge no more. The animals seemed confused.

"Seeing this, Aarohan threw off his white chador and took up his double arched bow. He shot a flaming arrow then, which was followed by thousands of others. The night sky lit up like the Diwali night. The arrows fell all around the Dhoni cavalry, and onto the oil pits which ignited in a great orange flash of light. As the pits ignited several of the Dhoni were set ablaze.

"I was watching all of this happen when I heard Aarohan say, 'Ratan! Release the tigers!'

"And so, we did. I gave the signal, and the men pulled the cow hide covers and opened all eighty-seven cages. We brought up the cage doors from above and the tigers charged into the light of the burning field. As they came out, they turned back toward us for a moment, but the elephants stepped forward and began trumpeting again. As they did so, I saw Manu up close. He was in Maast, and amazingly he still followed Aarohan's command.

"In the face of the great elephants, the tigers had no choice but to turn, and further they smelled the blood, and so they charged as a group toward the scent. They Dhonis were in total disarray by now, all the while our archers pelted them with flaming arrows, and the tigers picked off any man separated from the group.

"In spite of the chaos and the tigers, the Dhonis were well trained and managed to kill several animals and fell back into a peculiar formation holding their shields together in the shape of stupas. Soon, however, the tigers ceased to be a threat to the enemy, as they stopped to feast on their kills, whether beast or man. But it seems Aarohan had predicted this outcome all along because at that moment he began to chant, Surji mama er Teeyeta,' and Manu charged!

The Gangariddi warriors began to chant the same as well and all the elephants with their warrior riders followed Manu and Aarohan into the field. These behemoths smashed the stupa formation, crushing and scattering the men like ants. Each elephant was supported by eight others, simply ploughing through the enemy formation swinging their tusks left and right with the massive blades, slicing the enemy soldiers like grass. And all the while the warriors released arrows and spears into the carnage below. I have never seen such a decisive victory."

His family remained silent as Ratan stopped his narration for the moment. By now, quite a few neighbors had joined to listen. He looked around at the men and women assembled there to see him. They were all listening to his story, while the others were filling in the late arrivals to what he had already said. Ratan paused long enough for them to get caught up and then continued.

"By daybreak, most of the Dhonis were killed. The surviving ones were led away in chains to our camp. There Aarohan bathed and took his time. In the afternoon he reappeared in a white Dhoti and Chador. From the center of the encampment, he called for a Gono Adalat (people's

Court). When we had all assembled there in a makeshift parade ground, he read aloud the crimes of the surviving soldiers.

"Those found guilty and had witnesses against them were killed. Can you imagine Dhonis in our people's court? Those who were found guilty of past rapes of Indian citizens were castrated. When other soldiers were determined to have simply been following orders, they were released on condition that they would take the Tibetan route out of India, never to take up arms again. If they broke their vows, Aarohan told them that they would be crushed under Manu's foot. After the sentence he gave the most eloquent speech I had ever heard to the captives and their commander. He clearly staked out the illegal warfare that Eskander had waged in eight years. His logic and decree were irrefutable. I have never seen such a just and even King. Yet he was no king."

Ratan now turned his attention to his audience and questioned them, "Listen, all of you. This was just a battle. The war is yet to be had. This is our land, our women, our children. A few of you have spoken of making a deal to recognize the barbarian Eskander as king. But I ask you why? This Eskander is evil. He is a murderer and a tyrant. Death and destruction follow his footsteps. So, I ask you: do you want him as king, or do you think Aarohan would be a just King? You have heard of his deeds before. We need to strengthen his arms. He and his troops are well marshaled and just. They do not plunder or rape women.

"For me, I plan to rest for three days. Then, I will take my two eldest sons and go to the plains by the Buri Ganga River to the east in Gangaridai. We will join Aarohan's Army. As we are not trained soldiers it is likely we will die, but Arohan says he will teach us the ways of the sword. This being so, I will fight to save my wife and my daughters from the barbarians. Who will join me?"

Ratan hardly finished his statement when he heard some youthful drummers outside drumming and singing and marching. "Akdoom bakdoom..." they said. And with that, he realized that these youths were already on their way.

Chapter 29

Training of the Minds

The two brothers sat within a group of fifty youths. On the ground, on the grass. It rained the previous evening. The ground was soggy. It had that after rain smell. The youths simply sat there. None of the individuals moved. Nor made any sound. They simply sat there, waiting for the instructions to befell them. If there ever was a human group that resembled the singular purpose of an ant colony, then this would be it.

Rattan had brought his two sons to the plains of Ganga (now called Buri Ganga, translated to old Ganga) , to join tens of thousands of others from the delta to answer the call from Aarohan. News of the victory against the advance strike group of Eskander the Dhoni had spread like monsoon rain over the plains. Youths showed up, in their teens, twenties, and thirties. Both sons and daughters from various locales. Farmers brought livestock to provide provisions for the growing populace, and tradesmen came to build battle chariots for the war that was soon to come. They all showed up.

"I am here as your friend, a friend of the nation," Aarohan had addressed the denizens of Pataliputra on that fateful day when Munshara had tried to usurp the throne of the Nandas.

"I come to you not only with the knowledge of the Dhoni invaders from the far western lands, beyond even the Persians, but with a path to defend our lands.

"A few of you were in the royal court the day I was banished from my titles and positions. That banishment still stands, for I care not a hair's width about titles or positions," Aarohan said, turning to where Munshara lay on his back. "Today I come to you, oh people and the Punchayak, to advise you. Advise you that this nation must mobilize, body, mind, and soul. I care for no titles, only that I am Aarohan of Gangariddi, the seeker of the parrot feathers of that barbarian Dhoni, Eskander. I seek no empire, no dynasty. I only seek **'Surji mama er Teeyeta.'"**

Aarohan looked at both Munshara and Dhana Nanda. "I have no interest in your petty power struggles. You are free to go, but only as yourselves. You no longer have titles, servants, or retinues compensated by the state. This land, Gangariddi, has revoked all your privileges because you have abused them. If I see even a hint of resistance or scheming from either of you, I swear on my dear departed daughter's soul, I will crush you under Manu's feet."

Aarohan slammed his spear hilt on the stone pavement of the town square as he stated his promised vengeance. It didn't matter whether Munshara or Dhana Nanda believed his threat; what mattered was that everyone knew Aarohan would do it. The crowd understood that Aarohan was back with a mission, and they rallied behind him.

Aarohan turned to the Punchayak, "Oh elders, your predecessors placed you in your position not because of your titles, family names, or wealth. They placed you here for your jurisprudence, conscience, and wisdom, which our society needs in times of great peril. Well, this is that time of great peril.

'Ohh Punchayak Prothoma, I advise in the manner of the first society of the first Punchayak Shabha, grant Jotayu the title, charge, and responsibility of chief of all the army corps '

Hearing this, Jotayu bowed his head, his right hand fisted and rested on his left brace plate—a sign that he was ready to take on the responsibility if the Punchayak decreed it.

The first of the Punchayak stood up and looked at the rest of his colleagues for approval. All nodded. Punchayak Prothoma stepped forward and declared 'In the spirit of the purpose of the Punchayak, we agree that your advice is turned into a decree of the realm.'

Aarohan than moved to the second of the Punchayak, " Ohh Punchayak Ditiya, I advise in the manner of the first society of the first Punchayak Shabha, declare the plains of Buri Ganga east of us , as the training ground of the army that will stand as the Prachi , the wall against the Dhonis.

The second Punchayak, like the first, did the same ceremonial procedures, and answered, " In the spirit of the purpose of the Punchayak , we agree that your advice be turned into a decree of the realm"

To this, a few in the crowd started to cheer with war cries. The drums began to beat to war tunes.

Aarohan then paced to the third Punchayak, " ohh Punchayak Tritiya, I advise in the manner of the first society of the first Punchayak Shabha , declare that all able bodied youth, nay all able bodied men, nay all able bodied men and women go to the plains of Buri Ganga to be trained into that awesome army that will became like a Prachi, a wall of 'Will' against the barbarian Dhonis, and that all provisions be provided for such an awesome army .' Even before the third Punchayak could utter its ceremonial historic decree the crowd began to cheer. And now the Conch began to blow along with the beat of the war drums.

Now Jotayu stepped forward, "O Punchayak, we are not done with the business of the hour". Some in the crowd already started to yell out Aarohan's name and the suggestion about his position. Jotayu went in front of the fourth Punchayak, "Ohh Punchayak Augroj, I, the chief of all army corps, advise in the manner of the first society of the first Punchayak Shabha, decree that Aarohan of the Gangaridai, Seeker of the Parrot Feather of Eskander the barbarian, be declared the supreme commander of Gangaridai Army !'

The fourth Punchayak could hardly finish his decree, that whole of the Putri crowd in the town square had begun to chant Aarohan's name .

Then the senior-most Punchayak, the Probin Punchayak, came forward. "We, the Punchayak, hereby dissolve this body of the Punchayak so that our decree cannot be changed, and that no new Punchayak will be created before the menace of the Dhonis is over."

That was a few moons ago, before the victory over the expeditionary forces of Alexander. It was the thunderclap that opened the floodgates for the monsoon of people answering the call to arms. They were not trained. They were farmers. They were weavers. They were potters. They were carpenters. They were the fisherman. They were the ironmongers. They were not soldiers. But they came. They knew nothing about Warfare. Knew nothing about stratagem. Knew nothing about archery. Knew nothing about phalanxes. Knew nothing about spear charges. Knew nothing about battle axes. Knew nothing about martial skills . Nothing about weaponry. Nothing about battle stamina. Nothing about defense. Nothing about assault. Nothing about blocking. Nothing about parrying. Nothing about courage. Nothing about starring death in the face and yet saying 'I am here to meet you , but meet you here on my own terms'. Not on Eskander's term. Nor any king that had forced them as spear fodder in the battle field. But They knew what their say will be in this war that had been thrust upon them. 'Surji Mama er Teeyeta'

'Jawans, why are you here?' Jotayu's captain in charge of this group of youths asked them.

'To answer Aarohan's call to arms' a few said

'To defend our lands' said a few others

The group had been corralled into this batch after their arrival the day. After the night's rest they gathered on vast training fields. There they were asked about their martial skills if any.

Most didn't have any.

They were then asked of their vocation. Fishermen, farmers, cattle herders, weavers and so on. Do they have any specific preference in picking up a weapon?

As each person chooses their weaponry, they were caroled into such groups.

This was a group that held the spears, and Ratan's boys opted for their weapon.

The trainer Marshall yelled back. 'Jawans, those are all fanciful words. But it does me no good!'

"You are here for one purpose, and one purpose only: to bring me the parrot feather of Eskander, Surji Mama er Teeyeta.' Either you will bring it to me yourself, or you will be part of the stratagem that brings it to me. All other lofty ideals are superfluous and serve no benefit. Get that into your thick heads. You have one purpose, & one purpose only: the parrot feather!"

'How many of you are here in this group? The marshal asked,

A few looked uncertain, others began to count, while someone called out, 'We are hundred .

The marshal yelled out, who was that? Step forward

It was Ratan's younger son.

'Good' the marshal had a look at the lad. 'Today you will be the captain of your cohort.'

Turning to the other ninety-nine, the marshal continued, "It is very important to know how many are in your group. This is as important as your life, and your cohort's lives depend on it. You should also know how many are left in your group." He paused. "Yes, that is even more important because a lot of you will die in battle—your friends, brothers, uncles, or fathers. They will fall. If not them, then you will. If that strikes fear in your heart, suppress it. Harden your hearts. Because if that scares you, the idea that your mothers will be taken as slaves and violated should scare you even more. So yes, know how many of you are left on the battlefield."

"So today, you will lead your ninety-nine others to your objective."

Then he turned to the larger group. "You will be given one eight-ghonta to plan your assault. Whatever this designated leader of yours comes up with, follow through." 'Your objective: you will seek out the parrot feather that will be well guarded in the center of the field.

"Your weapon: take one bamboo staff. In actual battle these would be your Ballam spears."

"If during your assault you lose your sand pouch attached to your vest or they rapture , then you have bled.

The field referee will take you out of the assault.

"Any questions?"

The designated captain, Ratan's boy spoke up, "Jadrel, we don't see the parrot feather in the center of the field "

The marshal answered, "that is because ..." as he said so, he wore a battle helmet with the parrot feather, "Here it is. I will be in the center of the field. I will be guarded by twenty of my jawans. They too will be wearing jute apparel with sand pouches, if you in turn can dislodge it or rapture it they will be taken out of defense. Snatch the parrot feather from me if you hundred can!'

With that the marshal gave the sign, and the drumbeat began to pick up the space. He began to trot in battle pace and picked up his bamboo staff. He made his way to the center of the field where 10 of his jawans encircled him in battle defense formation. While the other ten divided in two groups began to float around as pods in assault formation.

Then after the prescribed time the drums changed its beat that signaled the start of the assault or rather the charge. All hundreds of the lads rushed towards to the center formation, all individual disorganized charge. A few within the crowd got caught up in the floating assault pod from the marshal defense team. Those caught up lost their sand pouches within moments of engagement, and summarily taken off the field. The veteran jawans did not go easy on the rookie lads in training, they punished them with their martial skills using the bamboo staff that bruised the lads. Bruising that would last at least three days. The rest of the crowd seemed to at first overwhelm the central ten-person jawan defense of the marshal. But the jawans were well trained, held their ground, worked in unison, and picked out each individual as they came crashing onto the formation. The field referees were busy, they began to pull, tap out all the lads who had lost or raptured their sand pouches in their disorganized assault. After a while, it became clear that none of the defense jawans had lost their sand pouches, or ' died', whereas the lads were falling like flies. And in the process were beaten black, blue with significant bruising. The floating pods become more effecting as many of the lads were taken off the field. And then at one point the hundred strong lads become less than twenty. At that moment the defense guards made way for the marshal, and he came out along with his guards in perfect battle formation and decimated the remaining twenty. All the while the war drums picking up ever increasing tempo.

All of the hundred lads had fallen.

None of the jawans had fallen.

Everyone simply watched in silence from other cohorts.

The Marshal then took his feathered helmet & yelled out loud, "This is not Eskander's helmet. You have not taken down any of us. Yet in actual battle the Dhonis are far superior in skill than my jawans.

"So, this is not Eskender's helmet......but your severed heads! Do you understand!"

Chapter 30

Aristotle, the Greek Chanakkya

Aristotle was waiting for this day. His lad Alexander has done that no man in Greek history has achieved. Or one should say, in the history of all nations. Not only he crossed Anatolia but go into the heartland of Persia and now even now the bigger prize, India! He had taught the lad logic well, his method of reasoning that is the core foundation of battle strategy. And the lad simply took it to a level that he, Aristotle could ever imagine. The lad seems to make the best of any situation, and then some. The lad courted death, and he is ecstatic in the manner he does so.

But Aristotle knew, one day there would arise in the world a talent similar to that of Alexander. Yes,

Alexander was unique. But never in this world does talent come in a single instance. They may appear to be unique but move far and wide enough, and one would find duplication of such talent on this earth. And Alexander has indeed moved far and wide. So Aristotle's logic told him, wait for it, Alexander will or rather shall meet his match or even worse, his greater. And it was no surprise it was to come from India. Mysterious this land is, India.

It was time to initiate his third grand scheme. Aristotle thought. The first was to mitigate, manipulate Alexander to fix his gaze on the mighty eastern Persian Empire. That had worked out well. The second goal was to sustain & retain the gains of the lands. That too had worked out well. He did not want to initiate the third grand scheme, for it was precautionary and precautionary measures for the extreme. Aristotle expected Alexander to return after his conquer of the Persian lands. But the lad had been led to believe in himself in the manner of Demi Gods of mythical times and that had instrumented such behavior. He has now gone into India. And India had its own gods.

His third scheme, god(s) forbid, if needed to be executed would mean things have gone terribly wrong. And Aristotle realized it may well be the time.

His spies had given him the word that Coenus's entire crack team had been decimated with no losses on the enemy side. It was the brilliance of the battle strategy trap, executed in a manner beyond imagination, which was its beauty, if one believed the reports. Reports stated that the Gangaridai had trained full-grown Bengal tigers as their war pack, along with the elephants. There was even mention of a 20-foot-tall monster of an elephant that led a pack of a thousand pachyderms. Rubbish. Whatever had happened on that fateful night had turned into mythical proportions.

Then again, Aristotle thought, behind every myth there is a certain amount of truth.

It was time for Aristotle to execute his third grand scheme and travel east.

Chapter 31

Open Palm to Fist

Deep Monsoon.

The training fields were ankle-deep in mud. With three moons of constant marauding by horse hooves and foot traffic, the ground had become a dust bowl when dry and a mud pit when soaked by rain.

Jotayu said, "I need more time, we need more time. They have improved, don't get me wrong. But more training is needed. '

Aarohan kept silent.

'I know what you will say my old mentor, that there was never a bad soldier, but bad generals. The jawans are motivated, they are. But they are no battle champions.... yet'

'Do you mind if I join the training drills tomorrow?'. It was FaMing. Jotayu was slightly startled. This companion of Aarohan seems to move in complete silence.

'Sure princess, when do you want to start?' Jotayu enquired.

'At your first ghonta. We will do the Surji mama er Teeyeta drill. You will be the barbarian, with the same twenty guard defenders that you had used against the lads. Paced out in twenty yards each in group of five, five and ten.' Fa Ming had said.

That was last evening.

The first ghonta was struck by FaMing herself. Thousands of jawans, assembled for the day's training, stood around the perimeter of the field. None had ever seen a female warrior.

From the far end, where the command tents were pitched, Aarohan made his way slowly, riding on Manu's back. The sun had not yet fully risen, and the silhouette of the large tusker made a powerful impression as it strode majestically to one side of the field.

Aarohan approached the station of the war drummers, with FaMing close by, holding her staff parallel to the ground within her folded arms. Aarohan instructed the drummers, "Start with ektal. When I raise my fist, move to tintal. When I slow down, return to ektal. When I circle my kill, sustain the trot rhythm. When I lunge, match me."

Aarohan glanced at FaMing. FaMing anticipated

Aarohan's query, 'your friend Balan tutored me. I am versed in the Kanti and the Kanji martial stances.

Aarohan let his chador fall. He was in full battle gear. He began the slow chant, ' akdoom bakdoon , ghora doom…' The three drummers began to pick up the beats from the Aarohan's chant.

He began to circle round the field with FaMing close by.

Chanakkya began to narrate the moves aloud to all who were present and within the earshot. 'We the Gangariddi strike right at the cusp of sunrise. Our senses are the sharpest now. The sun is always on our backs. Our eyes are already accustomed to the dark and now we ease into the daylight. Our enemies face the sun and have difficulty focusing on their alertness. The air is coolest and densest now. We modulate our breathing and build up our reserve. Breathing matters in battle motions, just like what a yogi will tell you.'

Aarohan began to speed up, his path tracing a wide arc, with FaMing meandering from right to left as if she were the orbiting planet to his sun. The arc tightened into a coil, and only in the last strides did Aarohan's target become apparent. The floating group jumped into action, moving toward Aarohan and FaMing. These were not the lads from yesterday but veterans from Jotayu's strike force.

Chanakkya continued, "We never show our intent. Keep the enemy guessing and exploit the ever-changing conditions of the battlefield."

Aarohan reached a striking distance of the first

group. The lead jawan swung fully at Aarohan, who seemed eager to engage. But at the last moment, Aarohan evaded the strike and pierced the sand pouch of the second jawan. The momentum carried the first jawan into FaMing's reach, where his pouch was promptly pierced. Two jawans fell in one maneuver.

"We never fight alone. No matter our skill, we fight in pairs, just as we have two hands," Chanakkya explained.

The remaining three took a more defensive stance.

Both Aarohan and FaMing stopped too. Stood motion less. The beat of the drums stopped too.

Aarohan turned his back on the trio and walked away. FaMing, meanwhile, circled to the opposite side, keeping the trio in the center. It seemed the trio were being stalked.

Aarohan raised his hand, and the drumbeat picked up on the tin taal.

'When you are the inferior number, we leverage our disadvantage through position stratagem.' Chanakkya narrated.

Both Aarohan and FaMing charged from opposite direction with the jawans in the center. Ferocious were their charge, and ferocious were the defense by the jawans. But they were forced to focus on both sides whereas the skilled masters on martial arts Aarohan and FaMing only worked what was in-front of them.

The sand pouches of the three jawans fell.

The observing jawans in training, couldn't believe their eyes. A woman fights better than the veteran jawans! In a culture where women are seen as frail and her merits are measured by her prowess in cooking age old family recipes to be dished & prepped for men, is unthinkable that, now that the same men are being dissed out by a woman in the battlefield. What in the flowing of Ganga!

The second floating group was now determined not to be the casualty similar to the first. They took the initiative, and the five fanned out, with the intention of circling the duo. Aarohan and FaMing responded by changing their location in the field as well, keeping all five in a line as much as they could. And they too began to battle trot towards the jawans.

'We never allow enemy forces to encircle us, and if possible, strike even before they have taken advantage of their battle formation ', Chanakkya added

Aarohan again raised his hand to initiate the Tin Taal drumbeats. This time the tempo was even faster. Aarohan and FaMing rushed the first in line of the Jawans, who were overwhelmed within moments. The rest four encircled Aarohan and FaMing, forcing them into a defensive posture now. Aarohan's back to FaMing's back.

The drum kept beating on.

Both Aarohan and FaMing were in a crouching position with their shield up. The four encircling them on all four sides. Neither did they make any move.

The drum kept beating on with an even faster

tempo. One could see both Aarohan and FaMing ever so subtly tapping their left feet, and then it happened. Probably triggered by some signal between FaMing and Aarohan, both swung around each other arm locked, developing a centripetal force and releasing each other to find gaps within the encircling four, in opposite directions. Both Aarohan and FaMing broke out of their micro siege. The Four kept on with their defensive shield-up posture but were too late to respond to this centripetal maneuver.

Even though this maneuver in itself was awe aspiring, what came next was unexpected. Both Aarohan and FaMing used their staff pressed into the ground to rebound back to the nearest Jawan, and having a swing at their back pouches. Pouches for both the Jawans fell. And this all happened in the rhythm of the high tempo drumbeats. This was more of a choreographed dance move, rather than a martial arts maneuver, perfectly executed.

Only two Jawans of the second floating group remained standing. Jotayu, sensing the battle slipping away, shouted, "Jawans, to me!". The two jawans broke formation and began running back to the ten guarding Jotayu.

FaMing would have none of it, she took out two sling ties and one after the other sent it flying towards the Jawans feet. Both got tangled up and fell. FaMing and Aarohan ran up and finished off their 'kill'.

The jawans guarding Jotayu were in full defense formation after witnessing the cutting down of the two floating units. They will take no chance. Shields over lapping shield with spears piercing out between the shields.

"What is the strategy when outnumbered and the enemy has consolidated their position?" Chanakkya mused aloud. This time, even he had no answer.

Both Aarohan and FaMing paced back and forth at distance of thirty yards from the defense formation.

FaMing stopped pacing. She looked directly at the defensive wall of the Jawans, "so ohh great Aarohan, this is the army that will take down Eskander's horde? They can hardly stand up to two individuals with the eleven of you!"

Then FaMing did the ultimate lay down on the jawans, "Your women must be very disappointed." She almost hissed it out.

There was a low hum of 'oouuu' that rang around the whole field. The less experienced jawans, two in number couldn't take the humiliation and took the bait. They did not hear Jotayu say out loud, "Stay in formation you lot, don't give in to her taunts ". They rushed towards FaMing with full committed charge, mad with rage. And FaMing took full advantage of the blind assault by the jawans. All she had to do was dance and evade the swings by the two and pick off the sand pouches from the 'enraged kittens'. Thus, two more fell.

The drum beat now took on a more festive rhythm. The drummers were enjoying the foreground action, and they were only too happy to provide the background battle beats.

'You probe the defense of your enemy not only physically, but also psychologically,' Chanakkya formulated, witnessing the mistakes committed by the two jawans.

Jotayu yelled out to his guards, "keep your cool my jawans, we will not give them an inch of our ground anymore. HOLD your ground."

Aarohan smiled. "They will not give us the ground. Then let's not take the ground route." FaMing caught the meaning immediately.

Aarohan tossed aside his staff and signaled for two heavy bludgeons. The tension rose. Things were about to get serious.

'Get ready to fly,' Aarohan whispered to FaMing. He began a slow trot, gathering momentum. FaMing mirrored his movements, her strides quickening.

The tin taal drumming intensified. The jawans braced, shields interlocked. Jotayu knew his mentor well. "Steady, jawans. He is just one man."

Aarohan was in full jogging momentum now with his two bludgeons. Just five yards in front of the formation, he surges his speed and does a flying full one eighty rotation with the bludgeons and hands fully spread out in a centrifugal angular momentum. He transformed himself into a cyclonic form, with the heavy bludgeons crushing into four of the jawans. They fell like blades of grass under a lawn mower. But the adjacent four thrust their staff in 'spear plunge's formation into Aarohan. Aarohan just recovered from his cyclic momentum , and from a low crouching position simply jerk his shoulders up. Right at that momentum the staff hits his sandbags, and two of them dislodge. By the rule of the game, Aarohan is, thus 'dead'.

But not so FaMing.

As the jawans were scared, busy assaulting Aarohan, she in full run flies onto Aarohan's shoulder, taking advantage of Aarohan's shoulder thrust. She is airborne twelve feet above head and shoulders of the jawans, summersaulting above all else and landing behind even Jotayu. While Jotayu was about to turn, FaMing without even turning, thrust her two shorter staff in backward motion into Jotayu. Jotayu's pouch falls. Jotayu is, thus 'dead'. Too.

The whole crowd remains silent. They could not believe their eyes. Chanakkya was silent too. He was astounded, like the rest of the crowd. But he was also profoundly sad. He stated out slowly, "…. And sometimes we sacrifice our prime, to attain our objective." Jotayu was dead, but so was Aarohan. Eskander would be dead, but now Chanakkya was certain that Aarohan would stop at nothing to attain his parrot feather, even sacrificing his own life. This made Chanakkya sad.

Chapter 32

Balan the First Shaolin

Sun began to rise over the horizon. How eventful the previous night was! But if the night was eventful, the Sun would find this day even more worthy to shine upon. The Sun would say, 'I am glad I rose today!'

Balan gripped his spear, which was drenched in blood from tip to staff. His palm was wrapped in very fine cotton, that too was deep dark red with clotted blood. He would often use fine cotton wrapped around his palm so that he would not lose the grip of his weapon during battle, for blood can be slippery.

He moved the sole of his feet in the manner of the katana of the spear—a motion the Greek hoplites had never seen before. Fierce was his stance, fluid was his motion, confident was he in his technique. By now, it was only he who remained standing from his strike team.

His piercing eyes locked onto Alexander's. Balan smiled. "So here I am. Here to claim 'Surji Mama er Tyeta,'" he proclaimed loudly. One of Alexander's Indian generals from Taxila began to translate. "By the law of your lands, and by the laws of our land on which you stand illegally, I challenge you to a captain-to-captain duel."

Alexander said nothing.

"They say you have one eye blue in color, while the other brown. Well today I see both have turned Yellow", Balan retorted over the rows of regent guards between him and Alexander.

The Indian general kept translating beside Alexander's ear.

With the flick of his heal on the hilt, Balan swung his spear around his body with the perfect martial stance. The tip of the spear leveled straight between the eyes of Alexander.

"Well? What is the color of your eyes today?" Balan hissed & provoked again.

"Your challenge is that of a desperate man who is about to die" Alexander said, while the Indian general translated.

"Sure, your man can rush me at this very moment and be done with it. But the four who would die in the process would be wondering, were you worth defending.",

Balan replied with laughter.

Balan relaxed his stance, took his spear by his side as a leaning cane. "I have single handedly killed thirty three of your men today. I must say I am not that impressed. So, are you any better? I am thinking you, my Baccha, is simply a boy with an army, throwing tantrums. Hah!"

Alexander, filled with rage when he heard the term 'baccha '. The Indian general did not need to translate that word to him. He had heard that before. Darius too, had that coined against Alexander's name.

He gave the sign.

The guards and soldiers made out a large circle for the duel to take place.

"Your champion Aarohan had severed the members of my captured soldiers. I will slice, dice and fillet you layer by layer, while you are alive. What kind of Barbarian severs prisoner of war", Alexander tried to take the moral high ground.

To that Balan gave out a loud laughter, "so speaks the lad who rapes, civilian women, men, boy, girl and everything in between after he illegally invades our lands! Your men had a trial, those who were PROVEN'; (Balan yelled out loud the word 'proven'), guilty were sentenced as per OUR laws '; (another yell for 'laws'). What laws of your land allows you to come to India? Your quarrel was with the Persians, did India ever do anything to you? "

Balan paused. He lowered his spear. He paced, "Your teacher is here. The one you call Aristotle. Come out

Aristotle". Balan yelled out

From one of the tents nearer to Alexander's, a figure with a pulled-over cloak, observing the whole proceeding straightened up.

Balan said in Clear Greek, "let's see what your great philosopher has to say about your campaigns. O'Aristotle, will you show your face?"

There was a stir within the ranks. How did this barbarian know of Aristotle and, how did this barbarian speak the Greek language? And was Aristotle actually there? In India, right there and then?

Alexander, yelled out loud, "Enough! Are we going to stand here and talk philosophies or are we gonna give you a taste of my steel Blade when I cut out your tongue." With that Alexander lunged forward.

Alexander was trained in martial arts ever since his youthful days. Until this day there were none who was better than him, be it in skill or stamina and more important in courage. He exuded mastery of warfare over not only an individual, or a group but over an army. But all this would come to a reckoning today.

Swift, powerful and precise was Alexander's charge. But Balan simply mirrored the effort and received the kinetic motion. Twirled around three sixty degrees, like a cog in a wheel and let Alexander's spear pass him by. As the spear made no contact, Alexander sensed he over committed, and immediately initiated a turn to face Balan again. Balan, knowing very well what Alexander's move would be, and that was a first ever, he simply thrust the hilt of the spear between Alexander's feet.

Alexander tripped over backwards onto the ground, from his own motion.

Balan, took his martial stance again and with the authority of a martial instructor and stated out loud in Greek "Isn't it the first day of training that one finds himself tripping over backwards? Is today your first day of training? Baccha!"

Everyone was silent. They couldn't make sense of what to make of what just transpired. Alexander's guards immediately jumped in, in between Alexander and Balan. Alexander smiled. This is going to be fun! Finally, a guy who knew his trade. Actually, knew his trade.

Kneeling, Alexander spoke loudly, "So you know our customs. We will have fun today. For his valor, I invoke the protection right on him. If he defeats me fairly, you will all let him go. But win I shall, and I will make you an example for the Gangariddis."

Stating so, Alexander took up his spartan shield and spear.

So did Balan picked up his spear and shield, that he himself forged.

Alexander began to charge from Get-go. Speed and Vagary were his hall marks. He always kept his opponent guessing. They seldom could better Alexander for there was no strategy against Alexander.

But not so against Balan. He was THE quintessential

martial artist. He had trained himself in an art form that he and Aarohan had developed. Then throughout his travels to the Tibetan plateau he even perfected it, understanding and incorporating the nuances of all of the regional martial arts and style. Today it was in full display.

As Alexander thrust forward, Balan simply mirrored his movements, stepping back. Whenever Alexander swung side to side or combined attacks, Balan effortlessly evaded and countered with precision. This continued for several exchanges, with Alexander unable to land a single hit on Balan. Everyone around was amazed.

Growing frustrated, Alexander intensified his attacks, increasing the complexity of his strikes. He finally made contact. But it was as a block in perfect stance by Balan to Alexander's strike, measured, anticipated. And everyone knew it was so.

"I am disappointed, oh Dhoni," Balan said, mocking Alexander. "Who trained you?" His words cut deep as Alexander realized he was being outclassed. Alexander was large, using brute force and aggression, which made him a good warrior—but he lacked the refinement of a true martial artist.

"You have an ego as large as the mountains." Balan said, as he evaded and blocked a whole lot of strikes by Alexander, "But by the time this land is done with you, your ego will crumble to dust."

Alexander, recognizing his opponent's skill, stepped back, retreating to his corner. He threw his shield down, instead took up a sword on his shield arm. He was going in all-out assault, with little defense.

Balan went back to his perceived corner. 'Give me a bucket of water.' A soldier obliged. First, He splashed his face with the water, then he stood up.

"What's the matter old man, having your last drink?" Alexander Hissed.

Balan then dipped his spear head into the bucket of water. Then he did something that only he knew how, never will ever a martial monk will learn this technique. He slashed and crisscrossed the spear in air that led out uniform continuous streaks of water, three streaks altogether on to the ground. In perfect straight line, in perfect parsing angle. A few of the soldiers understood what it meant.

And Alexander knew. He paused. He has never seen anything like this before. He could only imagine the amount of training, or the rigor of the martial knowledge exercised to produce such a skill set.

"Be careful, baccha," Balan warned. "You know not what I know. You have spent your life destroying dynasties and empires. I, on the other hand, have spent mine building up kingdoms, not tearing them down."

The "baccha "word triggered off Alexander, he came prancing down with both the blades drawn and in piercing formation, like fangs of a viper!

Balan had enough. He now unleashed his full training of the monk order, the same skills that allowed him to cut through six bamboo stalks at one swipe.

Alexander lunged in. While Balan also lunged, but only with a reverse summersault. As Alexander was airborne, he saw what Balan was doing. He recognized the martial art motif, the same style that he had seen rendered to him by Aarohan in Komolaphuli, when Aarohan freed himself of being his prisoner. As Alexander dug in his sword fangs, centered on the torso of Balan, Balan swung out his shield and spear, negating the swords trajectory. But what was equally executed at the same time by Balan, was the crane flip kick, or rather a knee kick that landed heavily and squarely on Alexander's exposed center, right under the chin. They were both in such close formation that had Alexander succeeded in thrusting his swords, those blades would have been three quarters in within Balan's chest. Only now, Alexander experienced a full knee knock-out hook on his chin. Both Balan & Alexander tumbled over. Balan carried with the momentum and twirled around into a crouching attack stance, while Alexander lay unconscious on the ground.

Alexander's captain of his bodyguards and lover, Hephaestion along with two other guards immediately stepped between Alexander's limp body and Balan. Two other guards hovered over Alexander to see if he had any significant injuries, while Alexander's physician, who was witnessing the whole drama, rushed in.

Balan stepped back, with loud laughter. "Didn't your master say I would have my hands on him if I better him ".

"That's what he said, but he is not awake to enforce his command, is he?" Said Hephaestion, as he always made light of all situations. "Guards, all of you, kill this bastard"

Balan readied himself for the final fight of his life. So, this is how I go out, Balan thought. Pity—these so-called high ideals of democracy and honor vanish the moment these barbarians taste defeat. That has always been the nature of western civilizations.

"You pathetic cowards, I am entitle to my prize", Balan declared out loud.

Right then a spear with a banner of the Greek Lyceum landed in the center of the court. Everyone paused.

"Leave this man to me. He is now a prisoner of the Greek state", a booming voice rang out.

Balan looked around to see a man in a cloak come forward.

"This is a military matter, the state has no jurisdiction here", Hephaestion countered.

"I invoke state, & Lyceum, and military jurisdiction over this man", the man in the cloak answered. Then he withdrew the cloak from over his head. There was a loud gasp.

Balan gave out a loud laughter. "Hah, the plot thickens", he exclaimed.

"I invoke the state claim on this man, for he has intelligence on all of the realms, including Tibet and China." The man in the cloak declared out load....

"I invoke the Lyceum claim on this man, for he has

knowledge that no member of the Lyceum has. And I invoke military claim on this man, for he is the greatest metallurgist in the world". The man in the cloak concluded, "this man shall not die here today'

"He may have seriously wounded a monarch, and you expect us to let him go just like that?", Hephaestion hissed

"Yes, just like that. I do not care if your monarch has experienced a life-threatening blow or not. This was a dual by law . And that man is mine."

"Finally, the second in the assembly here who knows what he really is talking about, but what makes you think I would comply?", Balan retorted.

And right then a heavy blunt object hit Balan on the head from behind, and he fell unconscious.

Alexander lay unconscious on one side of the ground with his physician pouring over him.

Balan lay unconscious on the other side with two individuals in the Lyceum cloak guarding over him.

And in the center, the cloaked figure stood tall. "By the authority vested in me, I claim this prisoner."

World history had just taken a dramatic turn.

It was Aristotle!

With this move, Aristotle had averted an invasion on the West by India.

"Keep your precious prisoner for now", Hephaestion said, and then added 'For Now that is.'

A few maids in the kitchen of the royal enclosure witnessed all this event play out, astonished. They knew what they had witnessed something extraordinary, that Alexander was defeated by this general from the Gangariddis. The chief cook came in, "you all saw nothing. If you value your life. Careful in what you say of what just transpired." All of the maids scurried off. Among them a number extra to them. With all the maids having their hair wrapped in cloth for hygiene reason, no one noticed that one of them was not from them.

That number knew _ ie FaMing knew, she had to act now and fast.

Chapter 33

Fall to Rise

Part 2

Balan reiterated, I do not think this nation will answer your call.'

Balan walked around the hut, seemingly measuring the space, as if to expand his mind within it.

'They are farmers, fishermen, weavers. A sedentary life is what they prefer and live. They are not warriors.

"We have a better chance... you have a better chance if you take a crack team and go after the Dhoni warlord. We can formulate a plan, just as we did in China."

Aarohan was prepping an arrow stick to be added to his quiver. "In the depths of the forest, where I first encountered Manu, I came to a certain realization. When you are secluded for forty days at end, in mediation, with no human around, things start to speak to you, and realizations manifest in certain ways.

"You have seen how these very same farmers tend and zealously protect their crops. You have seen the very same fisherman studies the waves before he casts his net. You have seen how intricate the weaving pattern & shape a weaver creates such skills. They all cherish their way of life. That spirit of life is a warrior spirit. Thats what I seek to kindle.

"I must now head to Pataliputra. But you, my friend can proceed with your plan regarding Eskander. I hope you will be successful. But just in case it goes the the other way, I cannot afford, we cannot afford an unprepared nation".

That was a monsoon ago.

The Greeks had sent out an expeditionary force to look for, and hunt down Aarohan. And fate would have it, now Balan was leading an expeditionary force to infiltrate the Greek forces, and hunt down Alexander.

Balan had started out with eighty-one Jawans. At a place later to be known as Agra, he had an encounter with another expeditionary force of the Greeks. A hand-to-hand combat ensued, for Balan did not want any of the Greeks escaping and reporting back and giving away their position to Alexander. The battle was fierce, even though the Greeks walked into an ambush. The Greek's method of a shield wall for defense proved too much for the jawans.

Eighteen of the Jawans lost their lives, with thirty more wounded, though Balan and his Jawans were successful in killing all the sixty Greeks they encountered. It seems the Gangariddis needed the elephant corps to better the odds in their favor, for the hoplites were the best hand to hand combat force.

Balan had to reconsider, he needed reinforcement. In order to make his plan work, he needed FaMing at his side, to infiltrate, for she was adept in martial assault to charm assault and everything in between. She was an excellent strategic planner. Balan sent one of the jawans to send her word to join him. But in the meantime, Balan proceeded westward to intercept Eskander and his army.

That was two moons ago.

On the Eastern bank of River Indus at a location near current Bahawalpur, Balan and his Jawans took possession of an abandoned village. They fixed up the place and recruited local help to set up a sedentary life of a village, though whole thing was a reuse to lure in the Greeks. The Greeks had a large army, thus they needed to plunder, coerce, collaborate with local village populace to sustain their army. The village was set up seemingly with a regular image of a village life, men, women, elderly and a few kids and a lot of festivity and apparent provisions. Then a few of the Jawans masquerading as farmers were sent out and allowed to be interrogated by the scouts of Alexander's camp.

'Spare me and my family, I will tell you what you want to know, but I beseech you that my family be spared.' One of the 'farmers' would say in isolation from others. 'we have just completed our harvest and I can show you where our village is, as long as you leave me alone with my family, and provisions.'

The Greeks sent in their scouts to observe the village. And they are convinced that it would be a great soft target to extract much needed provisions. A contingent of hoplites numbering thirty were sent to raid the village.

The jawans were ready when the Greeks came to raid the village, once all of the raiders came into the central square of the village, all exit points were blocked. Mayhem ensued. Without any loss to the jawans, the hoplites were brought down in a hail of arrows.

Balan waited until evening to remobilize again. This time masquerading as the Greeks, with seven cart loads of grain, vegetable, and a dozen cattle and oxen. They reached the Greek camps in the middle of the night. They had argued at the gates with guards, "You can grow hungry tonight, but it will be my neck that the cook will have if I do not deliver these load of goods, for do you think our lord Alexander ever goes hungry? These are needed for the camp's breakfast. I want to get rid of this blood drenched smell now, or do you want to taste my steel this late at night, eh lads ?', Balan had growled at the gate keepers , with his muddied bloodied camouflaged face. The guards stationed towards the middle of the night are the less experienced ones. Seeing battle fazed hoplites, prisoners, cart full of food and provisions, and beef...ie cattle and oxen, the in experienced gatekeepers yielded, without any proper check, or identity verification.

The group of thirty-three Jawans then made their way around the camp to seek out Alexander. The Jawans took down a considerable number of hoplites in the quietness of the night. The Jawans along with Balan, however at one point they were spotted by roaming guards, the alarm rang out. And mayhem followed suite. The jawans had considerable amount of advantage as they were not the ones taken by surprise, but eventually the numbers of the Greeks overwhelmed the jawans, and every single one of them perished except for Balan. The personal bodyguards of Alexander lined up around his connected tents, three row deep. Once that happened, any remote chance the Jawans or Balan had to get to Alexander was now nil.

Balan pranced and bounced around the large camp of forty thousand. He knew his time has arrived and that he would not be able to get out of this infinite assault by the hoplites, the Persians, the Egyptians, the Indians who had allied themselves with Alexander. But he was not a single bit apprehensive, his motive was to demonstrate the skills that the Gangariddis may poses, take down as many hoplites with him as possible, and show them skills that they have never seen before.

How he mixed and matched, the sword, the shield, the spear, the flying knives. How effortlessly he killed anyone assaulting him, turning their own momentum into a lethal mistake.

The Greeks wanted to kill him savagely. But at the same time, they were full of awe. What skills this mad man possessed! In many ways they didn't want to kill such a specimen of a skilled man.

....and then Balan was truly surrounded.

And he didn't mind, he simply assaulted whoever

came near, striking out incoming arrows and spears. It was indeed awe-aspiring to watch.

And then Alexander himself engaged Balan. And Aristotle took Balan into custody. And FaMing witnessed it all when she arrived at the camp that early morning.

That was three days ago.

Today FaMing crouched silently at the thicket near the encampment of Aristotle. His flag flew over the central tent. That meant he was now present inside the tent. Did Aristotle have Balan in there as his prisoner?

FaMing was scoping out her strategy if penetrating the camp and formulate a plan to rescue her mentor, Balan, when suddenly a group of men, women and a few children ran to the other side of the tent. Few even shouted out, 'they are going to hang the Hassasin leader'

FaMing took off from her position, she traced a path through the thicket to the other vantage point of the tent. And what she saw simply gave her a deep chill down her spine.

A wooden platform had been erected and Balan was set on that platform with a black cloth pulled over his head. There was a concentric ring of hoplites guarding the proceedings. And right then the Hangman pulled the lever!

FaMing didn't have time to react consciously, but by reflex she knocked her arrow, three simultaneously, all the while giving out a yell. Some of the hoplites spotted her, raising the alarm, and started towards her. All the while another group of hoplites put their shield to protect the hangman. FaMing's three arrows bound for the hangman bounced off the shields.

FaMing had to turn and sprinted into the woods. She didn't know where she was going, but she simply sprinted as fast as a gazelle, all the while tears ran down her cheek. She didn't know how far she ran or if her pursuers were gaining on her, or she had lost them, she simply sprinted. As if she simply wanted to run away from that vision of Balan falling the distance that would break his neck.

Why? Why did he have to go out that way?

And just like that the legend that Balan was, was no more.

Chapter 34

The Battle for the Parrot Feather

"By the blood that you have spilled on these lands, you shall have no more nourishment from this soil, not food, nor water. How long your transgressing soul lives depend on how fast you can reach your ill-gotten lands to the west where you may eat from again. But not here. This Dharani (Earth) is done with you. I have spoken on her behalf" –

Aarohan (King Hasti)

There it was, not.

Alexander was pensive. He has thirty thousand men ready to take on the Gangariddis. He had divided his men into ten legions of three thousand each. Of which two were cavalry divisions and one consisting of mobile chariots. Battle-hardened, yet weary his men are. The Bactrians and the Persians were eager to engage in battle under his banner. They themselves had never taken on the Gangariddis, as smaller skirmishes often resulted in Gangariddis favor. But this time they are being led by the great Alexander himself. There was considerable amount of enthusiasm in his camp.

But Alexander always knew his enemies well. From Darius, to the Egyptians, to Puru, he knew their war game well. But this Aarohan has turned into something of an enigma. First the well-orchestrated ambush and decimation of Coenus's advanced company. Then the daring assault on him by this other enigma, Balan. Alexander was not pleased that Balan was taken prisoner & then hanged by Aristotle. He felt sure he would have defeated Balan had he a second go at the Assassin. Now his old mentor had cheated him out of this opportunity under the claim or guise of state matter. What could be more of state matter then an attempt on the life of a god? State matter nonsense.

The cavalry and the chariot divisions were kept behind the lines of the foot soldiers and the phalanx. The phalanx would be his main tool to neutralize the elephant corps he had heard so much about. His army possessed about five hundred war elephants, but would they match Aarohan's?

His thoughts were interrupted by the sound of the trumpet. The enemy formation has been sighted.

Through the early morning fog, the rustling of unison footsteps was first felt, then heard. And then a silhouette of a gigantic mass of men appeared through the veil of the fog. Only the sound of rustling footsteps in unison.

The trumpet for battle commencement was sounded from Alexander's Army. Which was followed by huge cheer and war cry from the thirty thousand of the Greek hoplites.

The Gangariddis remained silent. Stoic in their stare towards the Greeks and their subjugated Persian and Bactrian forces.

When the Greeks ran out of cheering breath after five long moments, they began to taunt and hurl obscenity towards the Gangariddis. With the rape and enslaving of the women populace a common thread in their insult.

Still, the Gangariddis remained silent.

Alexander observed the eerie silence and discipline of the defending army. He was concerned. He often use provocation to his advantage. But if the Gangariddis do not react to provocation then that technique is no longer in play.

In answer to threats to raping of women, a female warrior in attire of a Chinese war lord, and a warrior helmet with peacock feather plume came forward on a white horse, the exact antitheses to Alexander and Buchapelus .

The female warrior began to chant, " Akdoom bakdoom" , which was answered by the Gangariddis in unison "Ghora doom shaje"

The Greeks and their conquered comrades now they themselves went silent.

The woman warrior continued, " Dhak Dhol …." The whole of the Gangariddis answered, " Jhajor baje".

The Greek army went completely silent. They began to realize there was something else going on here.

The female warrior continued "Baste baste chollo Dhuli "…. Which again was answered by the whole of Gangariddis army " Dhuli gelo komola phuli "….

And now she turned her stead towards Alexander's station, "Kamal phuli er biyeta " pointing her banner spear to Alexander. The female warrior removed her helmet. It was the painted warrior-faced FaMing.

"SURJI MAMA ER TEEYETA!" The whole of Gangariddi army unsheathed its weapon and pointed to only one person and one person only. Alexander the Barbarian.

This was simultaneously picked up by a sky deafening trumpet of an Elephant. Over the ridge on the east stood on its hind leg the beast, with its six-footer blades attached to its tasks, Stood Manu.

And Aarohan riding Manu, firm and square towards Alexander.

Alexander then knew he was upstaged, for the second time in his hegemon career.

The Gangariddis were fully prepared for the Greeks. They were confident of their General King Aarohan. History will know him as 'King Hasti', with a distorted narrative.

The Gangariddis had a very defensive, formidable formation. The phalanxes in wedge formation with Elephants lining up in between the wedges.

'Let us wait and see what Aarohan's move will be', advised Hephaestion. Knowing Alexander was always on the move on the battlefield, provoking opportunities that would fall in favor of him, Hephaestion wanted to read the battlefield a bit better than previous campaigns. There was never an adversary who had such a formidable pachyderm force. And Aarohan had lost his daughter to Alexander's exploits. There was never a more lethal weapon than a mourning raging father bend on avenging his daughter.

But Alexander always had to be the orchestrator on the battlefield. That's how he thrived, that's how he won his battles.

Alexander gave the order for the Persian foot soldiers. They slowly began to jog to the Gangariddis' line.

' Let's see how does these clumsy beasts deal with arrows' Alexander retorted.

Two contingents of Persian archers, now allied with the Macedonians slowly begin to move in formation to the elephant lines, specially towards Manu. When their commander felt they were striking range of Manu, he awaited the command from Alexander.

Alexander knew from his campaign against Puru that his cavalry would not be effective against the elephant line. The horses simply didn't have the courage to charge up to the huge beasts. They were not trained in that manner. Thus, he wanted to bring chaos and disrupt the elephant line with easy picking of the elephants with volleys of arrows.

And he would strike with his cavalry when the elephants were in disarray.

Jotayu watched for the queue, for Aarohan had warned him, "Our elephants would be the prime target of their archers. We should use that to our advantage"

The archers came into formation and knocked their arrows. The moment they released their loads, Aarohan gave the maneuvering command. All of the elephants came to a sitting position at once and the thick jute rolled in a frame contraption belted to all the elephants back, were unfurled as a canopy over them, similar to the framework of the canopy that would one now see on Rikshaws in modern day Bengal. The Greeks had their tortoise formation with their shields, and so did the Gangariddi elephants had theirs, against the volleys of arrow.

The arrows came. Landed in the thousands. On and around the elephants. But all protected by the unfurled framed jute canopies.

FaMing saw her opportunity, she gave command to

the Gangariddi cavalry to charge the exposed archer regiment of the Persians, leading the contingent herself .

Alexander observed the Gangariddi maneuver. Cavalry! Now this was his expertise. He didn't want to miss the opportunity. He too immediately led the charge, with five hundred of his immediate contingent. He charged, they charged. Slowly gathering momentum, he was there and so was his best friend, bodyguard, and lover Hephaestion. Riding side by side. These Gangariddis have given him so much trouble lately. Today all that is going to change.

FaMing with her white garb, the white knight, charged with her contingent into the archers. She knew the flank of her charging column would be exposed to the devastating momentum of Alexander's cavalry.

But she didn't care. She knew even if her contingent was devastated, her objective was to neutralize the only potency that Alexander's army may have against the Gangariddi forces, Aarohan's elephants. The Archers have to go!

The Persian archers were in disarray. The swing of the Gangariddi cavalry was effective. The archer's broke formation, retreating. A good number of them slashed by the blades or trampled by the galloping horses. But so were the Greek cavalry, charging the rear of FaMing's Column. FaMing's orders were very specific. No matter what, her contingent was to follow her lead, and her lead only. The maneuvers of the two opposing cavalries became a matter of speed and momentum, rather than face to face fight.

Aarohan immediately sprang into action the moment the archer's breaking formation. Manu stood up, the jute 'awnings' furled up , began to charge towards the Greek Phalanx, the most formidable aspect of the Greek army. Jotayu and the rest of the elephants trying to keep Manu's space. Even though Manu was the largest elephant that history would see, he was much faster than the rest of the Pachyderm pack. The training that he was given on the plains of Lalakhal was now paying off.

Simmias, the Phalanx Captain saw the elephant's column moving towards the phalanx regiment. Good, he thought. History will now witness which of the war machination was superior, the Greek Phalanx or the Indian War Elephants.

Alexander saw that Aarohan had moved towards the Phalanxes. He was gaining on the tail of FaMing's cavalry. Does he disengage and square off with Aarohan or does he finish off what he has on his plate right now. Let's finish off our gain here, Alexander thought.

Manu kept on charging towards the Phalanxes. His six foot tusker blades gleaming and flashing in the sun rays.

Simmias, yelled out loud, 'My Greek brothers! Today we make lard out of these behemoths we have heard so much about. Today we make history! Who is with me? "

"Ahoo, Ahoo, Ahoo" the phalanx foot soldiers rang out.

Manu strode up to twenty yards to the tip of the phalanx, and then stopped. Aarohan half standing on top of Manu in his full battle gear, his eyes piercing through his helmets, full of rage, for these are the reckless youths that had taken his daughter's life three suns back, yet restrained, for today his win or loss will determine the fate of India. He simply stood there, in full command and full confidence. Silent.

Between all the yelling and harassing the hoplites began to quieten down. They too became silent. And in full awe. At the size of Manu and the presence of the Aarohan, the Great! Wait why does this man standing feel like he was the True Great! A few glanced towards the station of Alexander. And then back at Aarohan. Those few began to realize that they were indeed in presence of greatness. And it was not Alexander. One claiming to be great was raping, pilfering, destroying nations , while the other defending his people and land, and some say avenging his daughter's death.

Aarohan spread out both arms. He spoke in perfect Greek, "Here I am, I am Aarohan. You want to conquer my lands. Here I am, conquer Me!". None of the Hoplites made any move. Do you charge this behemoth? All at once?

Aarohan maneuvered Manu to sit down. The point of each and every phalanx following Manu's motion, lower the Eighteen foot long poles .

Alexander stopped chasing the tail of FaMing's cavalry and turned Buchaphelus towards the ridge overlooking the field where the Phalanxes and Manu were standing off. He stopped and began to see what Aarohan was up to. His cavalry of five hundred slowly coming to a standstill to observe what was going on. Why did Alexander stop. It is never like Alexander to pause in the thick of action.

'So here I am , ' Aarohan continued , " whom amongst you will claim glory today ?' Aarohan teased them.

Alexander slowly began to realize what was happening.

Aarohan said out loud, "well Simmias, will you be relegated to the captain of phalanx forever or will you claim glory today? Here I am! All alone. So Have your say" .

The Greeks were surprised, Aarohan knew of their captain!

Simmias steadied his nerves. It was only Aarohan and the beast of an elephant. The rest of the elephants were significant distance behind.

Simmias was under strict instructions not to go for the kill of the large elephant, only defend the line.

But Aarohan's fool hardiness is too good not to take advantage of. What would Alexander do? He would charge right now towards Manu.

So Simmias yelled," Brothers! Who is with me Charge! "and with that all off the phalanxes in the near vicinity of Manu began to converge upon the Pachyderm.

But Alexander knew what really was going on. He yelled out 'Nooo' as he saw that the phalanxes had committed. He immediately began to charge towards the battle formation, but he was a good five hundred yards away.

Aarohan and Manu Sprang into action too. But only after a few moments after phalanxes had committed their assault, but most importantly their posture in their charge.

The spears of Phalanxes are a good eighteen feet long. Which creates a considerable moment arm load at the tip of the spear. So they are kept upright most of the time. Or the point laid down at an angle to the ground. But only at the attack angle in the last moment to conserve energy.

As Manu was sitting down, the attack angle of the Phalanxes was set at low pitch.

Though Manu was the largest elephant the world has ever seen he was amongst the fastest and the most agile . Aarohan maneuvered Manu to lunged forward towards the charging phalanxes. As Manu did so, Aarohan turned the gear and all the six-footer blades came out of their wooden sleeves, like unfurled flower petals, only this time it were the large blades forged by Balan.

Manu dashed towards the phalanxes, which would have been a suicide charge. But the hoplites were having difficulty raising the long shank spears. Just Before Manu made contact, Aarohan maneuvered him to charge on its hind legs, coming down hard on his fore legs splintering a whole bunch of phalanx spears. That created an immediate gap in the apparent formidable porcupine line. Manu simply charged and kept punching through. When he was five row deep, Aarohan maneuvered a multi rotational move, with the blades all flaring out. The hoplites were being cut into pieces like vegetables in a blender. The phalanx assaults were designed in a way that they were most effective on a frontal charge, three rows of spear point stacked one over another. Thus, when they found Manu right in their midst, they couldn't maneuver with their eighteen feet spears and couldn't turn sideways towards Manu. Their sides were totally exposed. They couldn't avoid the blades as they were all hemmed in.

Limbs flew, torso flew, blood came gushing through. Manu swinging his tasks simply cut down bodies like crops in the harvester season.

Jotayu knew of Aarohan's strategy and now the whole contingent of the elephant brigade began to rush towards the gap that Manu had created. What Alexander had done with Bucephalus the horse at the battle of Issus, Aarohan had done the same with Manu the elephant here. Create that gap in the enemy line.

Alexander saw what was going on. This is not going to turn out great if his cavalry does not create a wedge between Aarohan and the rest of the elephant brigade. Will his phalanx be decimated, or will it finally be the downfall of Manu? This is that moment in History.

It is said that significant moment in history is marked by courage and rising to the occasion, but it is never mentioned that it is the female gender that tips the balance that determines the course of history. Always!

In his battle awareness and being focused on Manu, Alexander did not notice FaMing turned around with her cavalry came crashing down on Alexander's cavalry column at right angle with full momentum of galloping horses.

Ever since the day Balan was executed by Aristotle, that devastating scene etched into FaMing's vision, she had waited for this moment. Alexander caught FaMing at the corner of his eyes as she was charging in. She! Fully square on him, her saber unsheathed. Alexander ducked just in time. But bam!

First her horse Loong T boned into Buchaphelus. Both Alexander and Buchaphelus tripped to their sides but not totally thrown off. The impact caused Loong to go sideways and FaMIng too.

And then the FaMing's cavalry column crashed into the Macedonian cavalry. Hephaestion and the rest of Alexander's immediate bodyguards veered left right into the charging Gangariddi cavalry to give cover to Alexander. Mayhem ensued. One would describe the scene like that of two pythons entangled in a spiral of death choke.

Aarohan and Manu continued. The rage of a mad bull elephant paled compared to how Manu rampaged through the stalled Greek phalanxes, slicing and charging relentlessly. Aarohan and Manu had to maintain their charge; staying static would allow the phalanxes to regroup and ready themselves for a counterattack. Many were desperately trying to stay clear of Manu's swinging blades. But Aarohan caught in the corner of the eye, that FaMing in her zeal to avenge Balan had over committed.

The Gangariddi cavalry was no match for the Macedonian cavalry, that had perfected its battle strategy over a period of a decade. What Manu was doing to the phalanxes, was the same the Macedonian cavalry doing to that of the Gangariddis. The only one bettering the Macedonians was FaMing . FaMing gave the order to the troops to consolidate around her, so that she could offer up as much as valor, zeal , and most important act as an anchor to the battle line . But Alexander now had his sight on her. Aarohan can wait.

Aarohan saw what was happening to FaMlng's cavalry. He made eye contact with FaMing, and her expression told him that she was going to go for the godless, and spiller of blood Alexander's parrot feather! She very well might lose her life in the process, but that didn't matter to her.

But Aarohan cared! Aarohan had lost his daughter to this amoral leader of the Dhoni's , for nothing . Simply for the ego that western culture and philosophy had installed in an overzealous lad, that his daughter had to die. Because they had to stop this blood thirsty, war profiteering assault from the west that his childhood friend Balan had to die. And now he will lose FaMing. Aarohan looked back to Jotayu. Where was he. He should be here by now. He had asked Jotayu to hold back enough so that he could present himself and Manu as bait to the Dhonis. Aarohan looked back.

And sure enough, Jotayu arrived with a sizable number of his elephant brigade, crashing into the gap created by Aarohan and Manu. The Macedonian phalanxes began to crumble under the weight of the assault.

Immediately Aarohan steered Manu towards FaMing and in full trot. Will he reach FaMing in time, was his outmost concern now. History will bear witness to the fact that in all battles of significance, it's not the individual battle formation and powering of one over the other that dictated the outcome of the war, rather in how one wing or group assisting the other in moment of peril that shaped the final victory. Aarohan knew that. But this time it was the urge to save FaMing, it was as if FaMing now had precedence over the target of the parrot feather!

Alexander and his immediate cohorts made

mincemeat of the cavalry around FaMing. Ratan's two sons, who, after six months of rigorous marshal training had been handpicked by FaMing to be part of her five hundred strong cavalries, came into shadow formation to protect their leader. Giving her and her steed Loong enough space for mobility but give cover for all loose projectiles. They worked as a trident, the martial form of which was perfected in the pantheon of Indian martial techniques. Alexander noticed so, he and his cohorts along with Hephaestion began to converge in a spiral grind towards the trident formation, always forcing FaMing and the brothers to rotate their stance. Like flies, the periphery entourage of FaMing's cavalry began to fall. And the defenders did it willingly, as if they were protecting their queen! For they were aware what Alexander, and his cohorts did to their female prisoners. And FaMing was an extraordinary warrior. Alexander would want to make an example of her.

Aarohan knew FaMing's life moments were numbered. He trained Manu to follow his signs and gestures, but now he yelled out to the pachyderm, "Manu, Now! ". Aarohan knew FaMing's life is now measured in the stride of the elephant. And Manu knew too. He made a straight Bee line to the thicket of the two-cavalry clash, mauling and slicing down the tail of Alexander's cavalry. But will he be there in time!

FaMing's cavalry number was now down to five individuals. Knowing her time is near, FaMing charged with her spear towards the flank guard of Alexander, perching the flesh of the steed. But keeping the momentum, and using the spear as pole, vaulting over the guard and the steed. The airborne FaMing unsheathed her sword as she zeroed on to Alexander.

But Alexander had seen this maneuver before by Balan. With lightning speed Alexander placed his shield between him and FaMing, and then rolled down the side of Buchaphelus. FaMing's momentum simply carried her over, her sword thrusting a tangent strike over the shield. Sparks flying. Alexander fell and then rolled back to his assault stance. FaMing fell to the ground too but landed with her back to Alexander. And because of that stance, she knew she was at a disadvantage.

Before she knew it, she was pushed down to the ground by Alexander from behind, like so many little girls would be in school yards by school bullies. For objective analysis will bear out that Alexander was simply an oversized school bully. Nothing more in history.

Alexander now had his full body weight, thigh and knee pinning down on the back of FaMing. He would kill her right there, then. It would have been nice to have her as a war trophy, alive, revel in the pleasure of violating her. But she was too militant, a female version of him. No, she had to go. Now.

He saw his shadow over his prey. He thought, how apt. That his shadow would be the last shadow that FaMing would see before she dies. But he noticed with the corner of the eyes that all his entourage suddenly moved away. And he saw his shadow grow by so much. For his shadow, Now, was overtaken by that of, Manu! Now he was the prey!

Chapter 35

The Plucking of the Parrot Feather

"We have to spin these lies, for the truth will bury us Greeks alive"

- Aristotle

It is said that Alexander had these last three wishes on his death bed.

'I want the best doctors to carry my coffin to demonstrate that, in the face of death, even the best doctors in the world have no power to heal.' How absurd the historical treatises are on this request. A man who spent his life pilfering nations now talks of healing by doctors and

is getting philosophical about it. Why is his body not carried by generals or his crack team? Ever since ancient times, all great generals have been buried by their peers after observing certain military rituals. But for the greatest general of all time? Nah, we'll pass. We'll let the doctors do the honors. Or is the real story that his inner circle decided only doctors should be allowed near his deceased body? Why? What would others have seen? A bloodied corps?

It is also said that he wished his hands would be exposed and spread out from his coffin. Every single culture throughout history would consider exposing the dead in such a manner as extremely dishonorable and disrespectful. That's why we have, in so many forms, the quintessential burial shroud, be it coffins, mummies, or other coverings. And now, the greatest conqueror in world history is laid out like a 'Nanga Fakir' (naked beggar)? How absurd. Or was this forced upon his corpse? And by whom?

Then comes the most outrageous wish: The Macedonians, who were the first to turn war into a profiteering racket, saw Alexander's campaigns fuel Greek coffers. Pilfering the wealth of foreign lands was the main impetus for a whole generation of Greeks to rally behind Alexander. And yet his last wish—the most outlandish of them all—was, 'Spread all my wealth on the return road to Macedonia.' Really?! That's what the power-hungry conqueror's last wish was? To give up all the stolen wealth he had amassed through his ill-gotten campaigns. And his generals and army were so, so eager to follow through this absurd wish? Eh? To give up their share of the loot? They wouldn't listen to Alexander to accompany him to the eastern parts of India, but politely give up their spoils of war, because Alexander politely requested so? Makes perfect sense.

Not!

And then there is the even more absurd. Wasn't Alexander the greatest war strategist of all time? Then why did he -for we do not actually know if at that point in the campaign he was alive - take his army across the barren, waterless, featureless Gedrosian desert, where he would lose four fifth of his army? Historical fact this is! Some strategists he is! Or was it that he was forced to take that route?! An escape route?!

The Greek historian Megatesthenis wrote a version of Alexander's return from India, or should we say retreat from India?

LIES.

All Lies.

By the ever rushing of Ganga on sandy shores, by the winds that hold up the wings of the gulls that fawns these shores, by the grains of the sand that aligns with the patterns of the waves of Ganga - Oh, for I have run across those sand dunes in barefoot as a child, here is the story of what really happened.

Alexander turned to see the shape of Manu silhouetted against the glare of the sun. And then out of the glare manifested the flying Aarohan, with the point of his spear aligned center to the chest of Alexander's vergina Sun armor!

Alexander's reflex kicked in. He shielded himself. Aarohan's Spear pierced the shield and heavily scratched the Vergina Sun emblem. FaMing gained her footing in the meantime. The 'White Fairy' as she was now called by her comrades, made mincemeat of all the guards who came to Alexander's assistance.

Alexander's cavalry away from the immediate sphere of events began to realize what was going on and began to regroup in order to rescue Alexander. But as the cavalry charged in, and so did Manu. And did Manu charge in! With the blades attached to his Tusks, and the flared-outside blades mounted to his sides, no man nor beast could approach the behemoth and its guarding of Aarohan. The horses froze, refusing to budge.

Alexander, being the heavier- built, heaved Aarohan to the side, and began to roll and twirl. But Aarohan, who, in spite of being a decade older than Alexander, had grown stronger in the two years since they last met. Alexander fought with passion, but Aarohan had perfected his trade to absolute art. He not only fought with skill and might, but his situational awareness was paralleled by none, not even Alexander. Aarohan took two of his daggers and pegged Alexander's red cape to the ground in a flash.

The red cape represented the virility of Alexander, but at that moment it became his Achilles' heel. Alexander's twirl thus wrapped him up in his own cape.

Buchaphelus came rushing straight towards Aarohan to trample him down and free his master.

And right then Manu turned like a whip and grazed the length of the body of the horse with his tusker blade. History will record Buchaphelus falling in the battle with

Puru , but it was in this battle of 'Hastinapur' that Buchaphelus fell, never to rise again.

By then a whole contingent from Jotayu's regiment crashed into the remaining cavalry of Alexander. Now, the Gangariddi's had the clear upper hand in the battle.

Hephaestion, seeing his king and lover, netted within his own cape, came charging to his assistance. FaMing engaged him squarely, a one-to-one battle ensued. Hephaestion with his brute power kept gaining ground on FaMing, and FaMing with her superior martial arts skill evaded effortlessly all of Hephaestion's swings and jabs.

Hephaestion, out of his frustration over committed with his spear, FaMing evaded & came inside the swinging radius of the spear and slashed the tricep of the charging man heavily. Hephaestion fell, realizing he could no longer feel his right hand. He knew his military career had seen its last. Or perhaps even his life had seen its last. FaMing did not hesitate.

Alexander unwrapped himself from his confounded cape, but in doing so placed himself squarely exposed to Aarohan. Aarohan no longer had the spear with him, but he was filled with so much rage. He was brought back to the night he had lost Roshan. His grief was unsurmountable. But he did surmount.

He took Alexander's shield with the pierced spear, swung it around one full three sixty degree rotation and bashed the edge of the shield with full momentum into Alexander's parrot feather helmet.

The parrot feather helmet flung away.

All noticed. All paused. Alexander, again, was unconscious, as he had been with his encounter with Balan. But Balan had been the sole person and outnumbered by Alexander's vanguard. Now, it was the opposite. Aarohan had his whole army at his disposal. He could, in essence, finish off Alexander right there and then.

All waited. The decimated Macedonian cavalry waited. The Persians waited. The Gangariddis now surrounding and having the upper hand over the Macedonians and the Persians, waited.

Aarohan unceremoniously picked Alexander's shield with the pierced spear point again, ready to bash Alexander's face in. The symbolism of it not lost on anyone, the spear that had pierced Alexander's insignia of Vergina Sun - shield spear and all – will be used as the weapon that takes out Alexander's life. His shield is broken, and so is his fate.

Right then a spear landed in front of Aarohan. It had a banner wrapped around it. A banner that both Aarohan and FaMing recognized. It was Balan's.

'Your friend Balan is Alive! ', A voice declared. 'you will never see your friend again, if you kill this wretched warlord. If you spare him, I will spare your friend's life. Is this wretched warlord's life worth more than your friend's?"

Aarohan paused.

'You Lie!" Aarohan replied.' What proof do you have that Balan is alive?". Aarohan positioned the shield with the pierced arrow, ready to thrust the point through the unconscious man's chest.

FaMing came up to Aarohan, and softly touched his forearm and lowered it down gently. 'Master, I have seen this man before. Before, your friend Balan was taken captive. He was the one who took hold of your friend, before Alexander's men could kill him. He is what the Macedonians call Aristotle. "

Aarohan lowered the shield. He went by the limp body of Alexander, and tore out the parrot feather from Alexandr's helmet. 'He turned to Aristotle and said in Greek, "I will listen to what you have to say. But Macedonians must surrender now and unconditionally, else there will be distance between Alexander's head and his torso. And this will happen Now ". Aristotle replied in Pali Pakrit, "it will be as you wish. All I want is my student's life spared. "

Aarohan looked at FaMing. FaMing nodded. Aarohan turned to Jotayu, "Secure and bind this wretched man. You will guard him personally. Sever his head if any of his men come to rescue him."

Jotayu said out loud, "it will be so , Oh Dikbizonti (conqueror of the four horizons)'. This was a rare title bestowed upon warriors who achieve rare feats, the kind one sees once in a millennia .

Aarohan turned to Aristotle and said in Greek, 'Come with me.' Aarohan walked to Manu, whose tusker blades and side-flared blades were red with blood. He motioned for Manu to sit and got on Manu's back. Manu stood up. Aarohan blew out the conch. The tune was one familiar to warriors of all nations.

Aarohan stood up over Manu as he motioned Manu to stand up. He was a good twenty-two feet up in the air. All in the battlefield saw him. He called out to Aristotle aloud, "Translate what I have to say in your tongue "

' I am Aarohan of Gangariddi. I have pledged my life to Justice and Honor. And with justice and honor, I hold the fallen parrot feather of Alexander the Barbarian. "

There was quietness across the battlefield. Quietness from the Macedonian side, for they knew they had lost the battle. But there was also quietness from the Gangariddis side, for Aarohan had trained a quiet, disciplined army; and they always listened when their prophet spoke.

Aristotle carried on with the translation.

Aarohan declared, "lay down your weapons, oh Dhonis. You have been misled to a false purpose in this battle. Lay down your weapons and I promise you will see your motherland, your parents and family again. But by the very air that I breathe of these blessed lands, I promise you, if any of you carry on fighting I personally will slash and crush you under the feet of my ride! "

And as he said so, he motioned Manu . Manu stood up on his hind legs and bellowed out a loud and sustained trumpet. And then came down with a thud on the ground felt by all.

Each of the captains of the Macedonian army lay down their weapon. For they saw the body of Alexander limp and in custody of the Gangariddi general. Their contingents followed suit.

Alexander was bound to a post.

The post was within a circular encampment, the perimeter of which was lined with white curtain fence and guarded to the teeth

Beyond which were the elephants, interjected with the gangariddi phalanxes.

Beyond the elephants were the Macedonian camps, in a very uneasy state of settlement. And they, themselves, were surrounded by three thousand of Aarohan's elephant brigade, with Manu stationed in the front and center. His presence was imposing.

Aristotle was seated in front of Aarohan , besides him was Seleucus. Aristotle spoke:

"There are amongst us , who believe Alexander has grossly overreached his mandate.

"We are aware of your declaration at the first contact between our army and your army. And believe it or not, there are amongst us in the leadership who agree with you. Our grievance was with the Persians. The Egyptian campaign and the Indian campaign were unnecessary. Greed dictated those."

"....And yet you did nothing to stop him.." Aarohan interjected.

Everyone paused

Aarohan continued, "...know that the law of our lands, as decreed by the Punchayak is irrefutable. Justice will be exacted, no matter what. So, when you sue for peace, keep that mind."

Aristotle paused and then continued, " Do not listen to me then, but hear out what our generals themselves have to say in favor of peace. Please allow our most trusted general Ptolemy have an audience with you."

"But first there is the matter of my friend Balan..." Aarohan interjected

"He is in the custody of General Ptolemy....so let us go to him"

Aarohan rose. "Let us then"

Aarohan, Chanakkya, FaMing, Jotayu along with their guards, caroled Aristotle to the enclosure where Alexander was kept prisoner.

Seleucus stayed behind. Aristotle examined his former student. Alexander was bound and gagged. Guarded by Jotayu's men.

Then the group entered a different enclosure where Ptolemy's entourage camped. They were void of any heavy weaponry. Aristotle indicated to a tent and motioned everyone to enter.

Aarohan paused, "What kind of treachery is this, you think we will walk into an ambush? ". Jotayu stepped in, "Let us check, first, O master"

A couple of Gangariddis went into the tent along with Jotayu. After a few moments Jotayu reemerged. "All clear, master".

Aarohan and the rest of the group, along with Aristotle, entered the tent. There was only a single Macedonian general standing with his helmet on, along with the Gangariddi guards. Aarohan determined the general to be Ptolemy. FaMing began to pace and survey the tent's interior.

"Where is Balan? If I do not see Balan within this very moment, I will kill each and every deserving one of you by sunset today."

Aristotle carried on: "This is Ptolemy. He will reveal where Balan is, but he requests that everyone except you and FaMing remain here. All must leave our company, for what the general has to say is very sensitive."

Aarohan quietened for a moment. Then he motioned the guards. Jotayu with a grunt said to Aristotle, "One false step, and your body will need to learn how to breath without a head, philosopher."

Everyone filed out of the tent. Only Ptolemy, Aristotle, Aarohan and FaMing remained.

Ptolemy spoke, and surprised everyone when he spoke in perfect Pali, "I will reveal to you both where Balan is. But you will need to keep it a secret, for the success of his mission, …… my mission depends on this secrecy…"

FaMing Turned on her heel, for she recognized the voice, and so did Aarohan. Slowly, Ptolemy removed his helmet.

It was, in fact, Balan!

Chapter 36

"Roshan"

Balan, kneeled with his hands tied to his back. And blind folded.

He felt the warmth of a fire nearby and the air flowing towards it. He could sense three obstructions to the air flow. Were these objects, or were they the guards guarding him? With all the subtle movement of living creatures, he knew it had to be the guards.

Then he could sense a fourth person enter the...... tent? Was he kept inside a tent?

"Why don't you be done with it?" Balan said in a matter-of-fact way.

"You are more useful to us alive than dead." Replied Aristotle.

Balan observed, "Us? Who is us?"

"Tell me Balan, how do you think this is going to end?"

"Ahh, A thinking Greek." Punned Balan

"let's move beyond the taunts, shall we?"

Aristotle motion the guards to leave the holding pen.

"We know there is going to be a very ugly ending to what Alexander is doing to the world. Until now, nations did not pay much heed to this horde coming out of Macedonia. But your friend Aarohan has done a good job uniting your nation. Sooner or later, someone is going to wise up and actually make mincemeat out of the Greeks. What happens then?"

"Well, you Greeks should have thought of that when you ventured beyond Persia. You may have a legitimate cause to turn on Persia, but what about the Egyptians? What about us?"

"Yes, my pupil went beyond his bounds. Like his father he is reckless. Believe me, we do understand the consequences of the errant boy. But we want to rectify our mistake...."

"So, are you going to pack up and leave? You will spank your pupil in the bottom, and he will listen to you? Once the boy has tasted so-called glory, do you think he will stop?"

"No, he won't", answered Aristotle, "We know that. But we do believe your friend Aarohan is going to put a stop to him. So, we are more concerned about what will happen next, what will your friend do? He lost his daughter to our errant boy. What would a grieving, exacting father do?"

"Burn Greece down. You think Xerxes was bad? Wait till you see what Aarohan does to your nation."

"We know, and that is why we need your help."

"Hah, help? Under what zodiac lucky sign, do you think I would want to help you? You want me to betray the very man for whom I am prepared to sacrifice my life?"

"Please, hear us out, we do want Aarohan to win over Alexander. We know Alexander is aggravating a lot of nations. Once the Indians unite, which they have, they will field a much younger army than that Alexander is leading. But it is not only the Indians, but we are also aware of your success with the Chinese dynasty, we know of FaMing, your protégé. We know if your life is taken, she will unite the Chinese against us, for the newly restored dynasty is indebted to you & her. Two great empires angered by the hegemony of Alexander. No, we cannot afford that. So, we do want to preserve our gains, but we do not want the Indians and the Chinese at our doorsteps.

"So, is that why you spirited me away from Alexander when his guards were about to kill me?" Quizzed Balan.

"Yes and no"

"We do not want to replace one hegemon by another. So, our goal is to establish.... "Aristotle paused...

".... Establish a society, a secret society. A society made up of key individuals that have greater influence on their society than Kings and Queens. For we know kings and queens are beholden to politics, self-interest, and worse, their egos. They will not serve our purpose. As a matter of fact, they are the very entities that we are striving to counter. We need a secret society who would be a check to errant kings like Alexander. We know there will be conflicts between nations. But our goal is to minimize the buildup of power, so that we can mitigate bloodshed. We are not beholden to any nation or have allegiance to any warlord, nor driven by greed, fame, or wealth. The closest thing that currently exist to what we are thinking is your 'Punchayak', the council of five who does not come from wealth or power, but from wisdom. But we want to go beyond that. We want to establish that first society, where the 'Punchayak' is made up of all nations' representation, but free from the will of their leaders.

"This pan national 'Punchayak' will ensure that blood is not shed, that children are not orphaned, women are not raped, and civilization is not looted. This Punchayak will establish the Will of Peace amongst nations. It will secretly create the atmosphere that would allow for exchange of knowledge and wisdom.

"There would be five arms to this society, represented by the pentagram, and only the militant secret arm called the 'Hassasin' the world may remotely know about. This arm would do the bidding of the rest four, when all diplomacy would fail.

"For is it not true, if we had nipped Alexander in the bud, how many countless lives would we have saved? If Xerxes were never there, would Persia invade Greece?

"Nay, we need a check on all the ego maniacs of the world for now and for the future. '

Aristotle continued....

"We are aware of your achievements for not only now. We had been following you, and your activities in Tibet, and then in China. We were scoping out Aarohan even before when he lost his daughter, such an unfortunate event. We wished we had acted upon our cause before we lost Roshan....

With that Aristotle moved to a chest and retrieved leather bound collection of manuscripts.

"For you see, Roshan, the poet, the astronomer, the mathematician, the linguist, the humanist, ...and the daughter of Aarohan, was also one of us!"

Aristotle bowed down in front Balan, took his blindfold off, and cut lost all his bounds. And then placed the parchment at his feet.

"You are a free man, oh master Balan. We know of your wisdom, we know of your knowledge about Boddhisatva, we know of your impeccable martial arts skill, and we know of your unparalleled knowledge about metallurgy, and we know of your affection for your friend's daughter.

"You may at this very moment, leave, and no one

will harm you. But we say before you leave that you read through the parchments, authored by Roshan. For I have complete faith that you will join our cause once you have heard what Roshan has to say. For this child of Aarohan was years ahead of us, a true 'Soma '".

As Aristotle said those words, his tears ran down; as Balan heard those words, his memory of Roshan whelmed up in his heart, and his tears too ran down.

Chapter 37

"Ptolemy"

FaMing gave out a short gasp. In other circumstances she would have run to her master. For the last time she saw him, she saw him covered in the black head gear provided by the hangman. And then the trap door had given way.

Within the holding pen or tent only Aarohan, FaMing, Aristotle along with Balan stood.

Aarohan spoke, "When FaMing told me you were no more, it was hard for me to believe, for I didn't think you would leave this world so unceremoniously "Aarohan punned. Then Aarohan grew serious, "What is going on here?"

"Before I begin to explain, you must first have this. This belongs to you." Saying so Balan handed Aarohan the parchments bounded in leather. "I am sorry my friend, that you have to go through this. Again."

Aarohan opened the leather and began to examine the content within. It were papyrus sheets bounded together within the leather bound, written in the Greek form. But what hit Aarohan like thunder was the handwriting of the form, and a parchment written in the Pali.

It was Roshan's

Balan began, Yes this is from Roshan, addressed to you. '

Aarohan's hands began to shake. His eyes began to well up.

Aristotle politely interjected, "This is the total collection of documents we have from your daughter. All of it was addressed to me. Except one, which is addressed to you. We have not pried into it, out of respect for your daughter. And for you. "

Aristotle slowly stepped back, having delivered his message. "I am sorry for what our boy Alexander did to your daughter "

Balan now stepped forward, "My dear friend, I know this is your moment. You have achieved almost the impossible. You have succeeded in bringing down Alexander, where kings and emperors have failed _ Where I had failed. I know you want to avenge your daughter's death, and it is your right, no it is your Dharma. But allow a day's time before you make good on your decision. Allow yourself time, so that you can go through all of Roshan's letters, including the one addressed to you. You have the Macedonians under your thumb. A day more won't make a difference."

Balan continued, "I cannot be seen out in the open, for the world knows Balan is dead, and Ptolemy is here to negotiate Alexander's release. Ptolemy had died when I and my Hassasins attempted to kill Alexander. And now, with Aristotle's design, I have taken the identity of Ptolemy."

"Will you consider a day?"

Aarohan looked at FaMing's blood-stained face, and then to his blood-stained hands.

'We have a day," Aarohan answered.

Chapter 38

The Letter

"My dearest Baba, I hope you have been well. I know if you are reading this, then all has not gone well for me. It is probable that I am not there in person to have this conversation in your presence. I cannot imagine the pain you are experiencing because of my absence, and it is breaking my heart that there is probably no one consoling you.

Ever since Ma passed away you have been both a father and a mother to me. You took so much care and attention to my education that I have seen no other fathers do. I am lucky to be your daughter and have been blessed with all the love that a daughter could hope for.

But your love was even beyond that. You didn't nurture me as a son or a daughter, but as a complete human being.

So good this Earth is. The sky. The sun rays dancing on the clouds when it sets. The breeze. And the kites that float there upon. The scent of rajanigandha during its mid night bloom

With all this peaceful beauty, that we are granted for free, in unstinted amount, why do we have so much conflict? Why do we spill so much blood, for no real cause at all?

With your encouragement I had first learned the tantras and then even mastered and deciphered its wisdom well beyond what my guru was teaching me. I needed more to engage with. So, I spoke with the abbots in Tibet, where uncle Balan now practices & preaches his Dharma

.I spoke with the sages in Babylonia, about our astronomy, astrology and numerology and their astronomy , astrology , and numerology

I spoke to the Greek Lyceum tutor Aristotle, about medicine, and forces of nature. And I compare all this knowledge of nation with that of ours.

I spoke with the priest of the great Karnak temple in Egypt, and we shared each other's cultural wisdom of the tantras.

How amazing the complimentary nature of these wisdom of nations!

If you were wondering why my correspondence stipend was so expensive, now you know. But these stipends were spent well. For us scholars of nation have to come to realize, the so called magic of nature is all governed by wisdom, geometry and mathematics.

And Man is the reader of this wisdom, geometry and mathematics

But Man has become instead the practitioner of chaos, disorder, and bloodshed

And the reason why?

Because Man thinks its glorious to shed blood, to be 'War Heroes'

How wrong Man is!

So, I met with a few of my pan national colleagues in Taxila. And we debated with heart, passion, wisdom, and understanding what Man needs to become.

Man needs to become peaceful. He needs to become a peacock. And not a lion. And that is why we started to influence all monarchs to engage in culture and the tantras and set up peacock thrones of all that is beautiful. Not lion thrones.

And for those whose minds were deceased by ambition to have a lion's throne; to find glory in blood shedding, we had devised other plans for them.

We formed the secret society of philosophers. They are apolitical, people of faith, but not beholden to religious and ritualistic dogmas, and will strive for peace and knowledge. They will forever be hidden and span across the eons. They will have people of influence and extreme merit amongst their ranks, but they will never be from the status of kings and queens.

All kings and queens suffer from poverty in their souls. They start with the intent of providing unity & leadership, but soon get intoxicated by the very power they espouse to protect. The idea that another human being needs to bow down their head to them is proof that all queens and kings have fallen victim to ego, of the harmful nature.

So, we follow the best form of leadership, or should we say Guardianship? Fashioned in the form of the Punchayak. All members of this secret philosopher society have studied it, and we agree.

One of our first acts was to influence the events that removed Philip of Macedonia. It stopped the wars on the Greek isles. However, Darius grew emboldened in the interim power vacuum. And so did Eskander. Our peer Aristotle in the west influenced him to neuter Darius's blood spilling. But Eskander being the stubborn mule he is, has gone beyond his mandate, and now makes his way to Indiyaa. Baba you, independent of us, have already sounded the alarm . Baba, I know, we know, you will be the best bet against the ever-errant Eskander. I am your daughter; I am your biggest fan. But it was the society of the philosophers who has been impressed by your integrity. And now they request me to talk you to become one of the vanguards of this society

Please listen to Aristotle. Please listen to what he has to say. For if you are reading this it means I am not there in person to speak to you.

I hope you are doing well. And in the best of care.

…. your ever & ever-loving daughter, Roshan."

Aarohan walked the moonless night far from the camp. What was missing, as the charming light from 'Chandra', was replenished a million fold by the million 'Tara' , the stars of the Milky Way, that hung like a pearl neckless around the darkness of the night.

The words of Roshan hung on to Aarohan's conscience as a million-pearl neckless as well. He simply stood in the darkness of the night.

There was a rustling noise, and then something rested on his shoulder. He turned to meet the eyes of the closest soul he had known since he lost his daughter. He smiled, in this deep sadness of his, staring into the eyes, not of Chanakkya, or Balan, nor FaMing, but of Manu, the Elephant.

Chapter 39

The Trial

The Sun rises on the morning after, on Hastinapur. Aarohan and Manu stride down the riverbank, from the west, with the sunbeams on their faces. Manu is in full battle gear, and so is Aarohan. They enter the compound. Aarohan panned the courtyard. It was surrounded by the elite Gangariddi soldiers guarding their most prized possession, Alexander. A full battle contingent was assigned to guard Alexander, being replaced by an equal number of resources every phase of the day, a portion of them within the compound, and the rest circling the encampment.

Aarohan stopped in front of Chanakkya, "Is the Punchayak representative ready to present his case against Alexander?"

Chanakkya stood up. Aarohan continued, "We

have demonstrated that we are superior in force compared to the Dhoni's. But I am not here to set an example of brute force superiority to these barbarians. We need to demonstrate that our society, our laws, our religions, and our philosophies are so much superior that they fear to invade our lands. Never again shall they set foot in Vanga."

Chanakkya, stood up in the enclosed courtyard with Alexander in the accused box, "We call this assembly in session. This is not a unified body. The court recognizes the accused party of the Dhoni's, who have invaded these lands, and they will be tried only by the law of Punchayak, the law of this land will stand. We have a prime war prisoner, the lord of Dhoni's, Eskander.

Turning to Aristotle, Chanakkya addressed, "You come as an emissary of the society that seeks peace. You are vouched for by a daughter of this land, Roshan, though she is killed by the very person you seek to free. You have not taken any life from these lands, nor have you caused harm to anyone. Thus, you will be allowed to talk free and walk free..."

Chanakkya continued, "…. However, your leader…. ", Aristotle interrupted with the phrase, "Sovereign …"

Chanakkya paused, "Sovereign? Does he look sovereign to you? All bound and in chains …? "Chanakkya wanted to establish decorum in his court from the get-go and that he would not accept any deviation, either through semantics or change in reference to law.

Chanakkya continued, "…But we digress, we will begin the trial of your leader Eskander…. You may begin your plea

"Plea you say' Alexander thundered from his chained station, "When my rest of the army comes to liberate me, I will have each and every one of you torn limb by limb and I will ...."

"Shut the fuck up! You spoiled brat.... " Aristotle interrupted, "I will slice your tongue out myself if you open your mouth one more time ! "

Son of Zeus never had anyone ever talk back to him. He went absolutely red. And hissed back, "You son of a swine, had not my father picked you up from...." Alexander could hardly continue when Aristotle took out his cucumber-slicing knife and sliced the lower part of Alexander's left ear lobe. Alexander screamed out & was taken by surprise and confounded by astonishment.

"It seems you don't ever listen, so what's the use of your ear. We might as well cut that useless appendage, eh?", Aristotle said with a raised eyebrow and an enquiring gesture like that of the Lyceum master he was. "Patch this monkey face up," he instructed one of his retinues. The lad obliged.

Everyone was taken aback. Everyone paused. Aarohan looked at Balan with bemusement, for the first time in a long time he betrayed a smile, and said under his breathe, "the old philosopher has spunk, I'll give you that."

Aristotle came to the center of the assembly with two scrolls in his hand; he stood silent for a while. He looked towards Chanakkya, then on to Balan, then on to Aarohan. Then finally towards Alexander "Your father gave you to me when you were only but a lad. I gave you a good moral foundation in your education, turned you into a courageous leader. I encouraged you to tackle the imminent danger of the Persians. You did well to defeat Darius. That was your mandate. Then you overstepped your mandate. After Persia you went into Egypt. You succeeded, and then we asked you to return. But nay, you and your cohort were glory-drunk in the success of your campaigns and did not heed our advice. You went on to Central Asia. We were fearful you would be the cause to give rise to yet another nation and had you lost in your campaigns you would have caused such enemies at our doorsteps. We were fearful that your campaign would result in us not going to the east only, but east coming into the west. For the East too can come West. They are far more numerous than we are.

Aristotle turned to Aarohan. "We were fearful someone like you would eventually better this lad... but never ever had I imagined it would be both in the pleasure and loss of that radiant mind... Roshan... your daughter."

"I have known Roshan before the perpetual wars. She communicated to me on numerous matters, at first as a student, but soon in her own right. We were amazed, I was amazed at her acumen. And it seems she was a reservoir of knowledge not only of her nation, and our nation but also of the Chinese, the Persians, and of the Egyptians and Zeus knows how many more scholars were in contact with her.

"She wrote to me passionately. To stop the menace my student was creating throughout the world. We were getting information about the mayhem caused by our soldiers, but most of us ignored it. Why would we? We were winning our wars. Then Roshan stopped writing to me. And then one day I received a message from her that she is heading to the western fronts. For she felt she needed to engage with my student directly.

"And then as I feared it did not end well. I began my journey east immediately after hearing about Roshan's demise by Alexander.

"We heard of a man called Aarohan, Roshan's father, who had deposed of the Nanda king and yet had not claimed the crown for himself. We were hearing he was the Alexander of the east, yet this one was civilized and not errant like my student.' Aristotle gave a glance at Alexander as he said so.

Alexander replied, " You have developed a quiet the tongue old man. Don't forget I am still your sovereign. It would do you good if you kept that in mind"

Aristotle ignored Alexander's reply. He continued ......"I wanted to meet him. But I knew he wouldn't trust the very philosopher who had tutored this tyrant who had pillage blood in the conquered land, who had killed his daughter, ...and who still doesn't know how to keep his mouth shut", with that Aristotle gestured should he unsheathed his knife again.

"So, we bargained with the other esteem general and scholar in the east, your friend Balan. ..... "

With that Aristotle stepped aside. And Balan / Ptolemy came forward. "I cannot profess what is it that we should do with the invader and his crime, that is for you to decide, and rightly so to exact your balance for the grief of your daughter. But if you permit, I urge you to consider, if you would allow me?"

Aarohan never saw his childhood friend be so formal with him. This must be his high recommendation.

"Speak your heart my friend", Aarohan replied.

"The scale of this boy's atrocities knows no bounds. I have seen in all my travels countless unnecessary conflicts and murder mayhem, be it the tyrant Nandas or Tibetan warlords or the marauding Mongols or the ever-warring Chinese dynasties. But this deed is something new. I fear he has shown the world what atrocities of this scale look like. And the mere rebuke of it cannot be a defeat of it. It has to be something more. It needs to be a counter-method to this war mantra, and equally potent peace mantra.

'Roshan spoke of this mantra of peace _ Shanti Shur, Prithvi Shanti, Om Shanti. She thought of society of nations, where the learned and courage heart would act to neutralize the warmongers of our times, it would not be limited to a moment , but strive across the arc of time. She conversed with Aristotle, and few more others. They came up with the formation of these peace keeper, known as the 'Hassasin' , of which I have become the latest disciple.

To which Aarohan raised an eyebrow.

"Yes, a disciple. We were in our own way..." Balan glanced at FaMing, "...trying to achieve the same in Tibet, with the establishing of the monastery, and then the other one in the Lin Forest in Shao Mountain in China. We feel we have established a system that will have a check and balance and have influence in the monarchies of the region.

And we have already had success with reestablishing the Tao dynasty. But we need something pan-region, pan-continent, so that we may negate the propensity of individuals like the lad over here."

"...and then you had shown us another method where, you coalesced a whole nation, whose main vocation is peaceful farming, into a martially trained nation well capable of defending itself against such a vicious army known for pillage, destruction, & rape." This time it was Aristotle who added to the conversation.

Aristotle continued, "We wanted to reach out to you, but it is my nation who had invaded you and we are the belligerent. So, we needed to find a way to have a good faith connection. And then we had, or we have the opportunity to demonstrate that good faith. We had an opportunity to save your friend Balan.

"Treason! I am surrounded by traitors" hissed Alexander.

Aristotle continued, 'the fact that we bare our plan in front of this lad , should amply demonstrate that we have no allegiance to this lad and that should we fail in our endeavor , it is our heads on the pike'

'So, what is your proposition, ohh learned scholars of the west?' Aarohan interjected.

Aristotle took on a pleading note, "The tide has turned, and the great Alexander is defeated. But now the proving test of our group is whether we will be a viable force for good. We urge you, and we believe you can be of similar persuasion, given your wisdom, and that your daughter shared the same..."

"Speak plainly old man, get to the point, and leave my daughter out of this," now Aarohan hissed.

Aristotle paused, raised both his hand open palmed, "We say, take a different part for your vengeance, set an example in history, give us back this lad, so that we may try him in our own court of justice...

"Court of Justice?" Interjected Aarohan, 'THIS IS the court of Justice".

Aristotle pleaded, "Please, my lord," he continued earnestly, "We do not want the conquered nations to fall into chaos, nor another decade of bloodbath & people vying for power because you have decapitated the tyrant who conquered them. And we do not want you to be the next tyrant who goes the other way towards the west, to conquer the lands around the middle ocean of Europe, Asia, and Africa."

"There I have said it," Aristotle sat down, with an air of dejection knowing Aarohan would not pay heed to the proposition by the group.

Balan/Ptolemy came forward, "We have already set up organizations in central Asia through our Tibetan monasteries and in the east through our Lin temples in the Shao mountains. But now, we need India and all the conquered lands' potentate—that is, you—to be part of our effort. Please, my friend, be with us."

Aarohan began to pace around the group, very slowly, his strides smooth, as if he was floating around the group.

"What say you, O FaMing." Aarohan tuned to the only female in the group.

"You were instrumental in bringing down this tyrant in battle, he would have killed you, and given the chance, violated you. What should we do with this lad to show our civility? "

FaMing came forward. "I'd say let me cut off this lad's manhood, so that he may never rape again. But then again, a boy lover like him does not have the ability to satisfy a real woman."

Aarohan paced further, 'The woman warrior speaks the truth."

'Let not the Amazon persuade you. Her mentor, Balan agrees with us." Aristotle pleaded.

Aarohan turned to Chanakkya, "What say you O Punchayak law Reader? "

Chanakkya came forward, "O my guru, your wisdom surpasses mine. But from where I stand here, we cannot chance a return of this tyrant lad to power, he needs to be neutralized, beyond doubt. Though we can argue not to bother about what happens in middle Asia from the fallout in the conquered lands, however, we shouldn't allow for a power vacuum that would set up new dynasties that may be hostile to India. "

"Then speak on the charges that are brought against this tyrant lad" Aarohan took a stance. Though he was standing, he stood in the profile of the Himalayas , solid , grounded, immobile.

"You, son of mortal man Philip, Alexander the barbarian of the Dhoni's has been charged with the crimes against the Bharat Mata, the Indian people and against Roshan the daughter of this man who has defeated you in battle. The charges of your crimes are as per Punchayak law:

Trespassing, violating, and invading the land of India with fifty thousand belligerents. The Charge thus of Fifty thousand count

Destruction of sixty-three villages with nineteen thousand inhabitants murdered. The charge thus of massacring the inhabitants, destruction of livelihoods, and the environment.

Stealing of wealth, and caravaning them off to western lands to the amount of eighty thousand taka. Thus, you are charged with return of similar amount of wealth 'Ohh tyrant of the west, how do you plead?'

'I don't plead to anyone' answered Alexander, ' Seleucus and his army will arrive soon and then you will be lucky to have your own trial. I will cut your cunt and feed it to the pigs in every city bearing my name from here to Babylon' Alexander taunted

Aarohan tightened his grip on his dagger. Everyone could feel the tension rise in the tent.

Aarohan paced the tent. He took his Conca and the ceremonially blew into it. Two jawans let the side of the tent canvass unfurl and all could feel the stride vibration of the behemoth. In came Manu. With outside sun rays bouncing his blade

Aarohan Spoke, "I now speak in the order of Punchayak. No one should interrupt the following verdict, for sure I will allow Manu to cut the interrupter in half.

"The mantra of the Punchayak does acknowledge the argument of peace to be had after the demand of justice on this lad.

"The Dhonis will have the choice to give up all the potency of your army and leave this land. You will only have a short dagger as your tool to live within nature. If you disagree to this disarmament, we will consider you belligerent and initiate the kill mandate on you all.

"The Dhonis will have to leave this land immediately and this land will not give you any provision. For you have violated her welcome! You will be given a three-day head start, and then we will pursue you, and if we find you lingering or scheming, we will kill you all.

Aristotle began to protest, '..........' And Balan immediately 'shushed' him silent, reminding him utterance would translate into a death sentence.

"You will have to leave all the wealth that you have stolen from this land and the lands of Persia.

"And finally, this man will be neutered, if not killed outright. Your choice.

Saying so Aarohan unsheathed his dagger, went

over to Manu's blades and sharpened it. He twirled the dagger with couple of martial moves and then turned the hilt to FaMing, and said what will echo across millennia 'Avenge all women!'

FaMing took the blade and walked towards Alexander, who now realized what was to happen. Alexander did not care about death. At all. But cared about his image of manhood. And this would be the ultimate castration of his manhood image. Literally. Alexander's eyes began to widen up in horror.

FaMing had no expression on her face. Her eyes did not blink. She slashed open the waist guard of Alexander, his wrapped loin robs, and slashed his manhood, ball sack and all.

Alexander screamed.

Only to find his freshly cut rare meat manhooh shoved into his screaming mouth.

"Guess we won't hear the screaming of all the princesses you raped after each land you conquered. I guess your childish war games are over. Glory boy." FaMing hissed.

That shut Alexander up. Before he passed out, horrendously bleeding onto the floor.

FaMing turned to one of the jawans, and said in a Non challant way, "Fetch the Kabi Raj, and stitch this bleeding pig up".

Aarohan turned to Aristotle. "You have your deal

and the three-day head start. On the rise of the third day, we pursue you, and if we find you, we will kill you. Until you have left our lands, then we will not pursue you any longer. Then we can talk about this pan-national community of peace makers you spoke of."

With that Aarohan, turned and left the tent. FaMing, Balan & Chanakkya stayed behind

Chapter 40

Flight from Truth

It had been a couple of nights since the disastrous Macedonian expeditionary forces left the plains that would soon be called Hastinapur. The rag-tag army kept marching south along the river Indus. Alexander, who by now had lost a significant amount of blood, was not able to sit up, let alone ride a horse. Even if he had not lost blood, the fact that his castrated loin had not healed would make it impossible for him to saddle up. That was the Just penalty imposed on Alexander by Aarohan, the fact of castration had neutered or cured Alexander of all his sexual misadventures and rapes, to wage war from the back of Buchaphelus. And that also ensured that the bloodline of Alexander was eliminated.

One could argue that is what is needed for world

peace in subsequent history, castration of all war mongering leaders, and generals. That's all one needs for world peace. Isn't that humorous!

Aristotle was dumbfounded. He knew, Alexander's life was at peril. But the suddenness of the events had taken him by surprise.

Balan / Ptolemy , had come forward and touched the forearm of Aristotle. "It could have been much worse. You've been allowed an escape route. Take it. Now," Balan said.

"We have no weapons. We can't return the way we came, through the conquered lands. We'd be torn to pieces by the Bactrians and Persians," Aristotle replied.

"How did you think this would end? 'Balan queried, 'However, Aarohan wouldn't actively campaign to rally against your retreat, as long, as long you keep up your end of the truce. Besides, you do not have any choice. The way I see it, you have only one way out, with your three-day head start, go south and then take the sea route to the mouth of Tigris & Euphrates."

Aristotle pondered, "we would need a whole flotilla, and all our wealth to conjure up a navy that would take forty thousand of us back to Babylon. That is madness."

"You need to decide, fast and now. Aarohan will destroy your army, horse, donkey, and men, and everything in between if he catches up with you," Balan advised.

"And what about the absence of Alexander from the commanding post?"

"You guys will figure it out, you are the spin doctor. I am sure you will come up with something".

Now it was a full moon, and the army marched south to the mouth of the Indus delta. The army was restless. They had been told, just as with Puru, that Alexander had made a deal with the Gangariddi general. But there was no sign of Alexander. Surely, he wasn't dead. Or was he? They were told he had fallen ill with the Indus fever, which would later be known as malaria. Ptolemy had taken the reins of Alexander's bodyguard corps, always seen in his body armor. He made it clear there would be zero tolerance for anyone seeking an audience with Alexander. The doctors had advised against it, and Alexander needed rest. Soon, the edict came: only doctors were allowed near Alexander, and no one could have an audience with him. Thus, the idea of "only doctors at his deathbed" was born.

Thus, the spin by Aristotle was, Alexander has declared, even the 'Great' had to return to his creator. And even the doctors cannot save him. So, he should be guarded by doctors alone, not by hoplites.

The whole of Alexander's army had to give up all of their arsenal before they would be released from captivity. No spear, No shield, no broad sword, or short sword. Only a welting knife. They were further given the edict, the moment they were spotted by Gangariddi jawans, they would be considered hostile entity and would be immediately eliminated. No questions or negotiations. In other words, the three-day head start the hoplites had been given should be utilized to the fullest. They would be given no food or water within the domain of India, for they have betrayed the hospitality of India, they had murdered and plundered its inhabitants

Chanakkya, on Aarohan's behest, took all the loot and tributes given to Alexander by various regional chieftains and returned it to the people. When the chieftains queried why the tributes were being returned, the Macedonians spun the second great lie regarding Alexander's defeat in India: "It is the wish of our wise and benevolent leader to return the wealth seized in campaigns, for he wants to demonstrate to the nations that no wealth can buy a man his health."

The Macedonians did not dare go back to Babylon by the same route they came into India, for in spite of the spin on why they are heading back and giving up all that they had taken, the Macedonian couldn't risk another assault and loss, for they no longer had their war weaponry. The rag-tag army traveled south along the Indus, hoping to take the sea route to Babylon, where they would have less chance of encounters with locals. They maintained their three-day head start ahead of the Gangariddis, knowing that every mile gained meant a chance of survival.

Ptolemy, or Balan, reached the coast ahead of the rag-tag army and negotiated a flotilla to carry forty thousand men via the Arabian Sea to Babylon. However, he could only secure enough boats for one-fifth of the army. Failing to secure the safe passage of the entire army, Ptolemy assigned Craterus to take as many men as possible on the limited number of ships and sail back to Babylon. The remaining army, left with no choice, turned west to attempt the journey overland, hoping to avoid any settlements to prevent conflict. Their only option was the treacherous Gedrosian desert, a journey that would take twelve days, but they dared not begin it. The Greeks never had to tackle such arduous journey with no food, water, or provisions. But their scouts reported that the Gangariddi army was only two days behind them.

Ptolemy / Balan advised, "My friend Aarohan did not kill you, even after losing his daughter to your invading army. But he will not hesitate to protect his country from the marauding horde your leader Alexander brought with him."

"The way I see it, you have two choices. Stay put and not cross the desert and stand your ground. Fight with my friend Aarohan and the Gangariddis, and in that case fight you will fight me, Or chance your lot across the desert. If I were you, I would take the desert, if you have the endurance, you'll live. You stand no chance against the Riddis.". All were silent.

"You are his childhood friend; can't you intercede on our behalf?"

"You still don't get it. It is because of me that you guys are not already dead. I have done my part.

"I will, however, be your guide across the desert. I will reduce the sixteen-day trek to twelve days. There is an oasis seven days out. If we can reach that watering hole, then there is a chance. If you agree, we will start in four hours.

"But that will be dusk!"

"Are you this stupid? Since when do you cross a

desert during the daytime? What military school did you go to, O slayer of Sparta." Mocked Balan.

"Well gentleman, you heard the man. We gear up in four hours." Aristotle said.

For four nights straight, thirty-five thousand rag-tag men, mostly on foot, trekked across the desert. They rested during the day, digging themselves into the sand or covering themselves with what little they had to protect from the scorching heat. By the fifth day, most had already consumed their water ration, hoping to reach the oasis within two more days. There was a lot of chaos. Only a few maintained their ration of water, while others fought with each other for the rations.

Balan steadied the army on the evening of the sixth day. They rested early and started early in the evening, hoping to reach the oasis at sunrise or before.

The army was thus stretched even thinner about twelve miles long, the head of this trek along with Balan reached the watering hole, right at sunrise.

As the hoplites rushed the water hole, there was a thunderous trumpet of an elephant. Everyone stopped at their station, for over a shallow dune in the sight line of the rising sun a large silhouette appeared. The oversized elephant and its rider that struck terror to their hearts over the past six months.

Manu & Aarohan was in full battle gear. With the six-footer of the blades tied to the tusks of the great tusker and the side blades all splayed out. Manu looked like a king a cobra ready to strike.

Balan / Ptolemy waved to the troops to pause. He then walked up to Manu. He patted Manu on the trunk.

Balan smiled. 'Looks like you beat us to the water. Is it only you?'

Aarohan smiled, "Do you think Manu can do the desert all by his own?"

Balan Chuckled, "Where are they, the Riddis? Beyond the dunes" ?

Aarohan kept silent.

Balan walked past Manu, began to climb the dune. Aarohan yelled, ' If I were you, I would remove my helmet, not be mistaken for the Dhoni's that you have adopted'.

Balan paused, then continued his walk up to the top of the ridge. What he saw baffled him. It was a sea of Gangariddis in the middle of this forsaken Desert. But how?

Balan trotted down to Balan, with a horrified look. "This is an impoverished army, with no weapons, no defense, you are better than this. "

Aarohan kept silent.

Balan kept silent too.

Then he spoke. "Yes, you are right, I have adopted these barbarians. But with the intention of civilizing them. That is what I do. I nurture societies when they do not know better."

"…… and that is why we will not kill your new protectorate army. However, I shall remain true to the Punchayak. Meaning, your protectorate army should never be seen by the Gangariddis on the others side of the ridge. So, you will advise the Dhonies to remain on the south side of the ridge line. And not to have a sneak peek 'into the eye of the Medusa' for their eyes will be taken out by my archers.' Aarohan said in a very measured voice even compared to his general demeanor

'Kindly wear this cape so that my men don't confuse you for the Dhonis.

'How is FaMing?' Balan queried

'Why don't you ask her yourself? 'Aarohan responded.

With that Aarohan nudged Manu. And Manu gave out a thunderous trumpet of a call. Within moments a contingent of Gangariddis appeared over the ridge. Aarohan gave the signal, all was ok. A few of them begin to lay out a roped planked treads on the slope of the sand dune, for Manu to climb out. And then a tall female warrior in colors of a battle armament never seen in this part of the world, and in beautiful contrast with the yellow of the desert and the blue of sunny sky, came trotting down on her white stead towards Balan and Aarohan.

'How are you, my master? ' Stern is her expression, but a slight welling of tears lined up in her bottom eyelid.

'I do well, my prodigy. My friend here treating you well?' Balan quipped.

'He is quite something, your friend here. In spite of losing his daughter, he restrains his vengeance, he restrains his ego. I still have a lot to learn.'

Balan looked back at the anxious group of Dhonis, Aristotle, Seleucus & all waiting for him, to understand what was in store for the rag tag army, did a massacre waited for them.

Balan looked back at FaMing, 'You will be shadowing us all the way to Babylon?'

'All the way to the frontier of India ' FaMing replied

'So, Persia is my goal now. …mmmm…. Some of them might still live to see their homeland again.

'I will see you around my friends…

With that Balan / Ptolemy retraced his steps to his dependent Macedonian army,

'You are not getting any water here. You are still in India, Let's move on' Balan / Ptolemy walked past the Macedonians and got on his steed.

But Seleucus protested, "Our men have run out of their ration of water, we will die crossing the wretched desert… you told us…" Balan / Ptolemy interrupted Seleucus, 'I promised you nothing, had you for once stepped out of your greedy Macedonian selves and had not consumed twelve days' worth of ration in five days we didn't need to stop here. Now if you are so incline, why don't you go over the ridge and ask the Riddis very politely for water and provision and maybe even the best 'Hammam' service, and maybe they will oblige, but don't come crawling back to me if they, as they saying goes in this part of the world, ' Tengree kete hathe dhorai dimu.'

"What does that even mean? ", protested Seleucus.

"Why don't you go and talk to the Riddis and find out for yourself, and we can finish this conversation in the life after. You game? Now stop throwing tantrums and follow me …" with that Ptolemy / Balan began to trot west.

There were a few Macedonians who chanced their life to drink water from the oasis, only to find their skull pierced by the sharpest arrows. As the days passed on, and the stranglers in the army came upon the watering hole, saw the dead bodies, and the silhouettes of hundreds of archers on the ridge. At this point, few just moved on, simply took off their military attire and surrendered. All they had to do was a take an oath to become full citizen of Indiyaa :

"I saw the lushness of India, I enjoyed its fruits, fowl , & fish, but I sinned against her hospitality, and I want to cleanse myself with dipping myself in waters of Ganges and never ever betray, on penalty of death , the Gangariddis ".

These individuals would then be given food, water and provision to retrace their steps as sadhus to Hastinapur (most took this option), where they would be received by Chanakkya who had become a very able administrator. The seeds of future Artha Shastra are sown there.

At the end of Godresio desert and at the frontier of Baluchistan, the western domain of India, Aarohan & Manu Stood Guard, as the rag tag Macedonia army crossed. And that my readers with discerning intellect is the reason why Alexander, the most 'brilliant' tactician in the history of military strategies, lost four fifths of his army.

Balan / Ptolemy & Aristotle rode up to Aarohan

Aristotle spoke, last night Alexander passed away. We have not made any announcement yet; it seems the ruse of only doctors who can see him seems to be working'

Aarohan nodded, 'You hold your nation not to invade us. EVER. And I will hold my nation not to march west, now that they have tasted victory over the greatest army on earth.'

"You sound like you are a member of the secret society we talked about." Aristotle smiled, turned his steed and left Indiyaa and stepped into Persia.

Aarohan turned with Manu towards Balan. Manu kneeled and reached out to Balan. Manu was shedding tears. Manu knew it was goodbye with Balan. Elephants know.

Aarohan came down and removed his war helmet. Balan could see Aarohan was in tears, just like his ride. Balan began to well up as well.

'Thank you for letting these lads through. I think I will not be seeing you again. For we have to manage the Persians, Babylonians, the Greeks and the Egyptians.'

"I wouldn't let Eskander's body reach Babylon, for when he is discovered that he was less of a man when he died, and not a god, people from all parts of the world would rise up against the Macedonians. So. Make him disappear …. like a god." Aarohan suggested.

Balan smiled. "Maybe I will spirit him to Egypt"

"FaMing will follow you; you know that." Aarohan quipped. Wanting to assure his friend that his journey to the west won't be all by himself.

"That might not be the case, my friend. I have a feeling my prodigy maybe developing a liking for the ' Dikbijonti'."

Aarohan was taken aback.

"Listen my friend, 'Balan Continued, ' You had taken a lot of grief in recent years, if a woman does come your way , keep an open heart."

Aarohan simply sighed. "I am afraid if that was the case here, my prodigy , Chanakkya would be heart broken."

"I believe your prodigy has willed it for his master. He loves you too much and he says he has seen how you and my prodigy had tag teamed to bring the barbarian down. He sees the synchronicity of both your persona."

Aarohan chuckled, "Had I been twenty years younger, my friend."

Balan quipped, "…, who bettered the barbarian in physical prowess?"

"Your daughter would have wanted it for you. All I am saying is keep an open heart".

"What about you? 'Ptolemy'?"

Balan put on his mask, "My task by the council has been set for Egypt. I hear these Egyptian women know how to shake their bellies." Balan laughed as he said so.

With that Balan mounted his stead and turned towards the stream of sorry state of the Macedonian hoplites traveling west, and stepped into Persia.

Epilogue

Chanakkya had just finished his treaties and his magnum opus, "Aarohan Shastra ". He has had great success in establishing the young king Chandragupta Maurya after the days of Aarohan and the Greek wars. To further establish the foundation of the new Mauryan empire he wanted to chronicle the feats of Aarohan and his Philosophies, this he wanted to achieve as the first prime minister of the Mauryan empire and chief advisor to the New King. He had just finished the Complete treatise and was extremely elated to see his old mentor again. He hoped he would one day meet Aarohan again and he would be able to show his treatise to him.

"What is the matter with you, Chanakkya? Have you not learned anything from being with me all these years?" were the first words Chanakkya heard as Aarohan entered. His arrival was unexpected, but the sharpness in his voice was even more so. Chanakkya, the man behind the Mauryan throne, the architect of an empire, had not been spoken to in such a manner by anyone in a long time, let alone be admonished. But more so, if Aarohan was upset with him, then what is it that he did wrong, for Aarohan is seldom upset. And Aarohan gets upset only when mistakes have profound consequences. The trivial never mattered, so what is it that Chanakya did wrong?

'My Guru, please have a seat. Have you travelled far? You must have travelled far.' Chanakkya said, offering hospitality despite his confusion.

To this Aarohan smiles, for he couldn't help but bemuse at that thought. Chanakya had literally known how far he had travelled, and the things he had seen and the things that he had to deal with between the time of his victory over Alexander and Now. But then what is 'Time'? Well, it is better that Chanakya had not experienced it, there is only so much that a human mind can process at a time.

It's been about ten years since he had last seen Aarohan. So much has happened since their last meeting. Chanakkya was an older man now. But his guru of so much further years seemed to be…. younger looking, than him. The ascetic life that Aarohan has chosen must have bode well with him.

"You haven't changed a bit, my guru. I have had people sent to the four corners of our domain in search of your whereabouts. Nor did our emissaries in the east, west, north or south kingdoms ever hear of you. Where have you been all these years my lord? I have hoped and sought your companionship and advice on so many occasions. Why did you just disappear after our hard-earned victories? People awaited your leadership! Where were you when we needed you most!"

Aarohan smiled again. "And yet, here you are, Chanakkya. You've done well, establishing the Mauryan Empire, guiding its kings, and putting governance into order. You didn't need me."

"Yet you re appear again and admonish me. What is wrong? what have I missed?" continued Chanakya in wiser thought

"You haven't done nothing wrong……. yet" answered Aarohan. 'what is that you are writing?' Chanakya handed him the first of the Bamboo books, the first of hundreds of such compilations all staked in neat piles in his library. As Aarohan browsed over the first plates, Chanakkya went on, "it's about the Greek wars, it's about you and how we marshalled the nation to overcome them."

'Why are you writing about wars? What good will it bring?" Aarohan let the book down after mulling over the verses "Surji Mamar Teeyeta", squaring straight up towards Chanakkya.

Chanakkya now knew Aarohan was here because of the treatise.

"People need to know, these historians need to know, from firsthand witness. I have seen some of the works by the Greek historians and they are filled with lies. Aristotle, Seleucus, Ptolemy / Balan all lie about the account of your battles with Eskander. They deny even the Events. They portray him as great! We need to tell our story. We must!"

"… and what will that achieve my Chanakya? Tell me what will happen when people read your book?" Aarohan still squared and starring straight into Chanakkya's eyes. Chanakkya could see the reflection of the kupi flames from the wall niches in Aarohan's eyes. The same intense stare that Arrohan would have when facing the Dhonis (Macedonians).

"It will give them great pride to know their history …" stated Chanakkya

"And they do not know of their history now? how old is our history? how far does our history go back?" interrupted and retorted Aarohan. Aarohan never interrupted anyone. This was almost the first.

"It will give them reason to stand up again if the Greeks return…" Chanakkya continued

"The Greeks return?" Aarohan's voice was edged with sarcasm. "After what we did to their armies, their horses, and to Eskander himself? We have the numbers, we have the youth, and… we have the elephants. So tell me, Chanakkya, what more will people do when they read your book?"

This time, Chanakkya hesitated. He knew where this was leading, but he continued, "They will take up arms and set out to conquer the western lands. We've shown them it can be done."

Aarohan stepped forward, "And is that good?"

"It will be good for our nation and our resources,"

Chanakkya answered, though he hesitated this time.

Aarohan took a step forward. "Tell me Chanakkya, how will it be good for our nation? Walk me through what will happen when we decide to better the western lands?"

Chanakkya went silent.

Aarohan continued, "Don't disappoint me Chanakkya or Kautilya as they call you these days. Don't fall into the trap of the Ego of warlords and self-grandiose kings; trap of the sick western philosophy of waging wars on other people's lands thinking it is patriotism, yet it has nothing to do with patriotism but simply ugly heinous greed. These western nations call themselves civilized yet their history is bathed in bloodshed. Nay, their Philosophy is fundamentally wrong. They think warriors are war heroes.

"War heroes? What are those? There are never war heroes, but spillers of blood. The whole lot of them. One can only be the defender of land and defender of one's people but the moment we step into other people's territory we become tyrants, the uncivilized.

"I ask you, was I not the one who defeated that barbarian kid Eskander and his hordes? Was I not the one that forced his troops to flee over the western desert? Was I not the one who commanded 40,000 troops, 6000 war elephants? Yet I disbanded them after the war. Why? I could have started my own dynasty. But I didn't. Tell me 'Kautilya' why I didn't?"

Had it been anyone else in the room, they would have said Aarohan was sarcastic with Chanakya, but that was not the case. Aarohan simply challenged Chanakya's premise.

"I had learned many years ago after my daughter's death, that everything in life is connected. There is no good in killing people, there is no peace. Tell me has there been any warrior or war lord or king in history who has been happy…. actually, happy at the end of their wretched lives after their conquering feats? They wage war on other people's land in the pursuit of happiness, resources and wealth, yet show me one that has been actually happy? Most battle-hardened warriors suffer from mental sickness. And let me not begin on the woes and grief of the innocent and the victims. Do you want their blood and ill will on your hands? Nay, you feel pride now because your Ego says you have done well in these past years but what will your Ego say when it is blanketed with greed? Your current pride will be replaced with guilt. I am here to spare you that pain."

"And that is just the beginning. I walked away from a kingship and pursuing the Greeks knowing that all that they had conquered in the past decades will again fall into chaos and death. Let them own their deed. We are far better than them. We don't need to be on other people's land, we have everything that we will ever need……. here. I had stopped another generation of bloodshed and if you heed me, your book will do nothing but create greed for another generation of bloodshed and vain glory. Let us not set that bad example in history."

Chanakkya pleaded, "But the people need to know of this history, your history, our history. If you think people do not need to know of you, for sure they need to know of your principals. Yes, Bharat's history is old, but this new kingship is young. We need a rallying point, a constitution...."

Aarohan interrupted, "Then write that constitution of governance! Write your philosophy of good governance and of ways and means. Write your "Artha Shastra "for the new administration and for the good of history, but for sure do not turn our history in 'hour of need' into something ugly and bloody because that's what your ego for recognition says so.

Listen, I cannot tell you what to do with your book but if I still command your respect then take my name and reference from all the narratives in your book."

"But then there will be no meaning or context to anything I have written", exclaimed Chanakkya.

"Exactly. And there is your answer. Your book has no purpose if it is simply talking about a person. If you write about me then how are we different than that Barbarian Eskander?"

"Then what about the events that happened?" pleaded Chanakkya. "Someone needs to record so."

"It is already recorded as long as people speak the Pali (Bangla). Tell me, what does your daughter sing as nursery rhyme to your grandson?"

"Surji Mamar Teeyeta!" answered Chanakkya

Aarohan smiled. With that Aarohan stepped back. Knowing Chanakya will do the right thing. He went away towards the door, "I will visit Manu and take him back. His time has come. I hope his current rider will be as humble and wise and give up the throne as did its previous rider!".

Thus, the birth of the 'Sadhu, Brindabon' kings.

Chanakya simply wept, knowing he will not see his old mentor again.

With that Aarohan steps out into the veil ......of time.

Epilogue 2

Aarohan stood at the top of the hill, gazing down at the Yellow River, or "Holudiya," as it was known in the local tongue, winding through the dense forests and high hills of the Arakan. A large banyan tree spread its massive canopy over him, its shade providing relief from the humid air. Moisture-laden breezes swept up the slopes, rustling the vegetation in waves that seemed to rise towards the sky, carrying with them the scent of the earth.

It's been ten monsoons since the Gangariddis defeated the Greeks. Ever since then Aarohan had sought seclusion and avoided public life. All denizens in Pataliputra wanted Aarohan to pick up reign of the kingdom. Aarohan would have nothing to do with it. Politics, power, and position had cost him his most precious treasure—his daughter, Roshan.

Aarohan's grief was an ever-present companion, a weight he carried long after the battles were won. His sorrow had driven him from the lands of Kamalaphuli to Pataliputra and back again. It had followed him through the court of the Nanda King, through the forests of Arakan where he had formed a bond with Manu, the elephant who found him in his darkest hour. For a time, during the training, the war, and the unification of his people, Aarohan had been able to push the grief aside. But once the war was over, once the victories were claimed and the nation united, his grief returned with a force that no battlefield had ever known.

Chanakkya became the lead participants in all matters state and governance. History will bear witness that he would become instrumental in setting up the Maurya Dynasty. But that is another story to tell.

Balan set up his Ptolemaic Dynasty in Egypt, but that is another story to tell.

Aristotle went back to Greece and took reign of the Lyceum and completed his treatise on science, literature, medicine. But that is another story to tell

Today in particular Aarohan felt a bit more grief. For he knew he had turned a new chapter. A chapter where his daughter, the most cherished person in his life, would no longer be part of his life effort. Aarohan stood there, in his white shroud attire. His right shoulder bared, one could see the muscular shoulder ball, that had developed from a life time of swinging & thrusting the spear, and pulling the strings of a bifurcated recurve bow.

The breeze ran over Aarohan's exposed hands. It gave goose bumps on his forehands, but this is not elation but sorrow. A sorrow borne out of loss but also sprinkled with the notion of joy, for out of this loss came the conviction to cleanse a nation. His daughter's blood, Roshan's blood, cleansed the nation of Gangariddi, today what we know as Bengal!

And this very emotion overwhelmed him.

And then at the distant horizon Aarohan saw it. A cloud formation, or is it because of the wind changing its pattern, whipping up moisture at the distant slopes. But he clearly saw it.

A towering human female figure, that had its knee planted within the high rolling hills as if it was wading through water. Its head touched the high clouds. It slowly walked towards Aarohan from the distant horizon. As it came nearer, the mist, the cloud, the wind, Aarohan's imagination, looking at it through teary eyes, he could discern the face of Roshan !

The Effigy of Roshan slowly walked across the Arakan hilly range, she was like a goddess who had descended to earth, and all nature around slowly bowed to her. A flock of crane flew across her shape. So grand this shape was, it took over all of Aarohan's field of vision. So overwhelming Aarohan was that he stretched his right hand towards the effigy of Roshan. His tears were running down all the while. Aarohan thought the shape actually blocked the sun rays when it walked past him. The shape kept walking towards the south and approaching the shoreline in the horizon, all the while Aarohan's gaze kept following it . Then as it approached the shoreline of Bay of

Bengal, it slowly laid down over the hills and took their shape.

And as it did there was a quake in the ground and all the birds of the forest flew at the same time with a rancor.

Others would say it was just a mild earthquake that is quite common in these regions, but Aarohan saw what he saw.

Aarohan felt a sharp pain to the right of his torso, and he gripped it hard with his right hand, tears running down his cheek at the sight of Roshan.

Aarohan kneeled to the ground, the weight of his sorrow bringing him down.

Then he felt a soft hand touch his left shoulder.

It was that of FaMing's. She kneeled beside him, and said, ' I wish I knew your daughter.'

Aarohan nodded, and slowly placed his hand on a baby's head that FaMing was carrying. Both Aarohan and FaMing touched their foreheads and in tender embrace while they cuddled their baby daughter.

Few would know that the people of the Arakan hill-tracts are descendants of Aarohan & FaMing

And in a distance the trumpet of an Elephant rang out and echoed through the Forrest, the gorge and the hills……. And across time. Manu!

AFTERWORD

It has been my privilege in researching and writing this story. I came to realization of what really happened in India at the time of Eskander the barbarian and Chandra Gupta Maurya and his mentor Chanakkya based on certain readings I came across in 2006. I ignored my realization for ten years, though it kept nagging me. That unknown character in history kept poking me in my side, why would you not tell the world my story? '. In 2016 I began writing & telling this story. I imagined his name to be 'Aarohan', meaning 'To Rise'.

At first the intent was that this would have been a peered reviewed research paper. Then I realized there would be a lot of naysayers and the whole absurd pushback from historians who, to this day have not fully explained, why Alexander left India abruptly, with his scanty army that was reduced to rubbles, taking the absurd return route and no spoils of war, and died within months of leaving India, inspite of being a strapping lad of thirty three !!!

So why not tell the story as a novel? Though we have availed artistic license in writing this novel, all the major events in this story are factually correct. So, something in this manner of the story did happen.

Thank you for your inquisitive reading.

Arman

Boston, Massachusetts
Saturday, June 29, 2024

ACKNOWLEDGMENTS

There are so many people, personalities, and events that give shape to a book. It is a daunting task to capture the presence and essence of all who influenced the storytelling of *Gangaridai*, a work that has been in the making for eight years, and even more so, the life experiences that have led to this endeavor.

I'd like to thank my ex-wife, **Anett Elek**, who was with me through the majority of writing this book, always critiquing it to give it more life, excitement, and flow. This is to you, Anett; I hope you like the final version of it.

I'd also like to thank my high school buddy, **Tahsin Rouf**, for giving the first cold-eyed reading of the initial writings way back in 2017 and being glued to the chapters, giving me the thumbs up and stating we have something worthwhile here.

I'd also like to thank a few of my mentors in life. The first is **Mustapha Khalid Polash**, a practicing architect in Dhaka, Bangladesh, who taught me visual composition, which, it turns out, is also applicable to writing. The second, **Dr. Nizamuddin Ahmed**, who was instrumental for me in completing my B. Arch with a bang! Third is **Franz Bauer** of GTZ, who taught me the art of cutting through the fluff and getting to the essence of 'Being' of any topic. The fourth is—oh boy—**Dr. David Leatherbarrow** of the University of Pennsylvania, whose advance courses in history and theory were, in essence, the act of splintering your brain into a thousand pieces and then collecting them off the floor. And my fifth mentor, the esteemed **Anton Germishuizen**, saw me through some of the difficult moments in my life.

This Acknowledgement section wouldn't be complete without raising a toast to **Dr. Afsarul Qader**, Ambassador, Govt. of Bangladesh, who had given me a physical copy of 'Artha Shastra'. A reservoir of wisdom, it is always a treat having a discourse with you! Thank you.

My gratitude also goes out to the folks at the **Dockside Pub** in Swampscott, MA, which turned into my own 'Hemingway' retreat for writing this book. **Keira**, **Becky**, and **Brandon**, thank you.

Also, gratitude and treats for my cat **Moonshee**, who has always been by my side—no, literally by my side in the apartment wherever I took up station writing the book. Moonshee, you are my mini 'Manu'.

Prayers for my late father, **Delwar Chowdhury**, who would when I was four, wake me up before sunrise in the town of Raj Shahi by the river Padma, and we would go for walks, and he would buy fish directly from the fishermen on boats, of their catches from the previous night. The mighty Ganga comes to me through those memories.

And finally, the powerhouse of prayers—*Mashallah*—my mother, **Sabiya Chowdhury**, a voracious reader herself who is one of the prime audiences and champions of this book. And you have given me that soft touch on the shoulder to carry on during very difficult times. Always!

And to all the memories in life I am grateful to have – both the joyful ones as well as the ones of sorrow & heartbreak, for all the events in this book I could relate to because of these memories and experiences.

About the author

Arman Chowdhury, AIA, is a licensed architect practicing in Boston, Massachusetts, USA. A nature lover, Arman can often be found exploring the backwoods of the White Mountains in New Hampshire. He wishes there were thirty-six hours in a day to accommodate his varied interests and passions within the confines of the circadian cycle. Arman adheres to three daily wins: exercising, engaging in creative pursuits such as reading, writing, or drawing, and meditating.

Arman considers himself a natural-born Sufi, a polymath, and an empath. As a voracious writer and keen observer of the human condition, he channels his diverse experiences and insights into his storytelling.

Arman dreams that there would be one day - even if only for a single day - that there would be no war or violence, so that humanity can finally claim its mantle of being a peaceful species.

Arman.Chowdhury@armanarchitecture.com